PINKERTON'S GOLD

A JOHN WHYTE NOVEL OF THE
AMERICAN WEST

PINKERTON'S GOLD

THOM NICHOLSON

FIVE STAR
A part of Gale, a Cengage Company

Farmington Hills, Mich • San Francisco • New York • Waterville, Maine
Meriden, Conn • Mason, Ohio • Chicago

LIBRARY OF CONGRESS CATALOGING-IN-PUBLICATION DATA

Names: Nicholson, Thom, author.
Title: Pinkerton's gold / Thom Nicholson.
Description: First edition. | Waterville, Maine : Five Star Publishing, a part of Cengage Learning, Inc., [2017] | Series: A John Whyte novel of the American West | Description based on print version record and CIP data provided by publisher; resource not viewed.
Identifiers: LCCN 2017007830 (print) | LCCN 2017012660 (ebook) | ISBN 9781432837198 (ebook) | ISBN 1432837192 (ebook) | ISBN 9781432837181 (ebook) | ISBN 1432837184 (ebook) | ISBN 9781432837341 (hardcover) | ISBN 1432837346 (hardcover)
Subjects: | GSAFD: Western stories. | Adventure fiction.
Classification: LCC PS3614.I3535 (ebook) | LCC PS3614.I3535 P56 2017 (print) | DDC 813/.6—dc23
LC record available at https://lccn.loc.gov/2017007830

First Edition. First Printing: August 2017
Find us on Facebook– https://www.facebook.com/FiveStarCengage
Visit our website– http://www.gale.cengage.com/fivestar/
Contact Five Star™ Publishing at FiveStar@cengage.com

Printed in the United States of America
1 2 3 4 5 6 7 21 20 19 18 17

Dedicated with thanks and admiration to
Five Star editor Hazel Rumney.
Her dedicated professionalism has made me
a far better writer than I ever dreamed I could be.

CHAPTER 1
A PLEA FOR HELP

"These damned robberies have got to be stopped!" Rafe Wallace slammed his meaty fist down on Sam Philpot's desk with a satisfying *smack!* A stacked pile of papers scattered at the impact, and Philpot scrambled to gather them up again. Rafe's face was effused with a red blush, he was so agitated, as he paused, almost startled at his outburst.

"Sorry, Samuel . . . Mr. Pinkerton. I didn't mean to get so carried away. It's so damned aggravating to think that a bunch of damnable outlaws are about to shut down the fastest growing gold mining operation in the territory. My company has sunk thousands of dollars building the smelter in Denver, and I'll have to close its doors soon if I can't transport gold from the diggin's back to Denver."

Wallace brushed his hand against his forehead in a worried gesture. He shifted his weight on his feet and tugged at the tight collar around his neck. "That's why I made this trip to St. Louis. When Samuel wired me that you'd be in town on yur way to Memphis, I knew I had to come. I'm gettin' desperate."

Philpot smoothed the last of the papers down and smiled at his new customer, in what he considered calm reassurance. "I understand how frustrated you must be, Rafe. I agree, the situation is damnable. I'm sure Allan agrees with me."

"I absolutely do. And please, Rafe, call me Allan. To your credit, you have come to the right place, Rafe. Pinkerton's Detective Agency has been solving problems like yours since the war. Don't fret. You now have the world's best and most dedicated detective agency standing at your side. Hell, as far as we're concerned now, it's Pinkerton's gold as much as yours, and we'll get it to your smelter, no matter what scurrilous efforts the lawless try to keep us from succeeding."

Rafe brushed his dark beard in agitation and frustration. "I appreciate the sentiment, Pinkerton. But in my world, it's results that count, not fancy speeches."

The general manager of the Denver branch of the Guggenheim Mining and Smelting Company struggled to calm down. He had made the long train trip from Denver to hear these words. He exhaled in quiet relief. "These bastards seem to know more about my plans than I do. Nearly every shipment from my branch offices at the diggin's in Georgetown or Central City has been attacked. The last shipment got through all right, but at a cost of five dead and ten wounded. Now, I can't find men willing to ride as guards for less than one hundred dollars a trip. As many as it takes to fight through lately, why, I'd go broke in shippin' costs alone."

Philpot nodded his silver-haired head, as if wisely digesting the disturbing news. "Is any gold at all making it to your smelter?"

"Some, but only what individuals sneak across themselves. I've set it up so my agents at the fields buy the gold from the miners and then store it at the assay office until there's enough fer a run into Denver. That way, we get first crack at the ore and the miners get their money at the claim sites, where they need the cash. Then, they don't have to leave their claims to bring their diggin's over the pass to Denver. Most prospectors don't want to leave their claims fer anything, fer fear of claim-jumpers, you know."

The chief of the Pinkerton Detective Agency nodded his head, his mind already weighing the various detectives he employed that he could send out west to work with the burly mining engineer standing before him. The answer was easy to decide upon and he smiled reassuringly at Wallace. "I know the man to handle this problem, Rafe. I'll telegraph him immediately and let him know you and Samuel are coming out to see him tomorrow. You can accompany him back to Denver and provide him all the particulars on your operation and the troubles en route." Pinkerton looked at the rotund Philpot. "This jobs calls for one of my very best men, John Whyte. Don't you agree, Samuel?"

"Absolutely right, sir. That's exactly who I was thinking of myself."

"Meanwhile, Rafe, why don't you retire to your hotel room and freshen up? I'll send the telegraph off and then pick you up tonight, say about seven, for a meal at our St. Louis version of Delmonico's in New York."

Rafe Wallace nodded. "Fine by me. But I want to have the right to reject your man, iffen I think he's not man enough to do the job. Fair enough?" His look challenged Philpot and Pinkerton to agree.

Philpot smiled and stood, his pudgy hand outstretched. "Not a problem, Rafe. You're going to be more than pleased when you find out who we have in mind."

Rafe Wallace enveloped the soft hand in his hardened paw, satisfied for the moment. The two men, although both were short and stocky, were opposites in appearance. Rafe was hard as the rock he mined, with a weather-worn face framed by a gray-streaked beard and a sturdy body, sculpted with the heavy muscles of a deep-rock miner. His brown eyes flashed with the fire of a man who knew the trials of life and did not surrender to them. In contrast, Philpot's face was ruddy, and his flaccid body jiggled with fat. His complexion was reddened not by sun and wind, but by drink and easy living. His time behind the polished desk had softened him. His gray hair and beard showed the careful ministrations of a skilled barber, and his hands had seen nothing harder to hold than an ink pen in years.

The florid-faced Philpot called for his office clerk. "Max, escort Mr. Wallace to his hotel. There's a room reserved for him already. Rafe, we'll see you about seven."

"Good enough, Sam, Allan. I'll be anxious to hear more about your detective that will be working for me."

Pinkerton smiled. "Believe me, Rafe, you'll be more than satisfied with our choice. See you around seven." He watched the old miner leave his office and reached for a pad and pen. Humming softly, he started composing the instructions to be telegraphed to the chosen detective. When he finished, he handed the message to Philpot. "Send this right away, Samuel. I'm off fer my hotel to clean up before supper. Pick me up at a quarter before seven."

"I'll do it, Allan. Hell, I wish I could go with him, damn it all." He smiled at Pinkerton. "Still. Someone has to man the office, right?" Satisfied with his lame rationale, he followed Allan Pinkerton out of his office and scooted to the telegraph room. He scratched at the silver, mutton-chop whiskers that framed his rotund face and decided to have a shave before supper with Wallace and his boss. Although he was married to Pinkerton's wife's niece, it was necessary to maintain a favorable impression with the famous detective. He liked his job and the nice salary that went with it.

Wallace wore the same rumpled suit with the stiff, celluloid collar and old, white shirt sporting the same garish, flowered tie that he had worn at Philpot's office. To his credit, he had shaved and perhaps even bathed, but Philpot couldn't tell for certain. He, Philpot, was freshly shaven and smelled of lilac water. His silver-gray hair was slicked down, and he wore a fresh shirt from a supply he kept at his office for such occasions. Pinkerton had changed as well, but apparently took no notice of Wallace's rough appearance.

The rock miner's unruly hair had been pushed down a bit, although it had not faced the serious application of a comb or brush. Philpot hoped the man's country-bumpkin appearance would not be held against him if any important acquaintances saw them at the restaurant. "Here you are," he beamed at Wallace. "Feeling hungry?"

"I could eat a dead polecat, raw and unskinned," Wallace answered. "All I've had for three days is sandwiches and warm beer, at rest stops along the tracks."

"Then, my friend, you are in for a culinary treat. Come along with you." Philpot led the way outside to where a rented hansom carriage waited, with matching bays working on feed bags hung from their noses. Philpot climbed into the interior and scooted over for Wallace. Pinkerton sat opposite the two men. "To The Queen's Own Restaurant, Harry."

"Right away, Mr. Philpot," came the muffled reply from the driver, sitting on the driver's bench outside the enclosed cab. The driver grabbed the horses' snacks, climbed up to his seat, and snapped the reins against the rumps of his weary animals. The hansom cab clattered off on the cobblestone street toward the center of the city. Philpot took the opportunity to point out the numerous buildings and landmarks of the Midwestern metropolis that was St. Louis. He wondered if Wallace had even seen such a sight before. Philpot thoroughly enjoyed his self-appointed position as educator of the rough-edged, hard-rock miner from the West. Wallace merely grunted and politely looked where he was told, his countenance not registering any sign of surprise or awe, regardless of the proclaimed architectural wonder cited for his amazement. Turning down one of the crowded main streets, the hansom pulled up before their destination. "The Queen's Own Restaurant," proclaimed the bright red and black sign framed above the gilded-glass twin doors. Standing in imperious majesty, a red-coated doorman stood guard over the entrance, his face aloof. A cluster of patrons waited outside the doorway for an opportunity to enter, but Philpot swept past, greeting the doorman by name, Pinkerton and Wallace at his heels. They dropped off their hats at the check stand and entered the main dining room. Philpot walked up to a formally dressed maître d', flashing a smile of greeting. "Evening, Jacques. Is my table ready?"

Favoring Philpot with the sparsest of smiles, the man nodded. "Of course, Mr. Philpot." He snapped his fingers and regally waved at a waiter. "James, take Mr. Philpot and his guests to his regular table."

Wallace looked over the crowded dining area, every table filled with finely dressed patrons enjoying their food and company. "Looks busy. We're lucky to get a table without waitin' half the night."

"Not at all," Philpot smugly replied. "I have a standing reservation and dine here most regularly. This is reputed to be the finest restaurant west of Chicago and, in my opinion, perhaps even New York. I hope you're in the mood for a first-class steak, with all the trimmings?"

"Never pass up a chance to get some good food. Had too many times I ate what was available, no matter what the critter was."

Their waiter, tall, thin, with a crisp, white linen apron tied around his waist, introduced himself as James, then led the way to a small alcove elevated above the main dining room, with walls curtained in deep red velvet, drawn open so they could view the main dining room below. He pulled out a chair for Philpot to settle in. "I hope you enjoy your meal, gentlemen. Please signal should you want anything. Your favorite Burgundy to start, Mr. Philpot?"

From the alcove, the three men could enjoy private conversation and still see the small stage at the front of the room when entertainment was presented. Their table was covered by a heavy, white linen cloth with matching napkins, upon which were placed bone china and ornate, sterling-silver flatware. James lit the table candle and moved away, to return with a bottle of Burgundy, the dust from the wine cellar still present on the bottle. He pulled the cork, smelled its fragrance, then poured a tiny amount for Philpot to approve, before filling the men's crystal wine glasses. "Are you gentlemen ready to order?"

Philpot nodded, enjoying the attention and rapid service. "Allan, Rafe, allow me, if you will." At Rafe's nod, he regally commanded to the subservient waiter, "We'll have oysters on the half shell for appetizers. New York sirloin steaks, cooked medium rare, with potatoes au gratin, creamed pearl onions, and green bean almandine on the side. Hot rolls with honey and fresh butter. For dessert, we'll have fresh peaches in sweet cream, and Napoleon brandy after the meal. All right with you, Allan?"

"Sounds fine by me, Sam."

"Rafe?"

"A long as it gits here soon. I'm starved."

As their attentive waiter left, Philpot raised his glass. "Here's to your good health, Rafe, and to yours, Allan."

"Thanks, Sam. And to yours. And especially to Pinkerton's Detective Agency being the solution to my problem."

"Oh, you can depend on that," Philpot laughed. "I quit worrying about that as soon as Allan determined who would be the detective assigned to the case."

"Well, you sure sound confident about this hombre. I hope he's up to the task. Those boys play rough. They'll kill anyone who stands in their way, without blinkin' an eye. A St. Louis city-slicker might get his backside scorched. Why don't you tell me a little about this here hooraw you're so proud of?"

Philpot held up his hand. "As soon as we eat. Let's enjoy the food, and, over cigars and brandy, I'll tell you the dangedest tale you ever heard. Ah, here's the first of our order. Bon appétit, my good man. You've never tasted steak so delicious and tender as what is served here."

Philpot pushed back his chair and with methodical precision folded his soiled napkin next to the empty dessert bowl. "There, didn't I tell you? The finest food this side of Delmonico's in New York City."

Wallace took a slim cigar and fired it up. He watched the rolling smoke float upward and worried at a sliver of meat caught between his teeth. "Yep, I'd say about on a par with Delmonico's. Although, to be fair, I suspect Delmonico's does have a wider selection on its menu."

"You . . . you mean you've eaten in Delmonico's?" Philpot's eyes widened. "My word, that's been a dream of mine for many years. Is it as grand a place as they say? When were you there?"

Rafe held up a hand to stop the rushed questions. "Slow down; I'll come clean. I go to New York once a year, to make my reports to the head office and major stockholders. I usually eat there once or twice. There's lots a' good places to eat in a city the size of New York." Wallace briefly described some of the finer restaurants of the city to the now thoroughly awed Philpot and an amused Pinkerton. Eventually he maneuvered the conversation back to what he was most interested in.

"Enough about New York. What's the lowdown on this detective you've promised will solve my problems?"

CHAPTER 2
A TRIP TO FAIR OAKS

"Jeesus," Rafe grumbled mentally, as he sat beside Philpot on the west-bound train out of St. Louis. *"What a pompous fart this fella is."* He wondered how Pinkerton's ever allowed him to be a manager for such a prestigious organization. If Philpot's detective was as silly an ass, he would refuse his help and go on to New York, to beg the home office for assistance.

Philpot finished his story about his trip to Chicago, to Rafe's relief.

The crusty miner decided the only way he could shut up the man was to take over the conversation himself. "I reckon Allan is 'bout to Memphis by now. I wish he could have accompanied us out to your detective's estate."

"Allan has irons in a lot of fires right now. We're lucky to have had his company for an evening. He left me implicit instructions. You are to be given final say on whether or not John Whyte is the man to solve your problem out in Colorado. Don't you worry; you'll be as impressed with John as I am after spending some time around him. John's probably the best detective in Pinkerton's stable of outstanding men right now. I'm proud to say that he's a special friend of mine."

"Well, I gotta admit, he sounds like a lightnin' strike in a barrel a' gunpowder. I don't think I ever met the son of a duke before. Especially one that cussed out the cousin of the Queen of England."

"It certainly came back to haunt him," Philpot mused. "Still, the queen's loss is our gain. Before he was twenty, John was a lieutenant in the queen's Bengal Lancers. He had a knack for the military and was soon a commander of a special unit of Sikh cavalry that was assigned the most dangerous assignments. Seems these Sikh men take special enjoyment in fighting, much as our Sioux Injuns, and they took a liking to John 'cause of his bravery and daring. Before he was twenty-five, he was a colonel in the Union army under General Custer. And before that, he was a spy under Allan Pinkerton, working directly for President Lincoln."

"And he got the medal of honor fer shootin' Jeb Stuart, don't fergit."

"No, I won't. He was a true war hero and has solved several hard cases for the agency. Why, a couple of months ago, he broke up a ring of pirates on the Mississippi River by getting himself put in jail with one of the pirates, then busting the crook out and infiltrating the gang through him. It was very dangerous and daring, but he shrugs it off as doing what's necessary to get the job done."

Wallace listened intently. So far he liked what he was hearing. Philpot rattled on, relishing the telling as much as Wallace the hearing of the story.

Philpot blew a stream of cigar smoke upward, watching it billow and wave through the air. "When he established himself in America, he sent for all his old soldiers left alive in India. He'd determined to serve in the Civil War, so he calls on President Lincoln, like they were old friends, and offers to join up with the Union army. Well now, President Lincoln likes what he hears, so he commissions John a major in the Union cavalry and, before the war is over he's a colonel, commanding a brigade of cavalry under General Custer. He would have been made a general himself, if the war hadn't ended before congress could approve it. Then after the war, he moved out here and started his plantation, building one hell of a house on a high bluff overlooking the Missouri River. Now he owns a lot of land, even more money, and still he's not done."

Although Wallace had essentially heard the same story from the pompous Philpot the previous evening, he became engrossed in the story. Philpot paused to add suspense and then continued.

"Afore long, he becomes restless, so he joins up with Pinkerton's Detective Agency, as he had worked for Allan during the war. Now, he's the best detective in the agency. When Grant became president, he immediately gave John a federal deputy marshal's commission, so he can arrest law-breakers, no matter where he's working." Philpot paused, to ensure he still had Rafe's complete attention. "John likes the hard cases, where he can work undercover and he never fails. He's a dead shot with rifle or pistol, and he out thinks the crooks; that's why he always cracks the case."

Wallace let the breath escape from his lungs. "Well, that sure is some story. I can't help but be impressed, if he's all you claim. I'm lookin' forward to meetin' him."

"Yes, indeed. We'll be there before noon. By the way, don't call him Lord Johnnie. He doesn't like that name. He fancies himself a regular American now. In my wire I told him that we would be showing up today, so he's expecting us. There'll be a carriage waiting for us at the station. He has a telegraph wire connected to his house. Goes right into his parlor."

Wallace blinked his eyes in surprise. "What'll they think of next?"

"That's not all. He's got his own personal railroad car."

Wallace was impressed. "A personal railroad car? I read about them the last time I was in Chicago. They're supposed to be something to see."

"Well, if you go back with Johnnie to Denver, you'll probably have the pleasure of riding in it. Since that's the easiest way out there, I suspect he'll be using it."

Philpot took his ivory toothpick out of his mouth and examined it. Then he continued to probe his teeth. "I wish I could go to Colorado with you. But, someone has to mind the store." He ruefully grinned at Wallace. "A task for every man, you know."

"That's true, Sam. Besides, the food in Denver is awful. Not a decent restaurant in the whole damned town. Hell, you might jus' up and starve."

Philpot laughed, a bit thinly, not sure if he was being insulted. "Well, then. It's as well, I suppose."

Rafe agreed and then pulled his hat down over his eyes. "I think I'll grab some shut-eye. Putting Allan on the midnight steamer to Memphis made me miss some sack time last night. Wake me when we reach Whyte's plantation."

The train arrived at the Fair Oaks station a few minutes before noon. Along with two burly men, lumberjacks by the looks of them, a strangely attired couple, probably a man and wife, gathered together on the station's wooden walkway and watched the train chug off into the distance, its dark plume of smoke drifting high in the warm, late spring air.

Philpot whispered to Wallace. "See those two?" He jerked his head toward the couple, who had started to walk away. The woman was in a long, flowing robe-like dress, brightly colored. The man was bearded, with a sharply pointed handlebar moustache, his head wrapped in a maroon-colored scarf. "They are a couple of those Sikh folks that came here with John Whyte. See that thing on the man's head? It's called a turban. Sikh men can't ever cut their hair, like Samson in the Bible. So they hold it up with a turban. Fierce looking fella isn't he?"

Wallace smiled. "I wouldn't want to piss him off, that's fer certain. He looked me over when we first got off. How many of 'em live here?"

"Not many. Like I said, most were killed off in their last battle over there in India, with John. Some more fought in the Civil War with John and were killed there. Those that were left work here on the estate, including some up at the main house as personal servants. Ah, here comes our ride."

A handsome carriage, pulled by matched black horses and driven by a young man wearing the unusual turban, pulled up. Wallace and Philpot loaded their bags in the boot and climbed in. "Like I said, these folks love John Whyte and stay with him, doing what they can. Howdy, Kai Singh. How's Lord John and your father, Khan Singh?"

"Mister Philpot. Hello to you, sir. Thank you, my father and the good lord are both well. I am to take you there straight away." He snapped the reins and the matched pair of horses trotted off on the smooth dirt road, oiled to cut down on the dust.

Philpot leaned over to Wallace. "Notice the things going on, Rafe. Over there, the apple orchard. Beyond there, a lumber operation and a maple syrup grove. Ahead on the right, some of the best cattle you've ever seen. John brings Angus bulls clear over from England to improve his herd's bloodline. Down by the river bottom, he grows corn and beans, and he has the finest herd of horses in this part of the country. He breeds them from Kentucky and Tennessee purebreds, brought up the river by paddle steamer. Half the people in St. Louis won't have anything but Fair Oaks horses to ride or pull their surreys. On the far east of his estate, he even has a little town, where most of the people who work for him live."

Wallace looked around. "I'm surprised he ever wants to leave this place, Sam."

Philpot beamed. "He also has places in New York, Chicago, as well as in St. Louis. And, he also doesn't mind living outta his saddle bags as long as he needs to when he's on a case."

Rafe Wallace shifted in the firm, leather seat. He was ready to get off his butt and on his feet for a while. "I certainly am lookin' forward to meeting Mr. Lord John Whyte, with a 'Y', Sam. He sure sounds like a catamount on two legs."

"Well, it won't be long now. There's Oakview, the house, up yonder on the top of the hill. Really something, isn't it?"

Before them stood an imposing three-story mansion covered with white plaster. Six tall, white pillars supported the second-floor balcony. The porch overlooked a green expanse of rolling meadows, clustered with grazing cattle, and the dense woods beyond.

Wallace agreed, his voice filled with admiration. "That's some place, all right. Looks like a castle from England, brought here and put up."

"Thirty-six rooms and, imagine this, there're five indoor toilets in the main house and running water for the wash basins. More like a fine hotel in Paris or something than a house."

"Do tell. That is somethin' fer a fact." Wallace gazed in awe as the carriage rounded the graveled drive and stopped at the steps leading up to the main entrance. The young driver informed them he would take care of their luggage and drove off around the corner of the house.

Philpot led Wallace up the marble stairway to the polished, massive, oak doors and pulled a cord. Wallace heard the faint tinkle of bells inside announcing their presence. Shortly both doors swung inward, and a slight woman, wearing a loose but colorful, flowing dress, bowed low before them. She was of indeterminable age and wore a golden anklet above each of her bare feet. Her dark hair was tied in a cluster of tiny knots. "Gentlemen." Her voice was soft and accented, with a decidedly British lilt. "Welcome to Fair Oaks. The Sahib is out back, trying out a new pistol. He is expecting you."

"What do you say, Rafe? Want to try out one of them indoor

privies first before we meet our host?"

"The privie first. My kidneys are fuller than a gully in a Texas thunderstorm."

As soon as the men relieved themselves, they followed the petite servant outside to the broad expanse of a green lawn, which ended abruptly in a sharp drop off to the muddy waters of the Missouri River, seventy feet below. Two men were shooting at several man-sized targets nailed to trees at the far side of the lawn. From a distance, one seemed tall and imposing, making the other seem small in comparison. As Sam and Rafe approached, the smaller swiftly drew a pistol and fired five rapid shots at the target, which was about sixty feet away. The sharp cracks of the weapon rang in the still air, and the greasy gun smoke drifted away in the breeze. Wallace noticed that all the holes could have been covered by the palm of his hand.

Reloading, then holstering the pistol, the marksman turned toward the two men, watching their approach. As they neared him, he smiled brightly. "Ah, Khan Singh. Our guests have arrived."

CHAPTER 3
LORD JOHNNIE

Rafe Wallace's face registered a sudden wariness as a huge dog rose from his spot in the shade under a nearby table. It was the largest canine the Colorado miner had ever seen. The great animal walked at the side of his master, the brown eyes in his massive head locked on the two newcomers. The enormous dog seemed content to stay by his master's side, allowing Rafe to warily turn his attention to the smiling host.

Philpot's colorful description of the English detective was impressive, but Wallace wanted to decide the merits of the man for himself. The first impression was not disappointing. Taller than average, and thus much taller than Rafe, John Whyte was broad-shouldered, while slim at the waist. The sleeves of his shirt were rolled up, exposing strongly defined muscles. Long legs encased in tight whipcord pants ended in short riding boots, with the Texas heel. The face was open and friendly, with dark-brown eyes. The sun-bronzed skin of his face was contrasted by straight, white teeth. He flashed a broad smile at his guests. He seemed to be gauging Rafe as much as the old miner was him. Only a vivid scar, running from the top of his forehead to disappear into his raven-black hair above the tanned brow, marred the picture. The hair around the scar was silver white, in stark contrast to the rest of his sleek, black hair and served as a dramatic accent to the man's face.

Hair curled from the neck of his white linen shirt, and his muscular forearms were covered in fine, dark fuzz. His grip, as he took Wallace's offered hand, was firm and powerful, suggesting much greater strength.

Philpot jumped forward to interject an introduction. "John, this is the man I telegraphed you about, Rafe Wallace, of Denver, out in Colorado. Rafe, my good friend, John Whyte, the best detective in Pinkerton's Agency."

Whyte's voice was soft and his words, well mannered. It reflected breeding and education. The accent was decidedly British, moderated by the years in America. "Mr. Wallace, I'm honored to meet you, sir. I was reading last night about your marvelous mining operation in Virginia City and your layered support design that allows you to extract twice the ore of conventional mining operations. You'll have to tell me about it, when we have a chance to talk."

Rafe was impressed. "Where on earth did you read about that? And what on earth is that dog? It's as big as a damned bear, if ever I saw one."

John smiled. "That's Rajah. He's from a breed called Great Danes. A bloody magnificent animal, isn't he? And last night, after Samuel wired me, I telegraphed the head office in Chicago to send me everything they could find about you before you arrived."

"Well, I'll be double-dunked in a water trough. All that in such a short time? Gives a fellow pause to wonder, don't it? That a person could find out so much about a fellow, so quick-like, I mean."

"That's part of what makes Pinkerton's so good. We have sources available that most organizations don't." John smiled again and shook hands with Philpot. "Samuel, good to see you. Thanks for bringing Mr. Wallace out personally."

"No problem, John. I wanted a chance to visit with you anyways."

John motioned to the place where his tall companion waited,

busy reloading several pistols and placing them next to two rifles on a small table. "Gentlemen, won't you join me? I've been test firing a new brace of pistols I received yesterday. Would you care to take a look?"

Wallace walked over to the table with John, Philpot one step behind. Rafe took one of the pistols from the huge silent companion of John, politely acknowledging him, as he was anxious not to give offense. The man was probably six and one-half feet in height and two hundred-fifty pounds in weight. A fierce face was marked by a great handlebar moustache of salt and pepper that curled into a sharp point on each end. A dark beard with faint streaks of gray covered most of the rest of his lower face, and dark, intelligent eyes peered out from under bushy eyebrows. The crowning focal point was the maroon-colored turban that was meticulously wrapped around the man's head, signifying his caste as a Sikh warrior. "Thank you," Wallace murmured as he took the pistol, his eyes still measuring the huge warrior before him.

"Mr. Wallace, I am proud to present my old friend and retainer, Khan Singh, formerly Color Sergeant Major of my brigade during the late war and before that, Master Sergeant of Horse, Her Majesty's 12th Bengal Lancers, of Her Majesty's First Dragoons."

The oversized man bowed slightly and rumbled deeply, "Sahib Wallace, your humble servant."

"Pleased to meet you, Mr., er, Khan? Or Sergeant Major?"

"Please to call me Khan Singh, Sahib Wallace. I am now retired from active service."

John smiled at his Indian friend. "And still the best pistol or rifle shot I ever saw, as well as a first-class scout and tracker. A better man to go on the trail with was never born. You'll find, Mr. Wallace, that there is not much this grand old warrior can't do."

"Please, call me Rafe, Mr. Whyte. Or is it Lord Whyte? Mr. Wallace makes me think you're talking to my father."

"Right you are, Rafe. And please call me John. That which was my English title, I left behind when I came to America. Now, have a go at those targets there. You'll find that this pistol is one superb weapon."

Wallace aimed the six-shooter and squeezed off a single shot. The pistol bucked in his hand. He squinted through the greasy-white gun smoke and was relieved to see he had hit his target, although high in the upper-right portion of the silhouette. More, he fired the next four rounds, getting three good hits, although scattered about the target. John drew his pistol from its holster and placed five neat holes two inches below the neck of one of the targets. Smiling in satisfaction, he placed the smoking pistol on the table. "Your turn, old friend."

Without a word, Khan Singh pulled his pistol and, faster than Wallace could count, fired his five bullets into the same area that John's had gone. The clapboard target had a huge hole in it, when Wallace saw it as the gun smoke dispersed.

Rafe nodded in admiration. "These are fine pistols, all right. Don't think I ever saw one quite like 'em. What kind are they?"

John turned the pistol in his hand. "They are called Russian .44's, made by Smith and Wesson Armory for the czar of Russia's army. I don't think I ever saw a better balance or more accurate pistol. I was fortunate to get six of the few not going to Russia." John spun his pistol around his finger and set it aside. He picked up one of the two new Winchester saddle rifles, chambered for the new brass, .44-77 caliber cartridge, lying on the table. "Khan, toss a couple of bottles out into the river. I want to see if I can still hit a target with this."

Khan threw two empty bottles far out into the swirling brown waters of the Missouri River. John waited a few moments, until the current had carried the floating bottles about fifty yards

downstream, then swiftly tucked the stock of the rifle into the hollow of his shoulder, took aim, and deliberately blew the two bottles into bits, throwing up a white shower of foam as the bullets hit the bottles and water. For the next few minutes, he and Khan Singh took turns breaking floating bottles, churning up the river's placid waters. Satisfied with the results, John put the rifle down and turned back to his guests.

"Good enough, I suppose. Khan, we'll take the pistols, the rifles, and two shotguns with us to Colorado. Oh, yes, take two of the Spencer .52 caliber buffalo guns with the scopes on them. We may have some long-range shooting to do." John smiled at Khan Singh. "Old friend, shall we take Kai? He can be our cook and maintain the parlor car for us while we are about our business. Would that be all right with you?"

Khan Singh bowed his head in agreement. There was a brief but obvious note of pride in his deep voice. "Yes, Sahib. He will be most happy to share in our journey. I will tell him tonight."

John turned toward his guests. "I see it's almost time for afternoon tea, or coffee, if you would rather. Would you two care to join me in the library? We can start our planning for the operation in Denver. That is, if you are ready, Rafe. I suppose you still have to decide if you want me to represent Pinkerton's for you."

"You're the man, John," Rafe declared, resolutely. "I'll go along with whatever you say, as long as we can stop this gang of outlaws from ruining my smelting operations."

"Jolly good. Suppose you tell me all you can about what has happened. I want to hear everything."

They ambled toward the house, Wallace re-telling John what he had told Philpot the day before. They approached the rear entrance of the main house and crossed the foyer to the library. Khan Singh skillfully maneuvered his muscular body to deftly open the double wooden doors, stepping aside to allow John and his guest to enter the large room.

Wallace gaped in amazement. Two walls in the impressive room were lined with built-in bookcases from floor to ceiling, stacked with books. Every bare spot on the adjacent paneled walls held a flag, military guidons, swords, knifes, guns, animal skin, or mounted head, including a massive tiger, with teeth fiercely bared. A broad, cherry-wood desk was placed in front of the one wall containing beveled-glass windows, through which the afternoon sunlight streamed. Overstuffed leather chairs and couches awaited the weary visitor, and a large table covered with several opened maps stood to the side, awaiting inspection. Underfoot, intricately woven Persian rugs softened the oak wood floor. Wallace sighed; he wished he had such a place to retreat to at the end of the day.

John followed Rafe's gaze and casually waved his hand at the walls. "The mementos of my wasted youth, Rafe. If you have any questions about anything, please ask."

Rafe Wallace's eyes fixed on a faded, yellow cavalry flag, still on a bullet-pierced wooden staff. "That one there. Is that JEB Stuart's guidon?"

"Yes, one of them, anyway. Khan Singh captured it at Yellow Tavern. Stuart was a wonderful cavalryman. It was a pity he died so near the end of hostilities. Khan Singh was awarded the Medal of Honor for capturing that little strip of cloth. That is one reason it hangs in a place of honor in my home."

"Pardon me for asking," Rafe said. "Did you get JEB Stuart, himself, like they say?"

"I'm not sure, perhaps. It's not something I'm proud of. He was a worthy foe who unfortunately chose the wrong side. It was so confused, soldiers riding and fighting, smoke and horses running madly about, dust kicked up all over the place. Perhaps so. I don't really want to know. In truth, I hope I didn't, but who knows?"

Philpot jumped in. "John received a Medal of Honor there, too. You ever see one, Rafe? Show him yours, John."

"Yes, please do, John. I'd like to see one up close, iffen you don't mind."

A bit reluctantly, John opened a drawer of the desk and took out a small box, which he gave to Wallace. Rafe opened the box and looked in quiet reverence at the little bit of gold and ribbon inside. "Mighty impressive," he said as he closed the lid and returned the box to John, who immediately put it away.

"What really makes it special, is that General Grant gave it to me personally, shortly before the war ended." He looked up at the soft knock and entrance of the delicate woman who had greeted Rafe earlier, carrying a silver tray with a teapot, cups, and cookies. "Smashing. I see Madam Singh has our tea and cookies. Rafe, your wishes?"

John presided over their afternoon break, and then the two Pinkerton men spent the rest of the afternoon listening as Wallace reviewed everything he knew about his predicament in Denver.

As they broke to prepare for supper, John spoke to Rafe Wallace. "I have one more man I think will be of assistance to us, Rafe. I've instructed him to join us at supper. You can meet him then."

As they were about to enter the main dining room, the front door opened, and a stocky cowboy stepped inside, slapping the dust from his shirt and unbuckling worn, leather chaps from around his legs. "Howdy there, John. I got yer message. Am I in time fer dinner? I could smell the curry chicken a mile down the road."

John laughed. "You rascal, you. I never knew you not to make it in time for dinner. Rafe Wallace, may I present William Williams, my superintendent of horses at Fair Oaks. He is a skilled horseman and an even better man to have in tight situations.

28

Unfortunately for my Union soldiers, he rode with Talbot's Texas Cavalry during the war. I was fortunate to meet him on a trip to Texas soon thereafter and convince him to join my organization. Otherwise, he was headed straight for a hangman's noose."

"Now, John, what'll this good man think of me? Howdy, I'm Curly Bill Williams, the best rider in the sovereign state of Texas. Mighty glad to meet ya, Mr. Wallace."

Suppressing his amusement, Rafe shook the scarred, hard hand of Curly Bill. "Mighty glad to meet you, Bill. Call me Rafe." He glanced at the bald crown of Curly Bill's head, pale white above and berry-brown below the shade of a Texas ten-gallon Stetson. "Mighty odd nickname, ain't it? Curly Bill, I mean?"

"Naw. You shoulda seen me afore the war. I had the purdiest head of curly brown locks ever to grace a man's noggin. Lost it all chasin' Yankees, but kept the nickname." He grinned at Wallace. "What the hell, it makes fine conversation with the gals, once I take off my sombrero."

John interrupted the discourse. "Tell him all about it later, William. Let's eat now, and I'll fill you in on our assignment. As soon as we finish our meal, send word to have six horses re-shod for travel in the mountains, including Blaze. He needs a good workout, and what's coming up is just the ticket."

After their meal, the four men retired to the library, where plans were formulated, and decisions made. As the clock in the hall chimed ten P.M., John yawned and stood up. "That's it then. We'll leave tomorrow. Samuel, would you telegraph the station master in St. Louis to stop the west-bound train for us tomorrow? We'll have the private car and a horse carrier to add on, all the way to Denver. William, do you want one of the new Winchester Repeaters to take with you?"

"Naw, thanks, John. I'll stick to my ole Spencer Carbine. I

can shoot better with it than anything else, anyway. 'Cides, it's got seven shots to your nine. I won't need any more than that, nohow."

"As you wish. Please don't forget to load the new saddle blankets. It will be a grand opportunity to try them out." He turned to Wallace. "I recently purchased some new saddle blankets from a source in New Orleans. Made from the fiber of the hanging Spanish moss, which grows in abundance there. The moss is touted to be the best saddle blanket material ever. Allows air to circulate under the saddle and avoid saddle sores for the horses."

Wallace grimaced. "I wish there was something like that for people as well. Every time I ride to Central City, my butt's sore for a week."

John nodded absently. His thoughts were already in Colorado and the vexing problem presented by Wallace. He suspected it was more than simple robbery if there ever was such a thing. "Tomorrow, we'll take the first step," he murmured to himself. "And we won't stop until it's resolved."

CHAPTER 4
RIDING THE RAILS

Rafe Wallace prided himself on being an early riser. He often told friends, "To beat the sun up allows me a head start on the day." He dressed, packed his valise, and wandered down to the already busy kitchen before the sun had cleared the trees beyond the east meadow. A pungent odor of curry and ground coffee beans caressed his nostrils. The pleasant, yet busily efficient wife of Khan Singh served him a cup of steaming hot coffee and watched disapprovingly as he dumped two heaping spoonfuls of cane sugar into it. Rafe gingerly tasted the hot brew, nodded his satisfaction, and then carried it out to the front porch to feel the sun warm the earth after the coolness of the night. It was a particularly favorite part of his day, and, as he sipped and reveled, his eye caught movement coming up the road from the direction of the train station. "Tarnation," he muttered as the two dots became more discernable to his eyes. "Two fellas. And, they're runnin'. What on earth? By thunder! It's John and that warrior-servant of his. What the hell? Why ain't they ridin' horses?"

Rafe watched in silence as the two ran across the lawn to the base of the steps leading up to the front door where they stopped, laughing and gasping for breath.

"Morning, Rafe," John managed to blurt out between deep breaths. "Lovely day, what?"

"What happened, John. Why are you two running like that? You let your horses get away from you?"

31

John Whyte laughed and brushed the sweat from his forehead. "Not a chance, old man. Every day there's not snow standing in the drive, Khan Singh runs me down to the train tracks and back. He says it will keep me strong. Personally, I think he likes making me suffer."

"Good God Almighty. That's four miles or more. And you run it barefooted?"

"Every day, rain or shine. That's one reason I enjoy taking a case that requires my travel away from Fair Oaks. I finally get some rest." John grinned at the perspiring Khan Singh.

The Sikh warrior merely grunted. "Sahib may not always have a horse to ride. Sahib will not become fat and lazy as long as I am major-domo of his household." The old warrior took one last deep breath and then started up the steps to the house. "I will tell Madam Singh to bring your breakfast to the garden patio. Sahib Wallace, breakfast for you as well?"

"You haven't lived until you try Madam Singh's flapjacks, Rafe. She has mastered your American pancakes to perfection."

"Of course," Wallace agreed, acknowledging the hunger pangs in his stomach. "Thanks fer the invite."

"Follow the walkway around to the east side of the house, Rafe. We'll eat outside, in the east patio. I'll join you as soon as I clean up and get dressed. Take your time and enjoy the morning. I'll be there shortly."

"By gum, John. These are the best danged flapjacks I've had in a month of Sundays. This here, what'd you call it? Maple syrup. Man, it shore does go down smooth."

John nodded. "We make it from trees growing over by the east boundary. I can sell all we make and then some. I heard about it from some boys in my cavalry brigade who were from Vermont. After my men mustered out, I sent for a couple of cousins I particularly liked, inviting them to join my family here in Missouri. They started making syrup from the trees on Fair

Oaks. Now, it's a fine cash crop."

The two men ate in silence for a moment, until Sam Philpot wandered down, rubbing the sleep from his eyes. The pudgy manager ordered his own pancakes, then proceeded to monopolize the conversation, quizzing John on details of the report he had recently submitted after breaking up the river-hijacking ring. Rafe listened with rapt fascination as John described his investigation and final shootout with the meanest group of river rats Wallace had ever heard described.

As Philpot ceased his questions in order to apply himself to the heaping plate of flapjacks brought by Madam Singh, Wallace asked a final question. "What time do we take off fer Denver, John?"

"The morning westbound will stop for us about twelve, Rafe. I'll have a carriage waiting out front around eleven. We'll arrive in Kansas City about nine tonight."

Rafe nodded. "Somehow it don't seem right movin' around so fast, does it?"

John laughed. "I don't know, Rafe. Going it the hard way, on a bouncing wagon, making twenty miles a day rather than an hour . . . I think I'll take the speed and comfort the railroad provides."

Rafe laughed and held his hands up in mock surrender. "When you put it that way, I think I'd have to agree. My butt's spent too many evenings recovering from such days on the trail."

The three men joined Khan Singh and his son at the front of the house at the appointed hour. A large carriage awaited them for the two-mile drive to the railhead. As they arrived, Rafe saw Curly Bill, driving six magnificent looking horses up a ramp into a stock car. John's dog, Rajah, bounded up the ramp, right behind the last horse, barking in excitement. The weathered stock car was coupled ahead of an immaculate black rail car, with silver trim and numerous glass windows framed with velvet curtains. Even the handrails at the front and rear coupling transoms were gilded in sterling silver. A name, written in silver script, was prominent on the side of the rail car, *Star of India*.

"My word, that's somethin', all right," Rafe gushed. "It looks longer than a regular passenger coach."

"It is," John said as they pulled up beside the gleaming conveyance. "It is better than forty-two feet long, with oversized wheels and extra springs. It was made by a gentleman in Chicago, name of Pullman. He calls them personal parlor cars. It was outrageously expensive, but I have some interest in an iron-casting plant located nearby. I had to buy one of Pullman's cars before I could obtain the order to furnish wheels for the others he is building. It is the latest and most luxurious way of traveling by rail. Go on inside and look around. Make yourself comfortable. I want to talk to William before he finishes loading the horses."

"I'll stretch my legs until the train arrives, if you don't mind, John. Plenty of time to look, once we're underway."

John hurried over to the stock car and engaged Curly Bill in animated conversation. Khan and Kai transferred the luggage and supplies, loading everything in the front door of the *Star of India*. Philpot joined with Rafe, and together they walked back and forth on the station platform. "Well, Sam, it won't be long now."

"No, Rafe. I'll hate to see you all go. The office seems a poor substitute for the adventures you and John'll be having."

"There's still time for you to go with us, Sam." Rafe mentally crossed his fingers that he would not be taken up on the offer.

The corpulent Philpot sighed. "No, Rafe. To each his own. I'm an office man, and I know it. I'll leave the field to those who are best suited for it. Well, I hear the whistle. The westbound train's at mile forty-eight hill. He'll be here in five minutes."

John must have heard the same sound, because he stepped out of the stock car and strolled up to Rafe and Philpot. "Here we go, Samuel. I'll keep you informed by telegraph as to our progress. I've told the stationmaster to stop the eastbound for you. It will arrive about four-thirty this afternoon. Madam Singh will take care of your needs up at the house until then."

The Pinkerton manager shook hands all around. "Farewell, and good hunting to all of you."

The confusion of the arriving train halted further conversation. The steam-spewing engine slowed and then screeched to a stop, with billowing plumes of steam, smoke, and sound marking its arrival. The dapper engineer swung down, conversed with the stationmaster, and, demonstrating a youthful agility that belied his age, scrambled back into his steel cocoon. He skillfully backed the train and its four passenger cars and one baggage car to the siding track, where his brakeman coupled John's stock car and private railroad car to the string. At the brakeman's wave, he pulled the entire train back out onto the main track, where he cut the hot morning air with the piercing shrill of his whistle.

John and Rafe watched the engineer's maneuvering with admiration.

"He makes it seem easy, doesn't he?"

Rafe nodded and commented, "I ain't seen many better, that's fer sure." He fell silent, awed by the mechanical marvel of the engine.

John pointed at the hissing engine, its wheels spinning on the tracks as the round, iron castings sought traction. "That's a Baldwin 4-4-0 engine. That means it has four lead wheels, four drive wheels, and no wheels under the cab. Look at the size of those rear drive wheels. Made by Krupp Iron Werks, over in Germany. I have hopes we can cast wheels like that in my plant before long. This engine will do thirty miles an hour, on level ground." He pointed up at the cab. "That engineer takes pride in his work." The engineer, his moustache a fiery red to match the mussed red locks curling out from under his long-billed cap, had painted his name under the opening from which he was looking down the track. "Shamus O'Brian," it proclaimed to the world.

O'Brian waved at John. "Well, Rafe, time to load up." With John leading the way, the two men climbed onto the rear platform of the private car. They stood there as the train slowly and then faster, building up speed, chugged down the tracks bound for Kansas City, the next leg of their route to the Rocky Mountains and Denver, the newest boomtown in America.

Wallace whistled in amazement as he stepped inside the private car. It was as lush as any parlor he had ever seen, even more elaborate than the waiting room in Fifi's whorehouse in New Orleans. Plush furniture, covered by red felt, was available for relaxing. The walls were paneled in polished mahogany and shined from the light streaming in through the beveled-glass windows. Twin chandeliers hung from the wood ceiling, crystal facets and silver threads twinkling in the sunlight. Beyond, Rafe saw Kai Singh already busy in a small kitchen. The maroon velvet curtains swayed to the rocking motion of the car as it was pulled down the tracks. Built-in shelves with leaded-glass doors displayed plates and glasses awaiting the next meal. A brightly designed Persian rug covered the floor, and a game table ready for cards or drinks stood against the far wall. Hanging on one wall was a rifle rack, with the weapons Rafe saw in use the day before already positioned for ready access.

Rafe swallowed. "I'm almost afraid to put my feet down, John. Everything is so . . . so damned fancy and fine. I ain't seen nothin' so fine as this since I last was in Madam Fifi's whorehouse, down in New Orleans." Rafe was suddenly effused with embarrassment. "I'm sorry, John. I didn't mean to imply this place is—Oh, hell. You know what I mean."

John laughed and dismissed Rafe's embarrassment. "One thing's for certain, Rafe. You'll spend a lot less riding with me than at Madam Fifi's. Not to worry—that's why I got it. To get us where we have to go, in the least amount of discomfort."

"Well, I'm as comfortable as can be, fer a fact. Where about's is Curly Bill? I thought he was a'goin' with us?"

"William is with the horses. He'll ride about the whole way with them, to make sure they're not in any distress. He'll join us for supper and to sleep. Unless we get a card game going, that is. That's about the only way I can get him up here with me."

"We'll sleep in here, too?" Rafe was doubly impressed.

"There are four bedrooms on the other side of the kitchen. And a small convenience, should you need it."

"You mean we can take a leak on the go?"

"As you're inclined. We dump it on the tracks, once we are away from any habitation."

John settled into a chair. "Have a seat and enjoy the scenery, Rafe. Kai is already making our lunch. Meanwhile, we embark on our adventure."

CHAPTER 5
HAZARDS OF THE TRIP

Rafe and John spent much of the trip to Kansas City huddled over the game table, where a large map was displayed, depicting Denver and the surrounding area. While they studied the map, they considered numerous options, seeking some logical way to open their investigation. Rafe's frustration was evident as he pointed out the spots where his shipments had been waylayed. The burly mining engineer put forth several different ideas, all involving massive shoot-outs with the robbers.

"What are you going to do? You got some idea?" Rafe quizzed, watching as John traced his finger along the route from the gold camps to Denver.

"I'm not sure, Rafe. I wanted to see if there was some pattern to the location of the robberies; something, anything that we might use to our advantage. I do see one thing that is very interesting."

"What's that?" Rafe furrowed his brow in concentration.

"Look at the locations." John pointed with his forefinger at the markings on the map. "Every one is before the Georgetown Road from Central City crosses Eight-Mile Gulch."

Rafe nodded his agreement. "So they are. But, it may be because the outlaws don't want to get too close to Denver before they make their play. Fer certain they wouldn't want to alert folks in Denver that a robbery was happenin'. They wouldn't want to ride into Denver smack up agin a waitin' posse of armed men, alerted by the commotion and out after them."

"Or," John mused, almost to himself, "the outlaws get off the trail before they get to Eight-Mile Gulch. Possibly, at the gulch itself."

"Well, we've tracked them as best we could and never saw any sign that they didn't ride back into Denver after a robbery. The trail is pretty rough, but I don't believe we woulda missed the sign of 'em leavin' it."

John leaned back in his chair. "True, however, I would think someone would see a group of men riding in from the west, if they did return to Denver after each robbery."

"We never found a soul what admitted to seein' 'em, even though we asked everone we could find."

John flipped his forefinger against his lower lip, his expression pensive. "I think I need to see this Georgetown Road as soon as possible, after we arrive in Denver."

Rafe nodded. "I'll take you myself, all the way to Georgetown and back. There's only one route fit to travel, and that's the Georgetown trail. You'll want to see our operation in Central City and Georgetown anyways, I suppose."

"Most certainly. And, I want to look at Eight-Mile Gulch. Why would the outlaws always strike before there? It's an important clue, I'm positive of it."

The miles clicked away under the rolling wheels, and, as the twilight fell in the west, the train rolled into Kansas City, Missouri. The busy city was perched at the edge of the great Midwestern plains, funneling people west and accepting the fruits of their labors for transport and sale in the East.

"We'll stop here for wood, water, and more passengers, before starting out across Kansas," John informed Wallace. "We may as well have a bite to eat at the Mulebach Hotel. It has the best food in town. Especially if Denver has a deficiency in good restaurants, as you apparently told Sam Philpot, who told me.

We don't want to pass up the opportunity for one last good meal."

"In all honesty," Wallace admitted, somewhat sheepishly, "there's several good places to eat in Denver. I didn't want that windbag to even consider goin' along with us."

John laughed heartily. "Rafe Wallace, I like your style more with every passing minute. Come on. Let's get some food. Maybe I can convince William to join us. He has a thousand stories to tell, and you are a first-time listener."

After a hurried but excellent supper at the famous restaurant, the three men returned to the station. Bill hurried to check on the horses while John and Rafe walked up and down the wooden walkway, stretching their legs and working off their dinner. Several burning oil lamps cast a yellow glow, spotlighting the crowd gathered at the train station. Those who were boarding the passenger coaches ahead of them mingled with those bidding farewell to the travelers.

Rafe commented as he and John slowly walked toward their car at the end of the string of passenger and freight cars, "Looks like a passel of folks are movin' west."

John's reply was interrupted by the clatter of a heavy wagon, guarded by a dozen armed men, pulling up to the baggage car, behind the wood car filled with cut logs for the long trip across Kansas. The three men observed with interest as two heavy metal trunks were passed from the back of the wagon to the baggage car before the heavy doors of the car were sealed and locked. The wagon and riders galloped off, leaving three men outside the barricaded baggage car. A slender man with a heavy beard seemed to be in charge. He was dressed in a business suit with a beaver-skin tophat and a cape lined with red silk, which marked his gentility. His rather hoarse voice was easily heard as he gave his final instructions. "One of you men ride in each car. I'll telegraph Denver that the money's loaded and ready to depart. I'll join you at each stop, right here in front of the baggage car. Keep your eyes open, and be ready for anything."

John winced. The general had spoken too loudly. Several people nearby had to have heard him.

"Yes, sir, General Dodge," one of the men replied as the three men purposefully strode to the passenger coaches, leaving the speaker alone on the walkway.

John immediately approached the man. "General Dodge. Do you remember me? I'm John Whyte, late colonel, 3rd US Calvary, the Michigan Brigade. We met at President Grant's inauguration last March. I thought it was you."

The bearded man studied John, his dark eyes boring into the face of the younger man. As the memory of their last meeting surfaced in his mind he smiled, creasing his face. "Ah, yes. The young Englishman who became a hero serving in our army, fightin' the Rebs. You were with Custer's Division, a bunch of fighting fools if there ever was such. What a surprise, meeting you here."

"I am en route to Denver. This is Mr. Rafe Wallace, of Guggenheim Mining Corporation. He is accompanying me in my private car. Are you bound for Denver, as well?"

"Mr. Wallace." Dodge's formal greeting was accompanied by a slight bow. "Is that your personal car at the end of the train, Colonel Whyte? I saw it as we rode up."

"Yes, sir. It is mine. It's one of the new Pullman private parlor cars. Would you care to see it?"

"Yes, as soon as I send a telegraph off to Denver. I've got a payroll to deliver to track's end, on the Topeka to Santa Fe spur out of Denver."

Wallace spoke up. "That's what they was loadin' on the baggage car, I reckon?"

Dodge nodded. "Better'n twenty-thousand dollars on this run. That's why I'm personally escorting the shipment. I'll get the telegraph operator to pass the word on to Denver and then rejoin you gentlemen. I am most anxious to see your car, Mr. Whyte. Pullman's cars are among the most outstanding examples of workmanship riding the iron rails."

As Dodge left, the telegraph operator motioned to a man, casually leaning against one of the roof columns, dragging on a smoldering cigarette and watching the activity at the station. He whispered softly, "Pst, pst. Harry, didya hear? The payroll's on the train. Get aboard, and keep your eyes on it. I'll telegraph Slim and the boys in Ft. Hays and tell him yur a-comin'. You'll be there tomorrow morning."

Harry nodded, flipped his half-smoked cigarette away, and casually sauntered to the last passenger car, climbing on behind a harried settler family settling down in their seats for the long ride ahead. The plan, as worked out by him and the telegraph operator, called for his gang to board at Ft. Hays and then hold up the train at the first water stop west of the town. One of the gang would be waiting there with their horses, and everyone would make tracks into Oklahoma Territory before any posse could find them. The outlaws had planned for the robbery ever since the telegraph operator had learned of the shipment of money for the work crews at track's end.

Wallace and John waited for Dodge to join them at the steps to John's car. He quizzed John. "Who is this General Dodge fellow, anyways? I don't think I ever heerd of him."

Dodge approached them, his rapid walk an indicator of the internal drive of the man, as John replied, "He's the chief engineer of the Union Pacific Railroad. He's the man who headed their construction effort to join the nation by rail. He was also Grant's chief military engineer during the war. Quite a fellow. You'll like him."

"Ya don't say." Wallace focused his gaze on the approaching Dodge. "The man who built the railroad to the west. What an achievement. Wait'll I tell the boys at the smelter about meetin' him and ridin' in your fancy car."

Dodge joined the three travelers. "Now, let me see that car of yours before the train departs. When did you get it?"

"It arrived a couple of weeks ago. Actually, this is my first trip in it." John led the others to the *Star of India,* and gave Dodge a guided tour of the plush interior. The crusty railroad builder was impressed and warmly praised the private car, to John's concealed delight.

"Well, I'd better get back to the mail car, so we can depart. This was a fine treat, Colonel Whyte. Thank you for showing me around."

"Please, General, call me John. And, as you are traveling to Denver, please consider yourself my guest. Rafe and I would deem it a distinct pleasure if you would join us for the trip. Wouldn't we, Rafe?"

"You betcha," Wallace rapidly seconded the motion.

"Why, thank you, John. Allow me to inform my guards in the mail car, and I'll instruct the train engineer to get underway." Dodge swung down from the rear platform and hurried forward.

He had no sooner returned than with the screech of its steam whistle, the train chugged out of Kansas City toward the vast prairies of Kansas and the great natural barrier of mountains beyond, called the Rockies by all who saw them.

At that same moment, a message was received by the leader of four desperate men, hardened outlaws all, containing the long-awaited code from Kansas City. His stained and broken teeth were revealed by his sinister smile. He crumpled the paper in his hand and then hurried back to the flea-bit hotel where his men awaited. The payroll was on the west-bound train, due in the next morning. The agreed-upon plan was immediately set in motion. Hec Berger, the oldest and most reliable of his men, took five saddled horses and led them west, out of town. Hec was to wait at the water tower, down the line twenty miles to the west of town with the getaway mounts. The hard-cases bought tickets to Goodland, the next stop beyond Ft. Hayes. They returned to the saloon to plan how they would spend the money that was soon to be exchanged for the seven-dollar tickets stuffed in their pockets. The evening passed swiftly and enjoyably for them. The money they lavishly spent convinced the bar girls to forgive their unshaven faces, dirty bodies, and foul breaths.

As for the men traveling in John's private car, the miles pushed on relentlessly through the darkness and the rolling plains of eastern Kansas. General Dodge enthralled John, Rafe, Khan, and Curly Bill with the description of the challenges in building the first trans-continental railroad, and what the future held for the industry. "Yes," Dodge remarked, as he drew on his cigar, "last year there were better than 40,000 miles of railroad track in this country, and in ten years, there'll be 60,000 miles. As the railroad industry grows, so will grow the country."

"Most amazing," John remarked. "That is remarkable growth."

"If I were you, John," Dodge offered, "I would get myself financially involved in the railroad industry. The money the Union Pacific is going to make is almost unlimited."

"Oh, I am," John modestly announced. "I am a principle in both the Gary Iron Works and in the American distributor for Krupp Iron, in Prussia. Why, the drive wheels on the Baldwin Engine pulling this train are from Krupp. I also have purchased a small amount of stock in the Missouri-Kansas-Texas Railroad. Upon your advice, I will purchase some Union Pacific and Topeka to Santa Fe stock."

"Excellent decision," Dodge answered, obviously impressed.

"Krupp makes the largest and best cast wheels in the business." His young host advanced up a notch on his list of friends to cultivate and retain.

The train swiftly puffed its way along the silver tracks, making an almost unheard of time of thirty miles an hour. A full moon offered a glimpse of the vast, rolling prairie slipping past. Slender stalks of range grass, four feet high, swayed like ocean waves to the rush of the passing train. A yawn or two from the men signaled it was time to retreat to the waiting comfort of the bedrooms. Curly Bill made a last check of the horses in the next car forward, and, before long, all was quiet in the *Star,* except for rattling snores and the muted sound of the rails clicking and clattering below the floorboard. A lone coyote watched the steel monster roll by, smoke pouring from the bell-shaped funnel at the front, followed by the lighted windows of the passenger coaches and then the darkened car at the rear. The noise and fury of the man-thing caused a shiver of dread in the solitary hunter, but, as swiftly as it came, it was gone.

Breakfast of ham and eggs greeted the early-morning risers. The men had all finished their morning grooming before the train pulled into Ft. Hays. It was 8:30 A.M. Union Pacific time and 9:30 on Dodge's pocket watch, which he kept on Chicago time. "Right on time," he announced in satisfaction, snapping the watch's cover shut with a loud *click!*

John, Rafe, and Khan Singh disembarked to stretch their legs, while Dodge hurried off to the mail car to check on his guards. A squad of blue-coated soldiers got off the train and marched away, under the stern eye of a grizzled sergeant, his beard streaked from the juice of a thousand chaws of tobacco. Several new passengers boarded the passenger cars, including four hard-cases, their guns tied low. John's attention was on the soldiers, and he failed to notice the hard-cases' arrival.

With an elongated and loud "All Aboard" from the conductor to speed them back, John and his friends returned to the *Star* for another day's journey on the shining rails. The train pulled away from the station and almost immediately was swallowed by the loneliness of the prairie. Briefly, John stood on the rear platform, gazing at the tall grasses covering the land flowing past, rippling and waving in the morning breeze. The undulating grasses, rhythmically moved by the wind, reminded him of his oceanic voyage to India, so many years before. The others were inside, engaged in a friendly card game, casually talking of women, gold, and trains, as the mood struck them.

The train seemed to be plowing a furrow through the endless, peaceful prairie, and the quiet beauty was as soothing to John as a fine wine in front of a warm fire.

John entered the car and sat by a window, engrossed in the shadow of the train as it raced across the waving grassland. His reverie was broken by the outline of two men, running atop the last passenger car. John watched in fascination as the shadows of the two men split up, one back toward the *Star,* and one toward the engine. John's mind jerked to attention. Something was wrong. He was certain he saw a gun in the hand of the shadow streaking across the waving prairie grass.

"Gentlemen," he announced, with enough urgency in his voice to halt the game and discussion. "listen to me. A man is coming this way, a gun in his hand. Khan, stand quietly in the corner there. Do nothing until I say your name, then make your move. Everyone else, act natural, but be ready."

By now the shadow was directly overhead, and its footsteps could be faintly heard above the noise of the wheels. The men followed the sound of the footsteps as they watched tensely through the glass of the rear door. A long-legged man in soiled whipcord pants athletically swung on to the platform. The stranger threw the door open and stepped inside, six-gun in hand and a kerchief over his lower face.

"Don't no one move, or I'll fill their gut with lead. Everybody stay where ya are." He pointed his revolver at John, who was closest to him. "Anyone else on this here fancy car?"

John feigned consummate terror. Stuttering, he answered, "P-P-Please, sir, don't hurt us. We'll do as you say. There's only my wife, taking her bath. 'Dear, come out here immediately, do you hear?' "

The outlaw could not resist. He eagerly stared over John's shoulder toward the front of the car, hoping to see a naked woman walk out of the bathroom. It was what John was waiting for. "Khan," he whispered to the Sikh standing in the corner behind the opened door.

A big knife buried itself to the handle in the outlaw's back, the sharp point streaked with blood protruding through the front of a grimy vest. With a gasp of surprise and pain, the dying outlaw gingerly touched the point of the knife with a finger, and then fell into John's arms, the gun dropping harmlessly on the rug. John laid the outlaw down and questioned him.

"How many of you? What are you after?"

The dying outlaw, stunned by the attack and feeling his life ebbing away, gasped the answer involuntarily, "The payroll."

Rafe and Dodge stood transfixed, shocked into immobility by the sudden savageness that invaded the security of their car. Dodge was the first to speak. "By God, they're after the railroad money."

John nodded and stood over the outlaw, whose glazed eyes proclaimed his imminent fate. "This one is done for. The others are probably at the baggage car right now. I wonder what their escape plan is?"

As if in answer, the abrupt slowing of the train caused them to stagger. They rushed to the windows. Dodge shouted the answer to John's question. "A water tower ahead and a man with one, two, four, five extra horses. The scoundrels plan to ride away after they rob the train."

John moved to the gun cabinet and unlocked the glassed door. He handed one Winchester rifle to Khan and took the other. He gave pistols to Rafe and Dodge, putting his .44 in his belt.

"Khan," he directed, "you and I will exit to the far side of the train. We'll sneak as close to the mail car as we can. As soon as the outlaws show themselves, we'll have the drop on them. Rafe, you and William make your way forward through the passenger car of the train. As soon as you hear my call to the robbers, come running. If they try anything, we'll have them in a crossfire. General Dodge, you want in on this?"

"Damn tootin'," the dark-bearded engineer proclaimed. "How dare they try and hold up my payroll." His eyes flashed in angry anticipation. "I'll accompany you two and try to reach the engine. One of the outlaws must be there, holding a gun on the engineer. I'll wait for your signal to make my move."

The men each took a deep breath and split up, Rafe rushing out the front door, followed by Curly Bill. John, Khan, and Dodge exited the back door and jumped off the slowing train. As they ran toward the mail car, they could see the broken glass of the rear door. The outlaws had obviously broken it and entered the mail car from the passenger coach. John and Khan climbed up the ladder to the roof of the nearest car, flattening themselves from the view of the outlaws on the other side, busily trying to wrestle the heavy trunks out of the open side door of the mail car. Dodge hurried on toward the steaming and hissing engine.

John eased himself toward the opposite side of the roof. He saw one man standing beside the water tower, holding the reins of the horses and watching the action at the mail car. The outlaws below him were cursing as they struggled with the money containers. Khan wiggled away a bit from John and also peered over the rounded roof, waiting for John's signal.

John glanced back, but could not see Rafe or Curly Bill. He had to assume they were ready. Nodding at Khan, he raised up until he could see two men below, pulling the heavy trunks toward the horses. Another man was holding a gun on the guards inside the mail car, covering the first two. The horse guard caught the movement out of the corner of his eye, shouting as he tried to shift his aim.

"Hey, someone's on the roof!"

Khan's shot drilled the gunman center through the chest, and John shouted down at the others. "Federal marshal. Hands up!"

He snapped a hasty shot at an outlaw who darted out of the car and ran toward the wooden leg of the water tower, pulling a gun on the run. As the outlaw peeked around the side of the support, John snapped another shot, nicking the wooden beam and causing the man to duck back, before returning his attention to the two outlaws below. They were caught out in the open, their hands full of trunk and no chance to go for their guns. Both had their hands up, glaring up at him. With Khan covering them with his rifle, John shifted his attention back to the man behind the water tower leg.

It was too late. As John realized the gunman had him in his sights, a loud report from the far side of the tower dropped the hiding outlaw in the dust. Curly Bill had arrived. At that moment, another shot came from the front, and Dodge shouted his name.

"John, got my man. Everything all right back there?"

While Rafe and Curly Bill kept the two surviving outlaws covered, John and Khan climbed down. Dodge came up, leading a glum outlaw, one hand pressed against a bloodstained shoulder.

With a satisfied grin on his whiskered face and a smoking six-gun in his hand he crowed, "We got 'em all, didn't we? Good. The sheriff in Goodland can take these jaspers off our hands. Let me see how my guards are." He clambered aboard the mail car, ordering the men inside to jump out and return the money containers to the car. "Hurry up, or we'll be so delayed the engineer won't be able to make up the time, and we'll be late into Goodland."

John shook Curly Bill's hand. "Thank you, William. You saved my life. That scurvy bastard had me dead in his sights."

"Hell, Boss, twarn't nothin'. I was afraid you'd have all the fun afore I got here. Two down and two still a'kickin'. What'd ya wanna do with 'em?"

"Three down. There is one more in the *Star*, probably bleeding all over my good carpet. Tie these three up and put them and their horses in the stock car. General Dodge says we can drop them off in the next town down the line."

Curly Bill and Rafe marched the three surviving outlaws toward their first day of many to come in unhappy confinement, leading the six horses, three of them burdened with already stiffening bodies.

CHAPTER 6
DENVER

The train wheezed and squealed to a stop in front of the Denver station, located at the far northern edge of the ever-expanding city. The shiny, black engine spewed clouds of billowing steam and sighs of belched smoke as if impatiently waiting for the next leg of the trip. John stood on the rear platform of his private car, curiously looking over the city, absorbing his first impression of the town. Denver was actually twin towns, Denver and Auraria, separated by the muddy expanse of Cherry Creek but joined by a large, wooden bridge at Main Street. Both towns were as raw and untamed as any boom towns, but Auraria was especially so.

Clapboard houses rose up as fast as overworked carpenters could build them. New stores and public buildings bordered one dirt street after another. Tents and crude dugouts sufficed when the owner was unable to afford anything better. People crowded the wooden sidewalks, where available, hurrying to their destination or aimlessly strolling. Numerous saloons and bawdy houses welcomed a steady stream of customers, while drink-sodden men stumbled out, to recover from the whiskey and to earn more money to spend the following night.

Wallace joined John at the rear platform and shared the view. "You'll find this town growing faster than any place in the country. John, the mountains are filled with more gold and silver than ever was mined before, and it'll all pass through Denver on its way to the mints back east. Yes, sir, Denver will

51

be a real city someday, the gateway to the Rockies. Hell, it wouldn't surprise me if forty or fifty thousand people lived here someday."

"Sounds impressive, Rafe. But from what I can see, it looks like the place has a long way to go before that ever happens."

"Don't you worry, John. It's a'gonna, mark my word; Denver's gonna boom. That is, if the outlaws don't keep it from happenin'."

John swept his eyes over the bustling town. "We'll see what can be done about that, my friend. Yes, indeed. Would you show us around as soon as I get the *Star* situated for our stay?"

They bid their farewells to General Dodge, who departed with his payroll, after effusively thanking everyone for their help in defending the payroll from the robbers.

John and Rafe remained on the rear platform while John's car was maneuvered to a location at the far end of the yards, next to a stock barn and corral and right beside a muddy street that led straight into the heart of Denver. Kai Singh helped Curly Bill herd the horses into the rented corral, and then the younger Singh combed and watered the weary animals. Confident the horses were receiving proper care, the Texas wrangler ambled over to join John and Rafe at the rear of the *Star.*

After receiving Bill's report on the care of the horses, John spoke. "Now we're ready, Rafe. Why don't you take the lead and show us this wonderful town of yours?"

"Be my pleasure, John. Let's walk. My legs could use the stretchin'." Only Curly Bill offering a slight objection. "I shore don't see why we need to walk. That's why horses was born, to save the wear and tear on our feets."

"Now, William," John teased, "don't tell me you've never walked to a place or two in your time."

"Not unless I couldn't help it, that's fer certain."

Rafe and John led off, the still-complaining Curly Bill falling in behind with the largest of them all, Khan Singh, bringing up the rear. Rafe pointed with his thick finger. "We'll mosey on down Market Street and then take the bridge at Main Street over to Auraria. If we want to see the heart of Denver, that's the best way to go." He described the various local sights as the four men walked from the rail yard to the heart of Denver.

"Here we are," Rafe exclaimed. "The bridge over Cherry Creek. This here is the center of town."

The traffic-filled bridge crossed over the geographical divider between the relatively strait-laced Denver and the more raw and raucous Auraria. The street to the north of the creek was lined with shops, businesses, and public offices, including several banks. South of the bridge, the same street burst with activity where numerous saloons and bawdy houses ran wideopen, around the clock. Drinking, gambling, whoring, and general rowdiness seemed to be the order of business south of Cherry Creek. John was fascinated by the chaos of a boom town. Men of all types were going from one bar to the next, or to and from their jobs. Wagons passed each other on the muddy streets, carrying everything from foodstuffs to mining equipment to greasy men with wagons full of raw, smelly buffalo hides.

"Let's stop off fer a drink," Curly Bill proposed. "All this walkin' has plumb worked up a fierce thirst in my throat."

John smiled. It was vintage Curly Bill. "Pick a place, William. I'll stand all of us to a libation or two. Then, we'll have to get back to the *Star,* to make plans for tomorrow."

"Well, this place here is as good as any, I reckon," Curly Bill announced, turning into the flapping, bat-wing doors of the Criterion Bar and Gambling House. With a smile, John held the door open for Rafe and Khan Singh and followed them into the dim, smoke-filled interior. Several tables of card players eyed the strange foursome's stroll to the cherrywood bar, elbowing their way up to the brass rail front. "Beer and whiskey all around," Curly Bill ordered.

The rotund bartender, bald as Curly Bill, with a pocked face from childhood smallpox and a nose broken more than once, wiped his hands on a dirty, white apron tied around his thick waist. He swiftly set up the glasses and poured the foaming brew from a tapped barrel. The whiskey bottle had no label on it and was well worn, as if the current contents were not the first it ever contained. "I would hate to ask where this liquor comes from." John chuckled as he sipped from the glass of foam-topped beer. "I suspect it didn't travel far to reach the bar here."

Wallace laughed. "Cheaper to make the stuff here and save the expense of shippin' from Kentucky. These mountain goats drink it up so fast they don't taste it anyways."

"Well, if you don't mind, I'll wait until I get back to the *Star* to partake of any more. I've too much respect for my liver to strain this foul-tasting bilge water through it."

"Tastes plumb fine to me." Curly Bill smacked his lips as he put his empty glass on the scarred wood of the bar.

Khan Singh waited for the others to take their drink before he lifted his beer glass to his mouth. His hand never made it. A work-scarred hand, beefy and hard as the mountain rock it dug through, and just as dirty, grasped Khan's wrist in a vise-like grip. A raspy voice, deep and rough, still blurred with the drawl of the deep south, cut through the babble of the bar, causing instant silence. "Afore ya drink that beer, fella, you'd best tell me jus' what sort of people you might be."

Before Khan could answer, John put his hand on Khan's arm and turned to the man. He was a tall, muscular dirt miner, his boots still wet with the mud of the street and his face scarred from more than one bare-knuckle battle. A wild thatch of greasy hair covered ears that stuck out like clapboards in a west wind.

"Why should you care, my good man?"

The intoxicated miner's answer was little more than a sneer. " 'Cause I don't drink with niggers, injuns, or wops. That's why. And, Englishmen, fer that matter. I'm an Irish bull from Dublin, fought with Gennel' Longstreet's First Corps and never surrendered."

"Well, my Irish cousin, you have made a painful mistake today, I'm sorry to say. The man whom you have insulted is retired Sergeant Major Khan Singh of the United States Cavalry. He is a Sikh warrior from India, far from here or Ireland. He is as mild-mannered a gentleman as you will ever have the pleasure of meeting, yet skilled beyond belief in the arts of self defense." John smiled at the scowling miner. "I earnestly suggest you apologize to him and accept our offer of a drink, before I give you to him."

The half-drunk miner blinked his eyes suspiciously. The fancy talk had confused him, yet he was not about to back down, especially now that everyone in the bar was watching the interplay, eagerly anticipating the coming fight. "I ain't about to apologize to no darkie, and this fella with the funny hat is a darkie, whether he's a nigger or not. So what do you want to do about it, Englishman?" He smiled nastily, showing stained, broken teeth.

John's face tightened, and he nodded in resignation. "Khan Singh, our grimy friend here seeks a lesson in manners. Would you be so kind as to instruct him?"

"Of course, Sahib." Khan Singh moved away from the bar, his hands held loosely at his side. The only indication of his readiness was the precise way he balanced himself on his toes.

The burly miner launched a decidedly wicked roundhouse right, which, if it had landed, would have broken Khan's jaw. Only, to the miner's surprise, Khan was not there. The agile Sikh danced away from the wild rush and countered with a blow of his own. It would have put a normal man down, but it only jarred the drunken miner and stopped him for an instant.

That was long enough. Khan spun the man around and, using his hip for leverage, threw the miner heavily to the sawdust-covered floor. The room shook with the impact, and the hefty miner groaned in pain. Easily, Khan pulled the fallen man to his feet, and his hands chopped down, one on either side of the stunned miner's neck. The man dropped like a falling tree in the forest, crashing face first onto the floor, unconscious.

Another man, a friend of the downed Irishman, tried to rush Khan from the rear, but John grabbed his arm and spun him around, his fist impacting the man's jaw as he spun into the blow. The impetuous friend joined his friend on the floor. Again, the bar was silent, the patrons awestruck at the fierce reaction by the two strangers. Neither had been touched, and yet Mick O'Shay and his buddy, the toughest men in the territory, now lay sleeping in the sawdust, as whipped as any of their previous victims.

John confidently grinned at the silent throng. "Gentlemen, I appreciate a man who admits when he has made a mistake, and this gent lying here understands he has made a beauty. I would deem it a pleasure if you would allow my friend Khan Singh and me to buy a round of drinks for everyone in the house."

The unconscious Mick O'Shay was nearly trampled in the rush of thirsty men to the bar. The crowd jostled to speak to John, curious to find out more about the strangers with the fists of iron. "Thanks fer the drink, mister. That was some fight. Nobody's ever bested Mick before. Your friend here moves faster than quicksilver. What was that thing he done with his hands? Who'd you say you boys were?"

The questions came faster than John could answer them. John knew the story of the fight would soon spread over the town, and Khan Singh would not be troubled again because of his dark skin and foreign appearance by ordinary ne'er-do-wells looking for someone to bedevil.

Finishing their beers, John led the others out of the bar, leaving the crowd to retell the story to each other again and again. They crossed the bridge to Denver, walking north on the wooden sidewalk of Front Street. Shops, restaurants, retail stores, and banks lined the wooden walkway, compared to the saloons and brothels lining Auraria's walkway.

Denver pedestrians were better dressed and groomed. They paid scant attention to John and his party, although some cast a sideways second glance at Khan Singh as they entered and exited the shops and businesses. Few of the Denver citizens approached the bridge. All stayed to the north of Cherry Creek. Curly Bill peered through the fly-speckled window of a saddle shop, talking with Khan Singh about the wares shown therein. John asked Wallace, "Rafe, who stands to profit the most from men with gold in their pockets?"

"Why, the gambling houses and whorehouses, I reckon."

"And what respectable citizen?"

"I don't rightly know. Shopkeepers?"

John shook his head. "No, I don't think so. Who would be more likely to supply the needs of someone with lots of money. Whores? Gamblers? Land speculators? Anyone whose appetite for riches would drive him to get it any way he could, legal or not."

John stopped in front of the office of a land speculator. A clerk stood at the front counter, working on a plat map. In an office off the main room, another man was reading some papers, oblivious to the human traffic flowing past his window.

"Yes, indeed," John mused as they continued their walk away from the bridge. "Two different classes of citizen, gambler and whore, businessman and land speculator. Yet both might have answers to questions. Both might have answers."

Across the street, the city sheriff's office was located at the corner. "Rafe, we should stop off and see the sheriff. Please don't tell him what my role is here. Introduce me as an investor of Guggenheim's."

Their meeting with Sheriff Rance Gilbert was short and unproductive. The old lawman was still hard enough to manage a boomtown but had passed the prime of his life, years earlier. When John questioned the sheriff's response to the gold robberies, the hard-bitten Gilbert brushed his silver-streaked moustache and shook his head. "It's all I can do to keep the lid on here in Denver. My authority ends at Graveyard Hill, this side of Apex Pass, and that's that. They come into Denver, and I'll deal myself in, but till then, sorry, but I got other worries."

"You have my sympathies, Sheriff, but if we don't stop these gold robberies, the whole town might collapse around you." John stood, his point made. "Gentlemen, we may as well leave the sheriff to his duties. Thank you again, Sheriff Gilbert, for your time."

"Like I said, Mr. Whyte. If they come to Denver, I'll deal myself in. Not before." Gilbert had felt the sting in John's rebuke.

They casually walked back to the *Star,* satisfied with their first reconnaissance of the town. Kai had a hot meal and cool drinks waiting. The rest of the evening focused on discussing their plans and putting together the necessary gear for the horseback trip to the diggings, across the black ridge of the mountains standing stark against the sunset-painted western sky.

"Shall I send a rider out to Central City, tellin' 'em we'll be a-comin' out on an inspection trip tomorrow?" Rafe quizzed John.

"No, that won't be necessary. I would rather we dropped in unannounced and see what we find there." John finished packing his kit, gathering his blankets into a tight roll before stuffing it into the horse pack. He grinned at Khan Singh. "Tomorrow, we are taking a trip into the high country. The mountains remind me of those at the Kiber Pass. Remember, old friend, the day the sultan's men ambushed us?"

The Sikh warrior absently rubbed his left thigh. "The ache in my leg from that day never allows me to forget, Sahib."

CHAPTER 7
TRIP TO THE DIGGINGS

Rafe Wallace arrived at the *Star* as the morning sun painted a golden patina on the snow-covered peaks of the high Rockies behind Denver. John and his comrades were dressed and ready for the coming journey. They had already finished Kai's breakfast issue of ham, eggs, and fried potatoes. Curly Bill had three horses saddled and a heavily loaded pack on an extra horse to carry the excess gear. John wore his faded, army-blue cavalry pants, with a darker strip down the leg seams where his gold officer's stripe had once been sewn. He had on well-worn riding boots, a wide-brimmed hat, and a faded denim shirt tucked into his cavalry pants. He tied a dark-blue kerchief around his neck and buckled on a polished leather gun belt holding twenty cartridges and a holster, carrying one of the new Russian .44 pistols.

Khan was also in comfortable, old pants from his army days. The turban wrapped around his covered hair was a deep ruby red. Curly Bill was in his customary stovepipe leather chaps, with a newly purchased plaid shirt and faded yellow kerchief. His old Confederate cavalry hat sat squarely on his bald noggin, and twin Colt .44's were cinched around his slim hips. Rajah bounded past, excited by the activity and anxious to be going somewhere after the long journey in the stock car.

Taking his leave of Kai, with orders to watch the *Star* and to replenish the food stocks from the many general stores in the city, John climbed upon his favorite horse, a black Morgan with a white blaze on his nose that gave him his name. Wallace led the way out of town on the old Georgetown Road, up the long, sloping climb to Apex Pass, the first pass west of Denver, where Sheriff Gilbert said his responsibility ended.

As the four men climbed up the slope, the terrain became rougher. The red sandstone bluffs forced several deviations from a straight path, and the pace was slow. Massive boulders erupted from the sandy soil, giving the appearance of discord among the gods of creation. Above them, beyond the approaching summit, the darker mass of the high mountains beckoned them, as if daring them to tred upon them. Dark, impenetrable, and forbidding, the mountains rose up before them, dwarfing the riders in their immensity.

"This certainly looks like a twin to the Kiber Pass, doesn't it, old friend?" John wiped the sweat from his forehead.

"Aye, Sahib," the old Sikh warrior answered. "But the heat is not as oppressive, I think."

"You boys oughtta be in west Texas in the summer, iffen you wanna talk about heat," Curly Bill threw in his opinion.

The road to Georgetown was hardly a road compared to what John was used to in the East. As they penetrated into the black basalt and granite stone of the high mountains, the road became a twisting horse trail, diminishing to something more like a goat's path. The so-called road climbed again and then dropped precipitously into a deep valley framed within sharp rocks, forged by a swift flowing stream fed from a mist-shrouded falls tumbling from fifty feet above them. Only Rajah seemed content to be on the dangerous road. He darted to and fro, sniffing and thoroughly enjoying the new smells and adventures as only a frisky dog could.

"This is Guy Gulch, and that there is Clear Creek Falls," Rafe announced as they clattered over a wooden bridge spanning the raging waters below. "This here is the spot I was tellin' you about. Never been a robbery any closer to Denver than over the rise there, Eight-Mile Gulch." He pointed up the road to another low pass through the hills ahead.

"You mean we've only come eight miles?" Curly Bill complained. "It's taken us damn near till noon."

"No need to hurry in these here mountains," Rafe admonished. "We'll wear out the horses, ridin' too hard in these mountains. Going down hill, it gets a mite better." He looked up at the sun, high overhead in the azure sky. "It's close enough to noon to eat. We may as well take advantage of the good water and eat here. It's a bit dryer from here to Central City. We'll make it by tomorrow night, if we step it out a bit after vittles and don't stop till the sun sets tonight."

"The stars sure seem bright up here," Curly Bill observed that evening as they lay on their blankets around their sputtering campfire, after finishing the evening meal. Everyone was silent, relaxing from the day's hard riding. "I wonder why that is?"

John considered explaining the mysteries of the atmosphere to the unlettered Texan. He saw no reason to confuse the happy-go-lucky Texas cowboy and settled for an easier explanation. "I suppose we're that much closer to them, my Texican friend."

"Well, fer certain, we're a might closer. I can barely catch my breath, we're up so high. Why did I ever leave the warm bosom of Texas?"

"You're seeing things most Texas folks will never see," Rafe chimed in. "Count yourself lucky."

"Hell, we got mountains this high in Texas," Bill retorted. "It's jus' that they're laid out flat, like the rest of the country." He rolled over and spoke to Khan, lying on his back, his strong hands cupped behind his head, the turban tightly wrapped about it. "How does this compare to your neck-o-the-woods, Khan Singh?"

"America is now my 'neck of the woods,' as you put it, Sahib William. However, it does remind me of the land of my youth, and departed family and friends, now at honored rest for eternity."

"Yep. I share the feeling." Bill tossed a stick into the flames of their small campfire, sending a shower of fiery sparks into the night air. "Well, I guess I'd better check the horses one last time afore we go to sleep. Boss, we gonna stand guard tonight?"

John deferred to Rafe. "How about it, Rafe? We need to have a man awake, or is that unnecessary?"

Rafe settled into his bedroll. "I don't see no need, John. We ain't in no danger from Injuns, and the outlaws haven't started picking on individual travelers yet. 'Cides, we got your dog, and he should alert us iffen anyone comes pokin' around." Wallace pulled his blanket up around his shoulders. "I vote no, but it's your call, John."

John petted Rajah, stroking the sleek fur of the Great Dane, and made his decision. "All right. We'll skip the guard duty for the time being. Rajah, it's up to you. Let us know if someone comes calling."

Yawning, Curly Bill moved off, headed to the picket line where the horses were tied for one final check before calling it a night. The others were already asleep when he returned, and he wasted no time in joining them.

The next morning, they crossed a deep slash between twin mountain peaks that Rafe called Crescent Pass. As they rode down the winding, narrow trail on the west side, Wallace spoke. "This is where they hit us the last time, John. Right about there." He pointed up above the trail, to the brush and rock-strewn hillside. "They was waitin' fer us, and if they had held their fire a minute more, I don't see how any of us would have survived. As it was, I lost five good men. Damn, but it hurt to tell their families that they was gone."

John climbed off Blaze and studied the area. "It is a good location for an ambush, clearly enough. What happened after the outlaws shot up your column?"

Rafe pointed above them. "We abandoned the pack mules and gold and retreated down to the trees there." He pointed back down the trail. "They got on their horses and came off that goat trail up yonder, see it?" He cocked his head toward the steep bluff. "Then they grabbed the mules and rode over the pass behind us and got clean away. We did hit one of their horses though. It dropped up there, at the top of the rise. The outlaws stopped, pulled off the saddle, and then rode off, laughin'. By the time we got untangled and back on the trail, there was no chance of catchin' 'em."

Wallace dismounted. "At the first shot, we scattered to the far side of the trail and returned fire as best we could. There was so much smoke and confusion, we didn't do them any damage, I guess. We had horses, mules, and men down all around us, so we was too rattled to do some real shootin'. I had to order the retreat; we was losin' too many men."

John listened to the story while his eyes combed the ground, looking for evidence of any kind. "Where's the dead horse now?"

"We pushed it off the trail, up there." Wallace walked back, toward the top of the pass, John and Khan beside him leading their tired horses by the reins. "There's what's left of it, down there. You can see the bones, by that large rock there. See 'em?"

John looked over the sheer drop to the bottom of the steep mountain. The remains of the dead horse were scattered about the rocky ground, 150 feet below. The wild carrion eaters had consumed most of the animal, leaving some hide and bones scattered among the rocks. John kicked a small pebble over the side and watched it fall to the base of the steep cliff. "Khan Singh, on the way back I think we should go down and take a look at the remains. Rafe, you can get us some rope, can't you?"

"Sure can, John. But you ain't thinkin' about climbing down there, are you?"

"Certainly. Khan Singh taught me how to climb in the mountains many years ago. It's not hard, with the right equipment."

"By God, I wouldn't want to go down that drop, fer nobody." Rafe gulped as he looked over the edge of the cliff.

"Now I want to see where the outlaws waited for your column. Would you show me the exact location?"

Following Rafe, John and Khan Singh scrambled up the steep side of the hill back at the ambush site, Rajah bounding up ahead of them. They came to a flattened area about thirty yards above the trail. Animals walking along the side of the hill had used the area to rest and sleep for countless years. The outlaws had built stone barricades to cover themselves from the fire of Rafe's men. It was plain to see how they had deployed, and where they had waited for the column to arrive on the trail below them. John's view of Curly Bill patiently holding the horses below was unobstructed. Rajah raced about, sniffing every outlaw's location.

"This is where they were, fer certain," Rafe declared. "You can see their fightin' positions. Then they rode down, following this here game trail, until they got back on the main road."

John and Khan Singh inspected the different fighting positions, examining the spent cartridges, smoked cigars, and chewed twigs left by the outlaws. "Seems like a dozen or so men hit you, Rafe." John tossed a couple of empty brass cartridges in the air. "They were well armed. Henry's or Spencers; even found some Sharp's .52 caliber shells from a buffalo gun. These fellows meant business."

"Damned right," Rafe agreed, shaking his head. "Iffen we hadn't been at a spot in the trail where we could git off the road and into cover, they woulda kilt us all. As it was, they did plenty of damage."

"I see no blood, Sahib," Khan Singh announced. "None of the outlaws were badly injured, it appears."

"I didn't think we did much to hurt 'em," Rafe admitted. "We was too busy dodging their bullets."

The three men continued to poke around, but there was nothing further to be learned from the effort. John pocketed some of the spent cartridges and led the way back down the hill. "We may as well press on. There's no more to be gained here. Come on, Rajah."

They continued on their way to the first stop in their trip, Central City. For a time, the men rode in silence as they digested the carnage of the gun battle that had occurred on the lonely trail. Rajah loped ahead, enjoying his freedom. Curly Bill finally broke the silence as he proceeded to tell Rafe an outrageous story of the time he drove six horses to New Orleans for the Confederate army, only to find the Yankees had taken the city and how he had then sold the horses to the Union army. After spending all his profit in a bawdy house, he had stolen the horses back and returned to his Texas home, chased the entire way by irate Union soldiers.

Curly Bill's infectious good humor soon had Rafe and John laughing, and even the normally taciturn Khan Singh was smiling at the irrepressible Texan. Their mood lightened, and the time seemed to pass quickly. Now, the ride was mostly down hill, and their pace increased. They were deep into the high Rockies, with tall pinnacles of foreboding rock all around them. The leafy aspen trees were replaced by pine and mountain juniper. Marmots and small ground squirrels scurried about, and Rajah ran himself ragged chasing one after the other. By the time Central City came into view in a steep valley between two mountains, the frisky Great Dane was content to trot, panting from his exertions, beside Blaze and his master.

The raw scab of a town, haphazardly thrown up around a swift-flowing creek named after an early prospector, Moss Fraser, was bunched along either side of the dirty water. The main street followed the twisting creek bed for several hundred feet up the valley, while the width of the town was small, hemmed in by the sheer sides of the mountains to either side. Great expanses of upthrust rock framed both sides of the narrow valley and restricted what little living space there was until it felt claustrophobic. The few permanent structures, built of green, untreated lumber, were hardly worthy of the name, and for most of the 2,000 or more prospectors, tents and earthen dugouts were the rule.

The banks of Frasier Creek were alive with men, heads down, busy digging and panning, seeking the elusive golden dust of their dreams. Travelers were passing through the town, en route up the valley into the interior of the country, away from the mass of prospectors around the town itself. Dark thunderclouds rolling over the mountain peaks to the west foretold of a coming rain. Rafe spurred his horse on down the rocky path toward the town.

"There she be, gentlemen," Rafe announced. "Central City. We're getting enough gold outta the ground around here to pave the streets of Denver, if I could only get it safely there from the diggin's."

CHAPTER 8
CENTRAL CITY

The rainstorm caught the four men before they could complete the ride down the steep, winding trail into the haphazard jumble of buildings and tents that was Central City. Cold, slashing sheets of rain fell intensely, the big drops at first sending up puffs of dust as they struck the dry ground, then blending with the dirt to form a slimy slurry of cloying mud. The drops pounded in layered ferocity, shading the mountains beyond the town in a soft, silvery blur. As one drenching passed over, a second followed close behind, each rain squall more cold and miserable than its predecessor.

The riders struggled to get into their oilskins but found to their discomfort that the wind and rain made their effort a waste of time. The wind gusts whipped the slickers up around their thighs, while rain ran in chilled rivulets down their necks, soaking their shirts within minutes.

The drenched, clay infused soil soon became a thick, glutinous muck, slippery and dangerous for their horses to walk on as they gradually descended the final mile to the town. The horses' hoofs made a sucking *plop!* with every step. The gluey mess splashed over the legs and bellies of the animals, as well as the boots and lower pant legs of their riders. Rajah slunk along beside John, unhappy at the fate that had befallen him, his boundless energy sapped by the mud and gloom of the storm.

To John's amazement, he saw that only a few of the men so desperately scrabbling at the earth had taken cover from the cold rain. Most of the prospectors kept on digging or panning, oblivious to the chilling rain. He mentioned the phenomenon to Rafe.

"Yep, you're kerrect, John. As long as these men can see to work, almost nothin'll stop 'em. Some even rig up lamps and work on after dark, although most are so danged beat by sundown that it's all they can do to eat and wander down to the nearest saloon for a nightcap afore hittin' the sack. They'll be back at their diggin's afore full sunrise tomorrow."

Rafe led the wet, saddle-weary men into the heart of the gold camp as night settled over the valley. "There's the best place in town to stay, the Moss Fraser Hotel," he announced, pointing to a ramshackled building of unpainted green wood across the street. They turned over their tired and muddy horses to a one-armed, grizzled oldtimer, who was swamping out the only stable in town, with instructions to clean and feed the animals well. John tied Rajah to one of the six-inch-thick stall supports and ordered a healthy portion of scrap buffalo meat for him from the agreeable livery hand. Then, soaked and chilled, they tromped through the dank mud of the main street to the bright interior of the Fraser Hotel lobby.

John secured rooms for the four of them. The green wood of the building was already splitting as it dried, allowing the incessant sounds from the street to enter. The worn chairs available for the clients had seen better days, years earlier. The chandelier hanging from the ceiling was filthy with the dust the floated everywhere. The tired men parted to clean up. "I'll treat the supper," Rafe offered as they climbed the bare wooden stairs to the third-floor rooms. "Meet you all in an hour at the front desk. There's one nice cafe in town, up to the end of Main Street. I know the two ladies that run it. We'll get a good, hot meal in our bellies and then see what's up."

"Sounds good to me," Curly Bill grumbled. "My belly's been

rubbin' my backbone all day long as it is."

John held Rafe back, as the other two men entered their rooms. "Will we have any trouble with Khan Singh and the miners?" he softly inquired.

Rafe shook his head. "I don't reckon so, John. The miners won't let darkies or Injuns work claims here-about, but with the iron you boys are a-carryin', I don't figure anyone'll say much. Especially if they see you ain't interested in settin' up a claim and doin' any gold mining."

The rain had ended as they trooped to Rafe's café. It was all he promised. The two spinster women who ran it treated him, John, and the others like visiting royalty. Rafe even mentioned it to John, laughing at the way the two old women would have flustered up if they had known that John did have royal blood in his veins.

"I think it's best if you introduce me as a stockholder from your headquarters, to allay any suspicion as to the real reason for my visit here, Rafe."

After the meal and a generous portion of dried apple pie and hot coffee, the four men stepped outside of the cafe, pausing to light up the complimentary cheroots picked from the humidor by the cash register.

John looked over the busy street. A rivulet surged down the middle of the muddy road, while miners slogged back and forth across the street, disregarding the muddy expanse. There were at least five saloons going full blast, and several ladies of the night stood by the back doors, catching their breath between customers, or exposing their wares to passers-by. The discordant sounds of pianos competing for attention were an irritant to his ear. The rushing water of Fraser Creek could be heard above all else, and the smell of sewage offended his nostrils.

"Seems like there's an extremely active night life here, Rafe. I thought these prospectors would be so worn out from their

day's work that they would be dead asleep." Several men staggered from one saloon exit to the nearest entrance of another.

"Some are," Rafe agreed. "There's always some who want to
whoop it up till dawn, no matter how hard they work. And
that's all there is to do here-abouts. Usually, even the most
dedicated gold seeker will drink and gamble a bit afore hittin'
the hay. There's also some riff-raff who've drifted up here,
lookin' for somethin', anything they can git away with. They
hang around awhile, drink, whore, steal, and gamble until
they're cleaned out and get run off or hung."

John nodded. "It must be the same wherever a place like this
is, I suppose. Rafe, let's stroll over to your office and look at
your books." He turned to Curly Bill. "William, would you
mind making a visit to the local drinking establishments, sort of
nosing about? Listen for loose talk about the gold robberies and
ask some discreet questions. Rafe and I will be at his assay office if you need to find us. Unless you hear something of major
importance, we'll compare notes in the morning at breakfast."

"Why, shucks no, Boss. I'd be more than happy to take on
that assignment. Khan Singh, you wanna come along?"

"No, thank you, Sahib William. I will stay with Lord John.
You will be able to get back to the hotel without my assistance?"

"Hell's bells. I was making it home from saloons long before
you even knew what one was, thank you very much." With a
wave of his hand, he strode off, making a beeline for the first
saloon up the street.

As Bill entered the saloon, John turned to Rafe. "Let's have a
look at your office, Rafe. Will your office manager be there, this
time of night?"

"Yep. He has a room in the back, so's he can keep an eye on
the place after office hours. He's a fine boy. Son of the banker
who does the company business in Denver, Loren Krammer.
Tom, his boy, has worked for me from the first day I got there.

His pa was instrumental in gettin' the funds to build the smelter in Denver."

"Any chance this Tom is involved in the robberies?"

"Nope, I can't see it, John. 'Cides, he stays close to the place guarding the shipment until the convoy gets under way. He'd not have a chance to alert the outlaws."

"What if he sent word by some accomplices?"

"I doubt it, John. The boy's too danged—well, I don't know, too timid, I suppose is the best word, to be involved with outlaws. He's been to college, back in New York, and his pa is well off, so it don't seem likely."

"Just the same, I would like to talk with him. We don't want to overlook the obvious." John walked along the muddy boardwalk, passing other pedestrians. The foot traffic was heavy for such a small town, but John saw no woman of quality among the pedestrians. His eyes never rested as they walked and talked. His natural inquisitiveness was heightened by his years in detective work.

"Besides the working prostitutes, I don't see any women," he remarked to Rafe, as they paused to let a miner, his hands full of supplies, exit one of the general stores. In reality, it was a large tent with a wooden front, filled with mining supplies.

"I doubt if there are a half-dozen decent women here," Rafe answered. "The married men sure don't want their wives exposed to what's around here."

John smiled. "I take it you don't consider the 'working girls' to be decent women?"

"Don't tell me you do?"

"I suppose you're right. Only, in India, the profession was considered to be an acceptable career for some. Many poor girls earned enough on their backs to take care of their families and still save something to retire on comfortably. I met some who were truly women of integrity. A person you would want to have as a friend in other circumstances." He chuckled. "They taught me more than just physical gratification. It's primarily in the more so-called 'civilized' countries that I have encountered such animosity toward the working prostitute."

"Maybe so," Rafe admitted. "I never gave it much thought afore. I suppose some of the gals back of the saloons are all right, but be careful where you put your wallet afore you climb into bed with one of 'em."

The doorway to one of the saloons flew open, and three men, quite intoxicated, staggered out. They eyed the three strangers, gauging the chance they could have some fun with them. The short, stocky Rafe, the taller, almost slender, John, and the massive, bearded and turbaned Khan Singh stood their ground, calmly returning the stares of the drunks with an unflinching gaze. Recognizing that the chances of a successful confrontation were slim, the drunks passed on the idea and stumbled into the muddy street, headed for the beckoning lights of another saloon across the street.

"Here we are," Rafe announced as they reached the doorway to a modest office, roughly constructed of green wood, unpainted, and already starting to shrink and crack as the lumber dried. "Guggenheim Assaying and Smelting," read a sign hanging from the roof eaves over the entrance. An oil lamp burned behind the closed curtains over the single window, built next to the door, offering a view of the muddy street.

Rafe knocked heavily on the thick, wooden door. They could hear the thumps of footsteps as a man came up to the closed door and then shouted at them through the barrier. "We're closed, pard. Come back tomorrow, at eight."

"Hello, inside. It's Rafe Wallace. Open up. I want to see Tom Krammer." He rapped on the door again.

A face peered out from behind the closed curtain. A shotgun was plainly visible to the three men outside. The man's eyes

73

squinted as he looked at Rafe, then spoke through the glass. "Give me a minute, Mr. Wallace. I'll get Tom Krammer. He's in his office."

Shortly, a second face peered out. The man was young, with mousy brown hair and a weak chin. A sparse, light moustache covered his thin upper lip, not very adequately. Thick glasses magnified pale, watery eyes, which seemed pinched above his thin nose. They widened as he recognized Rafe. "Mr. Wallace. I didn't expect to see you. All right, Henry. Open up."

The door's lock was turned, and a rough, heavyset man with a blondish beard covering his sun-darkened skin opened the door. He casually held a sawed-off double-barrel shotgun. The slight, underweight Tom Krammer was inside, nervously holding out his hand in greeting, a pained smile on his boyish face. "Good to see you, Mr. Wallace. You should have sent word you were coming. Are you all settled in at the hotel?"

"Yep, Tom. We're fine. This here is John Whyte, from the home office, and his assistant, Mr. Singh. John, my office manager, Tom Krammer."

John shook the weak grasp of the young Krammer, taking note of the unmanly grip. Khan Singh nodded and stood off to the side, where he could watch the man with the shotgun.

"I'm happy to make your acquaintance," John politely responded. "I see you have some additional firepower available, in case it is needed." He nodded at the bearded man with the shotgun, who had returned to his chair, by the window.

"Yes," Krammer replied. "We keep an armed guard around the clock. Henry there, like most of my guards, ran out of money while prospectin'. So, he'll stand guard for a few days, until he earns enough for another grubstake, and then he'll head back into the hills."

John appraised the guard. His patched coveralls and worn boots showed the state of his finances, but he seemed a no-

nonsense type of fellow. He needed a good shave and haircut but was reasonably clean. His brown eyes showed a spark of intelligence, while his sun-roughened face was pleasant and friendly. He held the shotgun like he knew how to use it. The worn belt around his pants still showed the faint *USA* on the belt buckle. "Army of the Republic?" John speculated.

"141st Illinois Volunteers, fought with Sherman to the sea," the guard replied, shifting into a more comfortable position in his chair. "How 'bout you?" He pointedly eyed their old army pants, the dark indication of the cavalry stripe still plainly visible.

John smiled. "Khan Singh and I were members of the 2nd US Cavalry. Served with General Custer clear up to the end. Has it been quiet around here?"

Henry patted his shotgun. "It always is. This is my third stint at guardin' the office till I make enough fer a grubstake. I hope to make a strike on my next try. If not, I'll be back agin, I reckon."

Rafe chimed in. "That's one of the reasons we've never had a robbery here in Central City, John. We always have a man on duty, inside the office, day and night."

"What if one of them were part of the gang that's making all the trouble?"

Tom Krammer spoke up, his voice soft and slightly timid. "I screen my guards with care, Mr. Whyte. Most are repeaters, and I always try and hire men my older guards have recommended."

"A wise plan," John agreed. "Still, someone is working against us."

Young Krammer nodded, his face reflecting the bleakness in his voice. "You're right, sir. And damned if I can figger out who."

CHAPTER 9
MOUNTAIN INVESTIGATIONS

John sighed in feigned sympathy. "The stockholders are asking the very same questions, Mr. Krammer. The very same questions."

"Please, sir, call me Tom. My pa is Mr. Krammer." He squinted up at John and the great bulk of Khan Singh. "Is that why you've come out here, then? To investigate the gold robberies?"

John smiled. "Not exactly, Tom. I am a concerned stockholder, expressing my views. I don't have the faintest idea about how to oppose a band of evil desperados. I came to visit Denver on business, so I stopped in to meet Rafe, and, before I knew it, he'd talked me into seeing your town."

Tom laughed in agreement. "Well, it's something, all right. I'm grateful the robbers don't try to hold up my office. I don't know what I'd do."

"You don't think they would try that, do you?"

Krammer shook his head, emphatically. "No, sir. Not only do we have an armed guard on duty around the clock, but there's enough men around Central City at all times to guard ten times as much as I would ever have in the safe. The miners are sorry we get robbed on the way to Denver, but they won't stand for thievery around the gold camp. Miners' law is pretty definite about that. It's a hanging offense, those that aren't shot down on the spot."

Wallace chimed in. "We've had fifty to sixty thousand in dust

76

here and not the first inkling of any trouble. Why should they try and shoot their way in and out of town, when they can hit us on the trail to Denver with less risk and more confidence of success? There, they are up against only a few men."

John drew up a chair and sat down. Tom Krammer sat behind his old desk, and Wallace took the worn, overstuffed chair in the corner. John asked Tom, gauging the young manager, "Tell me, Tom. What is your idea on how these ruffians work? How do they know when a gold shipment has left here for Denver?"

"I can't figger that out, Mr. Whyte. I suppose they have someone watching us, day and night. As soon as they see us preparing to leave with a shipment of gold, they hurry off and tell their buddies."

John nodded. "That is a possibility, I suppose. Still, the outlaws are always waiting for the column at a well-prepared ambush site. Isn't that right, Rafe?"

"Yep. They're already there when we arrive. Somehow, they seem to know ahead of time, so's they can get ready fer us."

"But, didn't you say that you don't even tell Tom here when you are going to leave with a shipment?"

"That's true enough. Last time, we waited four days, here in Central City, after the shipment was made up, afore we left. Still, they was waitin' on us."

John nodded. "Then, it's my opinion that the outlaws are alerted after you leave, but in time for them to beat you to the Georgetown Road."

Rafe agreed, an unhappy look upon his face. "I suppose so. But, I know we've searched real careful like fer any place those fellas coulda cut our trail. We didn't see any sign of where they got on or off the road. It stands to reason they rode out from Denver. Somehow, they knew when we were a-comin. Like it was written on the wind."

"Sorry, Rafe. I don't believe in the supernatural. No gypsy is looking into a crystal ball and seeing your column on the trail. No, they are finding out about your plans after you depart and yet still manage to be ahead of you on the road. We'll have to insist that the authorities work harder. They need to poke around until they find an answer."

Rafe sighed. "I suppose you're right, John. I jus' don't see how they could do any more. There's not a clue to be had when it comes to them damned skunks."

John smiled at Tom, whose return smile was as weak as his receding chin. "Let's call it a day and sleep on it. Maybe tomorrow, we'll see things a bit clearer."

The three men bid their good nights and returned to the hotel. The soft bed soon captured John and Rafe, while Khan thought about what he had heard. He wondered if the Sahib had watched young Krammer closely, as he had, while the two of them talked. The young man seemed a bit too nervous to the wise, old Sikh warrior. Khan Singh shrugged and rolled over. Sahib John missed nothing. He would wait and see what the future brought.

The three of them were seated around a table at the cafe early the next morning eating their breakfast when Curly Bill entered, his step a bit tentative. Curly Bill's usually cheerful face was woeful as he showed the pangs of internal agony. To everyone in the room, he was suffering from a hammering hangover. Bill's pug-button nose was sunburned red yet paled in comparison to his red-streaked eyes.

"Mornin' to ya all," he groaned as he gingerly slid into his chair and motioned with his cup for some coffee from the busy waiter. The swarthy waiter, a half-breed Indian, wiped his hands on a soiled flour-sack apron tied about his waist and sauntered over, determined not to hurry for any hungry white man.

"Coffee, and some eggs or flapjacks, whichever you can git

first." Bill put the cup of hot coffee gingerly to his lips. He sipped the steaming brew, grimacing at the heat or the taste, John was not sure which.

"No eggs. Flapjacks and syrup," the dusky-faced waiter mumbled to the unfortunate Bill. The sour smell of last night's excess of whiskey permeated the air after Bill's exhalation, following his first big gulp of coffee.

"That'll do. Bring 'em on. I'll say when to quit." He rubbed his temples gingerly. "The skull-poppers these miners drink would scald the skin off an armadillo," he grumbled.

"Did you have any success?" John inquired. "I would hope the night's sacrifice would not have been a waste of your time."

"Well," Bill admitted, with a satisfied grin, "it wasn't a total flop. I won thirty dollars playing blackjack over to the High Spade Bar. And, there's a gal or two who will be lookin' fer me tonight, I reckon. However, I'm hungover somethin' awful."

John suppressed a grin. "How about our problem?"

Curly Bill shook his head and took another bite of hot flapjacks, washing it down with more of the coffee. "Not much of interest, Boss. The miners and prospectors all seem about as puzzled as we are as to how these outlaws are doin' it. The miners are a mite worried, too. They know if Guggenheim's pulls out, it'll be like in the old days, with every man for himself. They want the robberies to stop as bad as we do. I couldn't get a single hint that anyone here knows a pile of beans about what's goin' on."

"Yet, it is here that it all starts," John concluded. "Well, today, we'll scout around a bit. William, you and Rafe ride north along Fraser Creek. Look for trails that might lead outlaws toward the Georgetown Road. Or, any sign as to how these men learn about the departure of the column. Maybe a telegraph line or something. Khan Singh and I will follow the creek bottom south. Meet back here for supper."

The four men split up and rode out of the mining town in opposite directions, following the polluted waters of Fraser Creek. The runoff from the previous day's rain had added its complement of mud and rock to the daily contribution from the mining operations. Along both sides of the creek, the miners had their camps and digging sites located, their claims stacked side by side for several miles out of town. Then, the creek grew smaller, and the miners thinned out, until there was only an occasional prospector, scratching around the hard rock, looking for traces of the golden dust.

John and Khan Singh stopped to rest their horses. They had followed several game trails away from the creek bottom, but each proved to lead nowhere but up the slopes of ever steeper mountain bluffs. The only happy member was Rajah, who joyously ran wild, free to sniff and bark at leisure.

The two men climbed off their horses and stood about half a mile away from Fraser Creek, beside a gurgling stream of icy-cold water. They chewed on the jerky stored in their saddle bags and sated their thirst in the cold, clear water. Both marveled at the view, the purple spires of the mountains thrusting upward as if seeking to touch the fluffy clouds drifting overhead. The soaring cumulus clouds paid no attention as they played hide and seek with the noontime sun.

John was grimly chewing the tough jerky when a flash of reflected sun off an icy outcrop caught his eye. He remembered a similar occurrence, years before, during the Shenandoah Valley campaign with Generals Sheridan and Custer. "Khan Singh, do you remember when we campaigned in the high mountains of the Shenandoah? The way we kept in contact with the supporting units? What did they call it? A heli . . . heliograph, that's it. The army used a heliograph device to signal. Remember? Flashes of sunlight from a mirror directed at another location. Suppose that's how our bandits are communicating. An ac-

complice in the town could use the heliograph to send Morse
code, alerting the gang when a shipment is leaving Central
City."

"It was a most efficient device, Sahib. I would think it would
work here as well. The problem is to find a location where the
signal could be seen by those waiting for it."

John turned to gaze toward Central City. He appraised the
tall mountain rising high behind the town. "There's the place
our man goes, as soon as the column leaves the city, I'd wager
ten shillings on it. Then, somewhere out there, miles from the
town, the outlaws get the message and hurry to where they will
spring their ambush."

John threw Rajah the last of his beef jerky strip and took a
final drink of the cold water. "Come on, we only have a couple
of hours before we have to turn back. We must try and find
where the outlaws wait for the word from their contact in
Central City. It's out here somewhere; we just have to find it."

Their search proved fruitless, however, so, as the sun reddened and started its long slide down the backside of the day,
they returned to Central City. Encouraged by their hypothesis,
but subdued because they had nothing solid to build a case on,
they washed up and awaited Rafe and Curly Bill at the cafe. "I
can't help but believe we have made an important first step,"
John affirmed to his friend, as they seated themselves at the
small table in the cafe.

Rafe and Curly Bill came in after a wait of fifteen minutes,
brushing the trail dust from their pants and shirts. Rafe spotted
John and led Bill toward them.

"Howdy, Boss. Any luck?" Curly Bill signaled for the
barkeeper to send over two beers. "I'm dryer than a desert
jackrabbit."

"No, I'm afraid not. How about you?"

"Nary a sign. Rafe says we covered the only trail outta town, so we're busted short of a straight, I reckon."

John nodded, and waited until the waiter had deposited the beers, which Rafe and Bill attacked with relish. As soon as both men lowered their drink and wiped the foam from their moustaches, he added, "Khan Singh and I did come up with a theory about the outlaws, which I want to verify tomorrow."

Rafe was immediately alert. "What's that, John? Lord knows we deserve some sort of break."

"There's a possibility the outlaws are using a heliograph to signal when a gold shipment is leaving Central City for Denver."

"What's a heli . . . heligra . . . Hell, what's that?" Curly Bill asked impatiently.

"It's a signaling device, using mirrors to reflect the sun. We used them in the army to send messages. You may have seen them during the war. They work fine when the terrain allows it."

"Oh, yeah," Bill answered. "I recollect once when I was on courier duty fer General Talbert, I think I saw one. But I didn't know what it was called."

Rafe's face was clouded with suppressed rage. "That means someone who lives here, in Central City, and knows what's happenin' is in cahoots with the outlaws, damn him. Who do ya think it is?"

John shook his head. "I'm not sure, Rafe, but please don't mention what we are discussing to anyone, even Tom Krammer."

"Hell, John. You surely don't suspect him, do you? He's a boy, and I know him and his pa."

"Rafe, my friend, I suspect everyone. Even you. But," John smiled at Rafe, to soften the accusation in his statement, "not very much. However, we must suspect everyone until we can strike them from our list of possible suspects. Not a word, to anyone. That way, a slip of the lip won't damage our investigation."

"Certainly." Rafe's reply was a little stiff, as he accepted the implication of John's words. Then the sense of the order became clearer to the grizzled miner, and his face softened. "Even though it couldn't be, if it is Tom Krammer, then his pa is probably in it, too. The boy jumps when the old man barks, that's a fact."

John nodded. "Perhaps. We'll see. Meanwhile, tomorrow, William, you nose around some more. Talk to the miners. See if anyone remembers anybody riding out of town after the gold convoy leaves. Anybody who shouldn't be riding out, that is. Rafe, you must want to go over some things with Tom. Khan Singh and I will see if there is a way up to the top of that high mountain behind town. If the outlaws are using a heliograph, that would be the logical place to put it."

Rafe and Curly Bill returned to the hotel to clean up before they met to eat with John and Khan Singh. John walked over to the assay office, judiciously picking his way across the muddy street, filled with ruts and horse manure. Tom Krammer was busy weighing small piles of gold dust on a balance scale.

"Hello, Mr. Whyte. I'll be with you in a minute. I have to finish this weigh-in, before I can lock it up in the safe."

"No hurry, Tom. I'll watch you and perhaps learn something about gold assaying. It seems like interesting work."

"This is almost pure dust. From up Fraser creek, a ways. The prospector has already returned to his claim, he's so afraid of getting his claim jumped. He's got a good claim, all right. This stuff is nearly pure gold."

John watched as Tom Krammer weighed and labeled the dust, before putting it into a massive safe, along with numerous other small leather sacks of gold. Skillfully, John maneuvered his comments, changing the scope of the conversation, until they were talking about the isolation of Central City. "It seems like the miners could use a telegraph line into Denver."

"That would be handy," Tom agreed.

"Of course, they would need someone to run it who knows Morse code. Tell me, Tom. Do you know it, by chance?"

"Er, no, sir. But I've sure been meaning to learn it some day." Tom glanced up at John, spilling a dash of dust, which he had to brush into a tiny dustpan.

It was too late. John had noted the slight pause before Tom answered and the shifting of the young man's eyes. Tom Krammer was lying. About knowing Morse code anyway.

CHAPTER 10
MOUNTAIN CLUES

The eastern side of the morning sky was already fading to a pale blue, while the western half retained the darkness a few minutes longer. Curly Bill was fighting off a yawn and picking at his breakfast at the same time. His bloodshot eyes had bags the size of silver dollars under them. A pinched look on his face showed how faithfully he had followed his orders to mingle with the drinkers in the saloons the night before, seeking to converse with anyone who might have information about the outlaw scourge.

"Damn, Boss. If I have to drink much more of that Who-hit-John juice these saloons serve as whiskey, my brain'll turn to mush. I don't know where these boys get their whiskey, but they oughta sell it as horse liniment."

"I think they do," laughed Rafe Wallace. "The men who drink it hardly ever come down with colic or fetlock fever."

"Very funny," Bill groaned. "I'm only doing this fer the good of the investigation. And now I have to put up with breakfast comics as well. Especially with my head about to split open." Curly groaned and rubbed his throbbing forehead.

John looked with sympathetic amusement at his hungover horse wrangler. "Sorry, William. I know it's a burden for you, drinking and whooping it up all night, but it has to be done. If it's any consolation, I plan on returning to Denver tomorrow, so your travails will soon be over."

"Can't say that I'll be sorry to leave. What's my job fer the day?" Curly Bill again rubbed his face briskly, as if trying to scrape the effects of the night's investigation out of his thumping head.

"You are to talk to the prospectors who have claims closest to Central City. Ask if anyone remembers seeing a rider leaving town after the gold shipments left. Someone who would not normally leave Central City at that time. Khan Singh and I are riding up that mountain behind the town. If some person is signaling the outlaws about the gold, it might be from there. We'll meet for supper to compare notes. I'll agree that you deserve a good night's sleep, so you can skip the bar-hopping afterwards." They left the cafe and picked up Rajah, who was patiently waiting for them outside, his big head cradled between his paws. He took up half the wooden sidewalk, but no passerby seemed anxious to urge him to move.

"Fair enough, Boss. See you all later. See ya, Raj. Good dog. Now git. I don't need you gettin' mud all over my clean shirt."

The Great Dane was full of energy, lumbering about in his frenetic manner, sniffing the cool morning air and ready for the day's adventures. John led the way out of town, with Rajah once again bounding ahead. As early as it was, the determined miners were already at work, shoveling gravel, and swirling water in their pans, seeking the golden nirvana of their dreams.

The way out of town rapidly degenerated from a cart path to a narrow walkway to a rock-covered trail, scarcely fit for a mountain goat. Still, it wound on, climbing ever higher, until the two men were over 2,000 feet above Central City, almost as high as the pass into town from the Georgetown Road, across the broad valley to the east. John climbed off his horse and stretched his legs. Rajah romped about, sniffing and panting, happy as any mutt in a field of rabbits.

The view of the green valley spread out below them was breathtaking. The great height reduced the town to a miniature, overrun with barely discernable men. The stunning natural colors of nature softened the harsh intrusion of man and created a scene both serene and deceptively pristine. "A most impressive view," John remarked in an understatement to Khan Singh, standing silently beside him.

"Yes, Sahib. The scars of man are hidden at this distance." Khan Singh raised his leonine head and pointed farther up the steep trail. "The trail seems to end up there, near those rocks."

John squinted against the bright sunlight. "So it does. Odd, the trail up to here is rather well used for it to end so suddenly, wouldn't you say?"

Khan Singh walked ahead, holding his horse by the reins as they approached the barrier across the narrow trail. A large pile of rocks and brush blocked any further progress.

"I guess we've hit another dead end," John grumbled. "Let's go back down. It must be some other mountain top, if my guess about a heliograph is correct."

As John maneuvered his horse around for the return trip, Rajah gave a mighty bark and disappeared in the pile of debris. "Rajah, come here, boy," John called, but Rajah was gone. John looked at Khan Singh. "That's odd. Where did he go?"

Standing well above them, Rajah's throaty bark beckoned them. They looked up. The Great Dane was looking down at them, running up and down on a path. He barked at them as if urging them to come up and join him.

"If Rajah can get through there," John announced excitedly, "maybe a man can." He climbed up on a jagged slab of rock and looked over the barricade. A winding path emerged among the jumble of rocks and brush, and John saw the entrance into the maze. Off to the side, a huge bush blocked the way into the field of debris. The bush was strategically planted in the dirt to impede both view and passage. John pulled it aside and shouted in triumph. It was apparent that someone had deliberately tried to conceal the pathway through the boulders.

"Come on, old friend. We're on to something." Leading their horses, the two men followed the torturous route through the tangle of stone and brush until they reached the far side of the barrier, where the rough trail continued to curl upward toward the top of the mountain.

In due course, they reached the summit of the mountain. It was barren of trees, mostly jagged boulders resting on a rounded crown about fifty feet in diameter. The view was unobstructed, a panoramic scene of the sawtoothed mountain range in all directions. Even this late in the summer, white splashes at the peaks of the blue-black rock indicated unmelted snow. Central City could not be seen from where they now stood, but, from this peak, the outlaw gang's confederate could easily signal to a lookout twenty or more miles away, alerting them to the departure of a gold shipment.

"Look around. Let's see if we can find some sort of signaling device," he instructed Khan Singh. He gave Rajah a deserved pat on the head and walked over the rocky terrain, seeking anything of interest. Rajah was eagerly sniffing in front of him, darting back and forth. Abruptly, the big dog stopped. He nuzzled his nose at something lying on the ground. John moved to see what had caught the dog's attention. It was a discarded cigar butt, half smoked, the band still on it. It had not lain there very long, as it was still tightly wrapped and dry. "A Cuban hand-rolled El Supremo," John remarked to himself. "Good dog, Rajah. Now who around here could get his hands on an expensive cigar like that?" He put the band in his shirt pocket.

"Sahib, over here." Khan Singh motioned for John. The Sikh warrior had moved off the top of the mountain, to a small depression, below the summit.

Khan had found where the ground was scuffed and scratched. "Someone has definitely been doing something up here, and not that long ago," John observed. He looked around. There was no sign of any heliograph, but it could be hidden almost anywhere. "There are probably many small animal caves within a hundred yards of here where our suspect could stash something the size of a heliograph," he speculated to Khan Singh. "Still, good enough," John concluded. "We have what we came for. Let's get back to Central City. Come on, Rajah. Show the way. Good dog." John followed the dog down the trail, convinced he had broken the mystery of how the robbers were informed of a shipment. Now to discover who was the informer.

CHAPTER 11
A LONG RIDE BACK TO DENVER

The trip down the steeply inclined path was no easier than had been their ascent to the top of the high mountain. They continually fought sliding up against the saddlehorns, and it put additional strain on their legs. Both were relieved to reach a semblance of level ground, where they could dismount and stretch their legs. They walked for a while, leading their tired horses, while both mulled over the newly discovered clues.

"I assume they have the drill down to a science by now," John concluded. "As soon as the gold convoy leaves Central City, one of the gang hurries to the top of the mountain, sets up the heliograph, and signals a lookout somewhere beyond the valley. He furnishes the number of guards, amount of gold, and so forth. Then, the outlaws hurry to a predetermined ambush site and, like the cold-blooded vultures they are, wait for the gold train to ride up the road, right into their guns. Rather ingenious, don't you think?"

Khan Singh remembered something he had heard Rafe Wallace mention. "But didn't Sahib Wallace say they had even sneaked out of Central City as the sun was rising? That means whoever was the signaler knew what was happening. I suspect we both have the answer as to who that might be?"

"Tom Krammer, you mean?"

"It would seem he is the most logical suspect, Sahib."

"Yes, I think so. Still, Rafe thinks highly of him, so we must act with circumspection, at least until we are more certain. We won't say anything about this, for the time being."

"As you wish, Sahib."

Rafe waved from the wooden walk in front of his assay office as the two detectives rode down the muddy main street toward their hotel.

"Hey, John. What's goin' on? How was your trip? See anything out of the ordinary?"

"Hello, Rafe. No, it was a very nice sightseeing ride. Other than that, it was rather uneventful."

"Damn, I was a-hopin' you'd cut some solid sign to show who these owlhoots were. Or how to stop 'em."

"Nothing comes easy in the detective business, my friend." John grinned at the bearded miner. "We'll have to keep poking about. Little things come together, and, almost without realizing it, you have the answer."

"Well, I damn shore hope so. I've got to get a shipment to Denver soon. We're gettin' too much gold stacking up here in Central City."

"Not long, Rafe. Khan and I are getting closer to an answer, I assure you. I've already formulated a tentative plan that I have high hopes will work. I believe we will return to Denver tomorrow. You decided yet if you will accompany us?"

"I suppose so. There ain't much more I can do here, so I might as well git on back. I'll be ready, first light. Dinner at the restaurant, around seven?"

"Fine, Rafe. We'll be ready. Why don't you bring Tom Krammer along? I'd like to pay my respects before we leave."

"Good enough. See you then." Rafe cut away, crossing the muddy street toward his office. John and Khan Singh dropped off the horses at the stable and secured Rajah for the night, much to the dog's displeasure. They strolled back to their rooms on the wooden sidewalk, being careful to not trip on the uneven slats. The traffic on the walkway was as hectic as ever, with mud-spattered men crowding the boardwalk, with the ever-present discord from the busy saloons and bawdy-houses adding to the hubbub.

John and Curly Bill were waiting at the table when Rafe and young Tom Krammer walked into the restaurant. Rafe waved and threaded his way between the tables to join them, Krammer in his wake.

"Howdy, John. Bill. Where's Khan Singh?"

"He was tired from all the sightseeing and begged you excuse him," John replied. "He wanted to check over the horses before we depart tomorrow. Good evening, Tom. Have a busy day?"

"Hello, Mr. Whyte. Yep, we took in several hundred in dust and nuggets today. The safe is nearly full. We'll have to make a run before too long, I suppose."

"And risk another holdup?" John shook his head. "Sounds rather risky to me."

"Yes, sir," Tom answered. "But if we continue to build up inventory here in Central City, it will invite a raid against the office, and, should that happen, our company could be put in a bad light, especially if innocents are hurt."

"We're damned if we do, damned if we don't," Rafe groaned. "It almost takes my appetite away."

"That's a bit of an overstatement, judging by your attack on that buffalo roast," John teased.

"Well, I said, almost," Rafe answered, shoveling another spoonful into his mouth and tearing off a hunk of pan bread to sop the gravy still on his plate.

The talk shifted to more mundane subjects, first about gold, then the weather, and last the charms of a new singing gal over at the Red Nugget saloon. The main course was finished, and coffee was poured for the men, as they ate the last of their fresh blackberry pie wedges.

John pushed back his chair and patted his stomach. "Quite satisfying to say the least. That cook should be commended for his culinary skills." John reached into the inner pocket of his coat and pulled out a silver cigar holder. He pulled the top off and offered the contents for Rafe's inspection. "Smoke, Rafe? These are some of my private rolling, which I brought from Missouri. Tom, how about you? Do you enjoy an after-dinner cigar, at times?"

Tom's eyes widened at the offer. He was being treated as an equal by the affable Englishman. It was a good feeling. "Yes, sir. Thank you. I do enjoy a good smoke, every now and then."

John lit a sulfur lucifer and held it while Rafe and Tom fired up their cigars, before lighting his. The three men blew silvery streams of smoke toward the ceiling and sighed contentedly. Curly Bill bit off a small cud of chewing tobacco and worked it under his lip. Silence reigned as the four savored the after-dinner ritual. John's face showed nothing of the satisfaction he felt at the additional proof of his suspicions about the young Krammer. Tom Krammer puffed expertly on the round stogie. "Mmm . . . fine smoke. You grow your own tobacco at your place?"

"No, the climate and soil at Fair Oaks are not exactly right for good tobacco. I have it brought in hogshead barrels from Kentucky and rolled by one of my employees, an ex-slave and his family, who rolled them in the Carolinas before the war. I sell all he can make in St. Louis, at my restaurant."

As they strolled outside, Tom Krammer looked at John and the others. "Buy you gentlemen a drink, before bed?"

"No, thank you, Tom," John answered. "However, I'll bet William here has a thirst. Right, William?"

"Shore enough, Boss. Lead on, Tom. I'll let you choose the pizzen palace of your choice. 'Night, Boss, Rafe."

"Goodnight, William. Don't forget, we depart at dawn. Tom,

I expect you to get him back to his bed at a decent hour."

Young Krammer chuckled and nodded assurance before leaving John and Rafe at the door of the cafe. The two thirsty men turned toward the lights and noise of the saloons, while John and Rafe walked on toward the hotel. John had a bemused expression on his face, as if a prey had fallen into a predator's trap.

Later, as John finished washing his face over the bowl and pitcher sitting on the rickety washstand in his room, a soft tap announced Khan Singh's return. He dried off with the thin towel hanging on a nail next to the mirror and opened the door.

"Yes, Khan Singh. Any luck?"

"I am not sure, Sahib. I slipped into Master Krammer's quarters without the guards hearing me, but found nothing, except . . ."

"Yes?"

"I did find a letter from his father in his dresser drawer. It spoke of Denver and his mother and at the end were three lines of strange symbols. Perhaps a code, I think."

"But no cigars? No sign of any 'El Supremo' cigars?"

"Sorry, Sahib. Nothing but the strange symbols in the letter."

"Too bad. But still, I find it very interesting that our young Mr. Krammer receives a coded message from his father. Most interesting. Did you copy the part in code for me?"

"Yes, Sahib."

"Good. I'll study it between here and Denver. Maybe I can make something of it."

Khan Singh gave John a slip of paper. On it were three rows of tiny arrows, pointed in different directions, with tiny numbers where the feathers would be on a real arrow.

John studied the symbols until sleep overtook him, no closer to breaking the code than when he started. Still it was another nail in the coffin the Krammers were building for themselves.

The four men rode out of the grubby mining town as the first rays of morning sunshine streamed over the dark mass of the eastern mountaintops. Rajah romped ahead, joyful at his release from the confines of the stable.

They paused to look back at Central City, from where they had first viewed the town only a few days earlier. The miserable squalor of the town was still inescapable, but the vitality of the men who lived there had changed their perceptions. The place now seemed alive and vibrant, with a level of activity that was admirable in spite of the shabbiness. For a moment they gazed in silence and then spurred their horses on up the grade, riding toward the summit to meet the morning sun.

They made good time and reached the location of the last ambush by late afternoon. John reined his horse where Rafe had seen the outlaws push the dead horse off the trail. He and the others edged to where they could peer down at the remains of the dead animal below. John and Khan unloaded the rope that Rafe had acquired and tied it to a large tree trunk beside the sheer drop off. Carefully, he and Khan Singh roped themselves around the legs and waist.

"What are you two doin' there?" Rafe questioned.

"We're making what is called a rappelling seat. It keeps us from falling as we go down the rope. Watch."

John fed the tied rope through a knotted loop in his "seat" and, taking one last look down, backed over the edge, holding the tied rope and bracing his legs against the face of the cliff. The others watched with baited breath as he swiftly lowered himself down the snaking length of the hemp rope until he reached the bottom of the ravine where the remains were lying, scattered by the wild scavengers. As soon as he released the rope, Khan Singh began his descent and soon was at his side. They waved up at Curly Bill and Rafe, looking down from above in morbid trepidation.

"Man o' man," Rafe worried, "you couldn't git me on that there rope like that, fer no amount of money." He edged away from the drop to make his point.

"Hell, Rafe," Curly Bill answered, "I seen them two go offa higher spots than this on a rope afore. That John, he learned some funny tricks from old Khan Singh whilst they was fightin' together in India, afore he came over here to America." Bill continued to watch, fascinated at the seeming lack of concern John and Khan Singh had around heights. He knew in his heart that flat land was the best land, no matter how pretty the scenery was.

John kicked at the dried hide and scattered bones that was all that remained from the dead horse. He searched for a sign of a brand, but it was useless. That portion of the animal was gone, no telling where. The carcass had yielded no clues, and John was about to start back up the rope when Khan Singh motioned for him. The Sikh was looking at a lower leg bone and hoof, dragged a short distance away by a scavenger.

"Look, Sahib. This horseshoe. It is of a peculiar design."

John examined the horseshoe. It was the standard "U" shape, with an additional straight bar welded across the back of the "U," which built up the rear of the shoe.

"See, Sahib. The hoof was cracked. The rider had a support added to the horseshoe for protection."

"Yes," John agreed, digging at the shoe with his pocketknife, not heeding the stench from the scraps of rotting flesh still on the white bone. "This is a 'Memphis bar.'" His voice was excited at the find as he pulled the horseshoe from the remains. "Built up to protect the frog, while the hoof heals. And not too old, from the wear of it. Good work, old friend. With this evidence, we can visit the local farriers and see if anyone has purchased such a shoe. One step closer to the goal, I'll wager."

John tucked the shoe into the pocket of his leather riding

jacket and looked up at the top, where Curly Bill was still peering down at the two of them. John walked over to a scrap of hide, still visible beside some bared ribs. "Looks like the poor animal was a Pinto." He grinned mischievously. "I'll bet you I get up faster than you do, old friend."

"Sahib, not for a long time yet. You are still the child and I the master when it comes to riding the rope."

Laughing, John glanced at the silver pocket watch he carried. Then, nimble as a cat, he started back up the thin strand, scooting up the steep drop like a squirrel up a tree. He reached the top, breathing hard, and checked his watch before leaning over the edge and calling down to Khan Singh. "Three minutes, old friend. Show me your best."

As the quivering rope showed Khan's assent, John pulled the horseshoe out of his pocket and gave it to Curly Bill, who turned it in his hands, Rafe looking over his shoulder in interest.

"A Memphis bar," Curly Bill announced. "Brings back memories. Ain't seen one since the war, when we had to make horses last, no matter how bad their hoofs were."

"Is that important?" Rafe questioned.

"Absolutely," John answered. "Some farrier had to make it, and I plan to find him."

Khan Singh scrambled over the edge, barely breathing hard. John looked at his watch. "Two minutes fifty seconds, old friend. You win, at least this time."

"What's a farrier?" Rafe chimed in, scratching his furry chin.

"A blacksmithy," Curly Bill answered for John. "You gotta forgive John, Mr. Wallace. He talks in English 'stead of 'merican half the time."

"And pray tell what do you call talk, my fine Texas friend. The mush from your mouth hardly deserves the title of 'America English.' "

"It ain't. It's even better. It's Texican." And with that haughty rejoinder, Curly Bill swung into his saddle and started toward the summit of the pass ahead. John smiled at the proud posture of his friend and followed, unable to think of a worthy reply.

CHAPTER 12
THE SILVER BELL

Denver had not changed during their absence. It had rained the day before, washing the dust from the buildings and making the streets a gloppy sea of mud. After returning their horses to the stable by the tracks, John and the others walked down the street toward the creek dividing Denver from Auraria. It would be dark soon, and the working men of Denver were making their way home for their evening meal. They reached the start of the wooden sidewalks of Main Street. Knocking the cloying mud from their boots, they stepped on the wooden slats, grateful to be free of the muddy roadway. As expected, the pedestrian traffic increased immediately on the dry walkway, and they found it hard to keep a conversation going.

"We may as well find a quiet spot in some saloon," John announced. "We're wasting our time trying to discuss anything out here. Too many people out and about."

"I know just the place," Rafe announced. "Right over there. The Silver Bell. Denver's classiest and most refined bawdy house. Run by a feisty Irish gal named Belle Flanagan. I consider her as quality a lady as any of the matrons in millionaire's row."

"Can we find a quiet corner in there?" John inquired.

"Sure. That is, iffen you don't mind being seen in a cathouse. Like ya say, it ain't the first time you was in one."

"Not at all. I've certainly frequented my share of such places while serving her majesty's forces in India. During the war,

Washington D.C., was filled with such houses. I found them to be a welcome respite, where a man could leisurely release the tensions of command. Lead on, my good fellow."

Rafe turned down the street and directed them into the front parlor of the Silver Bell. He escorted them into another world, sheltered from the raucous city outside. The room was opulently furnished, with an abundance of thick velvet, cut glass, and crystal chandeliers. Intricately carved, cherry-wood furniture encircled an indoor fountain, where a stream of water rushed down the sleek sides of a marble maiden, nude and as shapely as a Grecian goddess. Several well-dressed and coiffured young women mingled around the room, delivering and sharing drinks with the men in attendance. A fine haze of cigar and pipe smoke floated below the chandeliers, which tinkled melodiously as the wind from the open door stirred the multi-layers of crystal teardrops into motion.

Rafe escorted his guests toward the far corner of the huge parlor, where a beautiful, young woman of regal bearing was laughing with a portly, older gentleman in a slightly worn business suit. She recognized Rafe and smiled brightly at the mining manager, revealing pearly-white teeth. She motioned for a young, blond girl and patted the older man on the arm. "Helen will be happy to spend some time with you, Mr. Davis, won't you, Helen? Now, you must excuse me. I see an old friend has arrived with new visitors to my establishment."

She hurried over and embraced Rafe, obviously delighted at his presence. "Rafe, me darling miner. It's been too long since you stopped by. Glad to see you, you old rock breaker, you." She stepped back and smoothed her hair, smiling at John and the others. "Who have you brought to visit me? Welcome to you, gentlemen."

"John, this here is Belle Flanagan, as sweet an Irish lass as ever you'll have the pleasure of meetin'."

John appraised the woman before him. She was tall, nearly to his eyes in height, and even more with her hair swept upward in the latest style. Hair as red as her Irish ancestors who still lived in the old country. Peaches and cream complexion, a slender nose perched above a generous mouth—painted too red for John's tastes, but still intriguing. A delightful cleft in her small chin and slender, long-fingered hands completed the picture of an extraordinarily beautiful woman, still well short of thirty.

Her most enticing feature was her green eyes, which were lively, intelligent, and friendly. She boldly looked directly at a man, in contrast to the demure fashion of "proper" women. Her hunter's green, silk dress was cut low enough to draw attention to her creamy skin exposed between the twin, soft mounds of her bosom. John took her offered hand as Rafe made the introductions and gallantly brushed his lips against her knuckles. John was pleased to see that her hands were well manicured. She accepted John's homage as deserved and curtsied ever so slightly. His overall impression was that of a young woman not yet too jaded by the harsh realities of her profession.

"My pleasure, Miz Flanagan. Please call me John."

"And you can call me Belle."

"These are my friends William Williams and Khan Singh."

"Jus' call me Curly Bill, Ma'am," Curly Bill interjected.

"Your servant, Mimsab." Khan Singh's formal replay caused Belle to arch her eyebrow and smile brightly at the silver-haired Sikh warrior.

"What kind of a fella are you, big man?" She turned to John for the answer, drawn by his handsome countenance.

John satisfied her unasked questions about himself and the others, helped by short interjections from Rafe. In short order, Belle knew enough to converse with everyone.

She smiled at Rafe. "You and your friends in the mood for

some company, Rafe? I've two new young ladies, recently arrived from New Orleans. You will find them charming and refined." Her eyes caressed John as she spoke. The continental flavor of John's speech and manners, as well as his handsome appearance and manly physique, attracted Belle. She savored the feeling. It was a welcome diversion for the practical, hardhearted businesswoman.

"No thanks, Belle. We need a quiet place to park while we talk. Maybe later, after we're through."

"Certainly. This way, gentlemen." Belle led them to a secluded room with rich brown, velvet drapes covering the walls and window and a solid, wooden door, which she closed as she left. "I'll send one of the girls with some wine. How about champagne, chilled on ice?"

"That'll do fine, Belle. Thanks." Rafe smiled at the woman, appreciating her attentive treatment before his friends. "I'll be looking forward to spending some time in your company, Miz Belle. I'd like to buy you a drink, jus' as soon as we get done with our parlaverin'. Where will I find you?"

"Oh, I'll be around, Mr. Wallace. Don't you worry." She smiled at Curly Bill. "Visit us any time, Mr. Williams."

"Please, ma'm, call me Curly Bill."

"Curly Bill. You and your friends are always welcome."

"Thanks, ma'm."

A long, lingering glance was saved for John. Favoring him with a smoldering look and a bright smile, she swept from the room, leaving a sudden vacuum in her absence. Curly Bill swung around to face the others, frank admiration in his voice. "Boy, oh, boy. Ain't she somethin'? I'm sure a-comin' back here later. Maybe I can engage her fer a few hours, jus' for myself."

John laughed at the exuberant Texan. "Careful there, William. You might be climbing on a wild bronco." He glanced again at the closed door, remembering the way she had spun around before leaving the room. Belle Flanagan was some woman, without a doubt.

"Yeah. And what a ride it'd be." Curly Bill laughed, stretched, and settled into one of the velvet chairs placed around the green, felt-covered table, rubbing his hand, almost seductively, over the smooth material.

"To business, gentlemen," John announced. Everyone gathered around the table, then waited until the pretty, young waitress whom Belle had sent to serve them filled their champagne glasses and coyly inquired, "Will there be anything else, gentlemen?" with a knowing smile on her painted lips.

John shook his head. "That will be all, thank you," he replied, driving the expression from her face. She flounced out, insulted at the perceived snub.

"What's the next move, John?" Rafe sipped his wine and looked expectantly at John, who was toying with his glass, his face solemn and thoughtful. Bill and Khan Singh focused their attention on John, curious as to the next step in their investigation.

"It seems fairly straightforward, gentlemen," John finally answered. "The gold robberies mean someone has money to spend. Lots of cash. I intend to find out who's been buying things, lots of things, with money he shouldn't have. Outlaws can't stand it when they have gold in their pockets. Some will be spending it, hopefully foolishly and, even more hopefully, around here in Denver."

"What do you want us to do, Boss?" Curly Bill pulled his chair closer to the table. The pale top of his bare head reflected the yellow light of the oil lanterns illuminating the room.

"We have two jobs, William. You will handle one. I want you to spend every waking moment visiting farriers in and around Denver. Someone had to have made that Memphis bar horseshoe. I want to know his name."

"That'll be my pleasure, Boss."

"What about you, John?" Rafe injected.

"Khan Singh and I will nose about, inquiring about anyone who appears to have too much money. Starting tomorrow, we interview the land agents, banks, and gambling saloons. If anyone does have too much money, we have to find out who it is."

John drained the last of his glass. "Now, we better get some rest. Tomorrow will be a busy day." He pushed back from the table and stood, looking at his friends with a smile of anticipation. Rafe, Bill, and Khan pushed back as well, satisfied grins on every man.

"I'll be along directly, John," Bill announced. "I think I'll stick around a while and see if that fancy, red-headed gal wants some company. You don't care, do ya?"

"Fine, Bill." John chuckled at Curly Bill's eager, boyish lust. "I wish you the best of luck. Be warned, it may take more money than either of us has to win her favors for a night." He led the way out the door, back to the front parlor. Belle was ushering a tipsy customer out the front door, smiling at his profuse farewell.

"Hello, Rafe, Mr. Whyte. All through with your meeting?" While she spoke to Rafe, her eyes were on John.

John nodded. "Yes, thank you. I appreciate your fine hospitality. You have an excellent place to gather, both quiet and private."

"My pleasure, I assure you. Rafe is a dear and valued friend. Any friend of his is always welcome in my place."

"And a very nice place indeed."

"Can I invite you back later, for some lighter entertainment with some of my finer gals?"

John laughed. "I'm not so sure that's a good idea, Miss Flanagan. You see, after meeting their mistress, they all seem bland and shallow by comparison."

"Why, Mr. Whyte. How gallant you are. One can tell you've

had training in the fancy homes of the London swells."

"Yes, I had the pleasure, and the duty, of spending time in London. Once long ago, it seems."

Belle stared at John thoughtfully for a long moment. Impulsively, she took a gamble and spoke her mind. "Well, my polite and interesting English gentleman, I don't become involved, in a professional way you understand, with my customers anymore. However, perhaps you might be interested in joining me for a late supper, say about ten this evening?"

John was not a prude and had, in fact, known many happy hours in the pleasure houses of Punjab Cross, when he served in India. A young prostitute, whose Hindu name meant Tiny Blossom, had patiently tutored and shown him the joys of what men and women could share together. She had taken pride in her profession and in John's increasing skill at providing as well as receiving pleasure from a woman. He smiled at the memory of the young Hindu girl and of the many others he had encountered while in Washington.

"Madam, I believe it would be a great pleasure to join you this evening. Until then?" At her nod, he took his leave, followed by Rafe and Kahn Singh.

"What on earth was that all about? You aiming to get friendly with Belle Flanagan?" Rafe asked as they walked up the wooden sidewalk, Khan trailing silently behind. "I thought you said you wanted to git some rest?"

"It's a good move, Rafe. She has access to an additional source of information. She can ask the girls of the bawdy houses who is spending excessively. You and I will never have their confidence. Yes, it's a good idea, to solicit the good will of Miss Belle Flanagan."

"But, John . . . she's a . . . a whorehouse madam. What will the good folks of Denver think iffen they hear you're hangin' out with someone like her?"

Thom Nicholson

"One, I don't really care. Two, I'll be discreet. It's a good plan and worth any risk. Now, let's go see Sheriff Gilbert and bring him up to date on what we've found."

"Why?"

"I've found that investigations usually go smoother when the local constabulary is kept appraised of what is happening. He may be able to offer us some help, if we keep him informed."

"Whatever you say, John. You know best."

The three men walked up the street toward the corner office, where they found the old lawman behind his desk, shuffling papers. He glanced up, grateful at the interruption.

"Howdy, Rafe. Mr. Whyte, isn't it?"

"Yes. Hello, Sheriff Gilbert. My friend and associate, Khan Singh."

"Oh, yes. The jasper what pounded Mick O'Shay into sawdust. The barflys are still talking about it over drinks. Thanks, Mr. Singh. You shut him up proper. I haven't had trouble with him since."

Khan Singh smiled, and his deep voice was soft and mild. "It was nothing, Sahib. My pleasure, in fact."

Sheriff Gilbert laughed, deep down in his ample belly. "Haw. Haw. Good answer, Mr. Singh. I wish I'd seen you in action. It must have been a sight." Gilbert pushed the offending papers aside. "I reckon you didn't come here to socialize. What can I do for ya'll."

John brought the Denver sheriff up to date on what they had discovered in the mountains. The crusty lawman nodded as John described his plans to follow up on the clues uncovered to date. After careful consideration, John decided not to bring up his suspicions about Tom Krammer and his father, Loren. The timing was not yet right, he concluded, as he sat across the worn desk from Denver's sheriff.

"A bar across the open end of a horseshoe." Sheriff Gilbert

106

scratched the stubble under his chin. "I'll be able to help you there. I'll question all the blacksmiths here in Denver. Your people can talk to those in Auraria and in the smaller towns surrounding Denver. That will cut some time off your search. There's a bunch, so I'll start tonight, while I make my rounds. As fer the land speculators, you best handle that, Mr. Whyte. If any give ya a hard time, jus' let 'em know I'm in agreement as to your questions. I figger most of 'em are on the up and up and will level with ya. Any that don't, we'll visit together. All right by you?"

"That would be most appreciated, Sheriff Gilbert. Thank you for your assistance. We will keep you abreast of any information we find."

Gilbert nodded. "I think I'll send some inquiries to the sheriffs of nearby towns. If they hear of anyone with more money than what seems normal, I'll find out about it. The crooks may not be spending it all here in Denver."

John and the others shook the old lawman's hand and left the office, content with the results of the visit. They walked casually along the wooden sidewalk, discussing their plans for the next day.

"I've got to spend some time at my office, John," Rafe announced. "I've got a pile of paperwork higher than my head, if I'm any judge."

"I understand, Rafe. You take care of business. William, Khan Singh, and I will begin our investigation. You can join in whenever you have time."

"Fine. And with that, I'll take my leave, if you don't mind. I'm tuckered out and tomorrow's a long day. Night, John. Khan Singh."

"Good rest, Rafe. Come on, Khan Singh. If I'm going to have a late night supper with a beautiful lady, I'd better grab a few minutes rest myself."

"As you wish, Sahib. Pity. Once you would have hunted the wolf until time for your appointment and then arrived at the lady's door fresh as a love-struck juvenile."

"And once my faithful man-servant would never have dreamt of insulting his master by noting his advancing years."

"Yes, sir, Colonel, sahib. I also see some of us get cranky, when we are tired, as we age. Twice the pity."

CHAPTER 13
NIGHT MOVES

Khan Singh adjusted the coat as John slipped it on his shoulders. It was cut in the current fashion, royal-blue wool, with deep maroon, velvet lapels and a belt at the waist. While it was indeed a fine jacket, it was more suited for a gentleman's smoking session than a late night rendezvous with a lady. John reasoned that Belle's taste was more extravagant than the ordinary hostess he might visit. His black trousers were pulled over low-cut riding boots, polished to a high sheen by Kai Singh.

"Well, what do you think? Do I seem the dashing blade, ready to call on the scarlet woman, sly as a fox in the night?"

"I suppose, Sahib. Remember to maintain your guard. Don't become careless, just because the woman is beautiful."

"Understood. I'll go alone. If William returns home before me, give him the assignment tomorrow of questioning the farriers in Auraria about the horseshoe with the Memphis bar."

"I will. And what are your instructions for me?"

"You accompany William. I'll spend the day visiting the land brokers and the county records office. I'll make a list of anyone who is buying large amounts of land for further investigation."

"As you wish, Sahib."

"And have Kai restock the larder. We may have to leave on a moment's notice."

"As you wish, Sahib. Everything will be in readiness."

John slipped his arms into a long drover's coat held by Khan Singh. He had no desire to draw the attention of the late night pedestrian traffic to his "dude's attire." He adjusted his broad-rimmed Stetson and opened the door of the *Star of India*.

"I'll be late, old friend. Don't wait up for me."

The rugged, old warrior smiled. John winked and stepped outside, whistling softly.

He rode Blaze through the muddy streets to the Silver Bell. People were still out in large numbers. Drunken miners and restless cowboys jostled back and forth on the sidewalks or crossed the street in front of or behind the dark horse and coated rider. Nobody spoke to John, nor did he try to engage anyone he saw in conversation. The horse was picking his way through the muddy ruts without John's help, allowing his mind to drift, thinking of other times, other places.

John admitted to himself that he was looking forward to the coming engagement with Belle Flanagan. She appeared smart, tough, and strong-willed. Their interaction across the dinner table should be most intriguing, he mused. The beautiful owner of the Silver Bell was probably many times more intriguing than the more reserved women of Denver. John remembered from his military service in India how interesting and delightful a companion a skillful courtesan could be. She would have no qualms in saying or doing what she damned well pleased, especially when she was not conducting business. She had no fear of men, nor of violating the mores of the day. Neither would she feel stifled by the tradition which muzzled "good" women and forced them into the background while in the company of men.

He doubted that Belle subscribed to any of the more current social customs of society. As a financially liberated woman, she, too, would say what she thought and do about what she wanted, the devil take the hindmost.

He tied Blaze at the rail in front of the Silver Bell, among several other horses, then stepped through the door. The parlor was nearly filled with men, smoking, flirting, drinking, and talking with the working girls of the house. He gave his name to the beefy bartender and was directed to the second floor, down the hall to the last room on the left. He could feel the eyes of the bartender on him as he climbed the stairs alone. A glance back indicated that nothing seemed to be out of place. The other patrons seemed to be the wealthy businessmen who would frequent such a place as this, and none seemed especially interested in him personally.

A soft knock was immediately answered by a rotund black woman, dressed in the black and white uniform of a maid. Her round, friendly face grinned broadly at John, and she opened the door wide. Her white teeth had a huge gap between the front two, making her smile seem juvenile and warm. Her dark eyes crinkled in pleasure at the fine appearance of her mistress's guest.

"Welcome, suh. Ya'll must be here to see Miz Belle. Come in and rest your bones, while Miz Belle finishes her makeover. She's near 'bout ready, I reckon, so it won't be long. You can call me Sally, if ya'll needs anything."

"Thank you, Sally. I'm not early, am I?" John's gaze took in the apartment of Belle Flanagan. It was at least two rooms, maybe more. The parlor and living room were furnished in an abundance of pink and scarlet. Lace doilies graced the polished wood tables and plump armchairs. The walls were covered with cream-colored wallpaper and pink-flocked roses. The baseboards and crown molding were painted a creamy white. While the furniture was more delicate than the heavy, leather furniture John was accustomed to, it was certainly elegant and well built. The parlor showed a considerable investment in all its furnishings, including a fine oil painting of an Irish country scene on one wall. It was decidedly too feminine for John's taste, but certainly impressive for a rugged boom town like Denver. To top off the impression, a delicate scent of floral perfume teased his nostrils.

"This is very comfortable, Sally." He smiled at the beaming black servant. "You been with Miz Belle long?"

"Since the war, Mister John. I was workin' in a black cathouse outside Petersburg, Virginia, when Miz Belle found me. I was a household slave afore the good Massa Lincoln done freed me. I didn't know what to do and ended up working on my back fer a dollar a throw. Them black soldiers was some randy fellas, I declare. Anyhows, I come down with somethin' awful sick. I was throwed out by the madam, with jus' the clothes on my back. Miz Belle saw me layin' on the street, 'bout half dead, and took pity on me. She nursed me back to well, and I decided right then, I was gonna stay with her the rest of my born days. So here's I be. Fat and sassy and happy as a tick on a coon dawg's back."

John laughed and gave the beaming Sally a generous hug. "Good for you, Sally, my dear. You keep Miss Belle out of trouble, and I'll be forever indebted to you."

"I'll try, honey, I'll try. But, iffen I know my Belle, them dark eyes and good looks you is a'carryin' will make my job all that much harder."

"One thing you can depend on, my loyal Sally. I'll never intentionally hurt your mistress."

"Honey, men's like you never hurt us gals, intentional like." She laughed loud and hard, her jolly countenance quivering and rolling with each guffaw.

"What are you two up to?" Belle Flanagan swept into the room from the next, resplendent in a pale, cream-colored gown. Glittering rhinestones outlined the plunging neckline and, once again, drew John's eyes to the stirring view of a soft, yet firm bosom. His fingers twitched—they wished to stroke the softness so desperately. Belle's auburn red hair was swept up in the latest New York fashion. Gold bracelets glittered on each arm, and a diamond ring flashed on one of her long, slender fingers.

John stood and bowed low, utterly struck by the statuesque beauty of the woman and determined to let her know it. "My word, but what is this vision of loveliness I see before me. Belle, you astound me. I am unaccustomed to seeing such exquisite beauty so far from London or New York."

Belle smiled, pleased. "Be off with you, you English scamp. And what blarney. Your tongue is as smooth as the old stone itself. Besides, I have been inquiring into you, John Whyte. Why would the son of the Earl of Bransworth be slumming around in the dregs of England's lost colonies, far from the glitter of London high society?"

"I've fallen a long way from there, my Irish beauty. I'm the youngest of four brothers. You know what that means—last in the pecking order. I don't have a farthing waiting for me in Great Britain. The States are my best hope for success, so here I am. What about you? You weren't born here, not with that brogue."

Belle smiled. "You're right, lobsterback. I came here in '56 with my father and mother and four younger sisters. We settled in Boston, and life was good until the Mick riots of '59. Pap was right up front, as usual. Some policeman shot him and left him lying in the street." Belle sat down at the table, where white tapered candles cast a soft glow on the china awaiting the serving of food. Sally was scurrying about, readying her culinary effort for presentation. Belle motioned for John to sit.

"I think you'll enjoy what Sally has prepared. I sent her to a cooking school in New York, right after the war. She has an appreciation for food and a knack for cooking, as you might guess from looking at her. In case you might think I am being critical, her heart is as big as the rest of her, and I love her as I did me very own ma."

"I had no doubt of it, Belle. You are fortunate to have her loyalty. I have a special friend as well, Khan Singh—you've met him—who taught me the skills of warfare and has stayed at my side, in war and afterwards. I appreciate how special such a person is and am grateful for his friendship."

Sally placed the first course on the table, motioning for both of them to test her efforts. It was everything Belle promised. "English roast beef and Yorkshire pudding," John exclaimed in delight. "And delicious, too. In fact, even better than that. My compliments, Sally, it's wonderful."

"You jus' hush up and eat, Mister Whyte. I's happy to do it. My Belle don't eat enough fer what's good fer her health. You come around anytime, iffen it means my Belle eats like she should. Now, pour the lady some of this here wine. It's been in ice fer two hours. Drink it while it be cold."

The two diners engaged in light conversation while they devoured the food presented by the beaming Sally. After finishing a delightful dessert of canned pears smothered in cream and brandy, John pushed back from the table and groaned in feigned distress. "My word, Sally. I'm stuffed. I doubt if I could walk across the room, I'm so full."

He shared the last of the wine with Belle and lifted his glass in a silent toast to her. "I must admit, I am most happy to find such delightful cuisine so far from the bright lights of New York or Chicago."

Belle bobbed her head at the compliment. "And in the boudoir of a whorehouse madam?"

"No, I did not mean to suggest that at all. You misunderstand me, madam. I meant no disrespect to you."

"Why not? I've been snubbed by the best of them. It doesn't offend me anymore." Belle sipped her wine. The muscles of her well-formed arm rippled as she lifted her glass. The subtle movement caused a similar ripple of desire to course through John, leaving a most delightful sensation in its wake. Raw desire stirred him and left him anticipating more.

"While in India, I was fortunate enough to become very well acquainted with a wonderfully sensual woman who was an elegant courtesan. It is an honored profession for poor women over there, and many girls use it as a stepping-stone to financial security."

"Well, if that's the way you feel, then you are in the minority, me bucko. The so-called good women of Denver would run me out of town on a rail if their husbands would let them. Since most of their husbands are regular customers, I can understand why." Her green eyes flashed.

John looked intently at the red-haired beauty across the table from him. "You are not going to allow that to happen, I take it?"

"You bet. I'm buying up property all over town and the surrounding area. If the good women ever succeed in closing the Silver Bell, I'll retire and manage my other business holdings. When I came here from Washington, D.C., I decided it was my last move."

"Good for you, Belle. I'm enough of a rebel to cheer for you. I admire your ambition and determination. I applaud your grit." He paused and then asked the inevitable question. "How did you ever get involved in this business, anyway? That is, if you don't mind telling me."

She shook her head, the red tresses bobbing, the ruby strands sparkling in the candles' glow. "After Pap was killed, my ma was destitute. I was seventeen and attractive enough, I suppose. Ma marched me down to a whorehouse that was run by an Irish lady Ma had met in church. Ma was one of the few women who would speak to Tilly Quinn, since she was a soiled dove. She never held it against Tilly, to her credit. Ma and Tilly decided I'd have a better chance there than trying to work as a housemaid or bar girl, which were my only other choices. Tilly took me on, taught me the business and how to stay free of diseases and so forth. I had some schooling and could cipher, so I kept the books and did the bills. The Civil War was a boom time for the business, and we ended up in New York and finally down in Washington, D.C."

John smiled. "You don't say? I was in the capitol off and on during the war. Just about every officer in the city went to one house or the other. Which one was yours?"

"A place called 'The Little White House,' over on west K Street. You know the place?"

"Certainly. It had a very good reputation—discreet, clean, and filled with quality ladies. It was probably the most frequented pleasure house in the city, especially for the higher ranking officers."

"How about you, John Whyte? You ever visit?"

John laughed loudly. "Now, Miz Belle, a gentleman never discusses his personal moments of that nature, especially with a fine lady."

"How gallant. I suppose I should expect nothing more from a rake like you. Are you married, John? Not that it matters, you understand."

"No. So far, I've avoided putting such a burden on any poor lady's lovely shoulders."

"I shouldn't think many fine young women of good virtue would consider it much of a burden." Belle hid a small yawn behind her shapely hand. "My, my. It's later than I thought." She coyly arched her eyebrow and delicately inquired of John, "I rarely make such an invitation, but would you care to have coffee and cognac? In there." Her eyes glanced toward the bedroom.

John shook his head. He saw the sudden surprise and even disappointment that momentarily shadowed Belle's eyes. "I'm afraid I must regretfully decline, my dear. I have some work that I must attend to tonight and a full day tomorrow. However, I wonder if you would allow me the honor of escorting you to dinner tomorrow night, say, around nine? We'll try the cuisine at the Western Stockman's Cafe."

Belle stammered in confusion. "Wh . . . why, I don't know. That is—"

"Consider it settled then. I'll call for you at nine prompt. Until then, I want again to thank you for a delightful evening and an excellent meal. I'll look forward to tomorrow night."

John swiftly pecked Belle on the cheek and took his coat from Sally, who was as perplexed as her mistress over the sudden departure. She was convinced the handsome English gentleman would end up in Miz Belle's bed. Goodness knows she deserved a little diversion. It had been a long time between gentlemen friends for her hard-working mistress.

John stepped outside and adroitly climbed onto his saddle. He trusted he had made the right decision, although his desire made riding the horse a bit uncomfortable. He suspected Belle Flanagan was not accustomed to being refused. Hopefully, her interest would increase from the unexpected response and, by the close of tomorrow night, the invitation would be repeated. John whistled tunelessly as he walked Blaze up the shadowed street. The incessant noise from the saloons didn't interrupt his musings of an evening in the company of a red-haired beauty. It crowded everything else out of his mind.

CHAPTER 14
DETECTIVE BUSINESS

The next morning, Curly Bill returned to the *Star of India* barely in time to sip a cup of Kai's hot coffee before they all parted for the day's business. His bronzed, weather-worn face was creased in a huge smile. He seemed anxious to tell his story, so John obliged the affable Texan. "Good morning, William. And how was your evening?"

"Oh, Boss. It were Heaven on earth. I couldn't find Miz Belle right away but did run into Claudette, a wunnerful gal from New Orleans. Arrived out here to Denver a couple a' weeks ago." Curly Bill sighed, like a love-struck adolescent. "She was wunnerful. A real lady and so danged purty. Why, it about takes a fella's breath away, jus' to look at her. We spent the whole evenin' together, eatin', dancin,' drinkin', and . . . well, you know."

Curly Bill had the good grace to blush slightly, forcing a wide grin from John, and even Khan's stern face softened, allowing a twitch of his lips under his fierce, pointed moustache.

Bill took a sip of his hot coffee and leaned over to whisper in John's ear. "Boss, she went and kissed me good-bye this mornin' at her door, and she was baby-butt nekkid. How 'bout that?"

John had to laugh and clapped his friend on his muscular arm. "William, my fortunate friend, you seemed to have found a rare treasure, indeed."

"Yep," was the smug reply. "And I only spent twenty dollars fer her company fer the whole night."

"My word. How, er, how interesting. At that rate, you will

118

have spent your entire month's wages in only four more days."

"Well, it's shore worth it. If my pap could only see me now. Seein' a twenty-dollar-a-night whore and not worried 'bout the cost."

"Frankly, William, I doubt if you would want your father aware of your behavior right now. He'd likely take a razor strop to your hind end. Not that you don't deserve it, my good fellow."

"Well, there's that, too, I reckon. Say, do ya think I oughta explain to Miz Belle that I'm already took? I sorta left her thinkin' I'd be comin' back to visit her."

"Why don't you let me handle that for you, my love-smitten friend? I will be seeing her tonight. I'll convey your regrets. I'm certain Miss Flanagan will understand."

"Would ya? Thanks, Boss." Curly rubbed the underside of his droopy moustache with the top of his forefinger. "What about today? What's the plan?"

"You and Khan will visit all the farriers in Aururia and the surrounding area south of Denver, seeking the one who made the Memphis bar horseshoe. Sheriff Gilbert will be checking the shops in Denver for us. I plan to go to the county clerk's office and look through the land registrar's records. I hope to discover someone buying large amounts of land, spending money beyond a reasonable income level. Then, I'll stop at the banks, to learn if anyone has been depositing unusually large amounts of cash. I'll save our friend Krammer's bank for the last."

"Sounds fine by me. Ya ready to ride, Khan Singh?"

"Yes, Sahib William. As long as you promise not to burden me with endless stories of your newly found love life."

"Fine by me, ya old mossy-back. I'll jus' keep my thoughts to myself and not let you enjoy 'em at all."

The two men left the railroad car, still arguing good-naturedly about whether it was a loss or gain not to hear Curly Bill's colorful description of his escapades the previous night. John smiled at his two best friends while putting on his gun belt. He pulled the pistol several times to ensure its smooth release. Then he twirled the chamber of the Colt to ensure the weapon was loaded and went outside, leaving Kai to clean up the morning dishes. Blaze was already saddled and tied at the wooden fence that separated the corral from the rail yard.

"Morning, Blaze." John stroked the animal's velvety nose, talking softly to the black stallion. Then he smoothly vaulted into the saddle and rode toward the downtown area of Denver, slow and easy, enjoying the warm morning sun and the bustle of the awakened town. He stopped, tipping his hat, to allow two busy homemakers to hurry past, shopping baskets in their hands and talking together so intently they hardly noticed the courtesy. John watched as the two women hitched their dress hems high and skirted a muddy puddle before stepping onto the wooden sidewalk across the street. They turned into a millinery store still jabbering, while John pointed Blaze toward the doorway of Rafe's office. He could see that the burly mining engineer was already at his desk through the wavy glass of Rafe's office door. He dismounted, tied a rein to the hitching post outside the office, and tapped on the glass until he attracted Rafe's attention.

Rafe grinned a hello and waved John in, pushing back from the cluttered desk. "Howdy, John. Take a load off. Want some coffee, or somethin' more substantial?"

"No, thank you, Rafe. I stopped by to warn you not to overwork yourself this wonderful day. And, I'll be wanting to speak with Mr. Krammer at his bank this afternoon. Say about four. Will you accompany me? Sort of an introductory visit."

"Be happy to, John. Say, you're not still thinking he's involved in these gold robberies, are you?"

"Nothing like that, Rafe. I want to probe about, see if he has noticed any men who are spending more money than perhaps they should. That sort of thing."

"You still want to keep your real purpose in Denver a secret?"

"As long as possible. The more we nose about, the more people will eventually figure out what we're up to."

"Whatever you say, John. I'll be ready about four. See you then. That is, iffen this pile of paperwork don't fall over on me and break my back. And John . . ."

"Yes?"

"My financials look pretty damned bad. I gotta get a shipment of ore from Central City to my smelter soon or shut down. You understand?"

"Certainly, Rafe. Within a few days, I promise."

"Fair enough. Well, see you at four." Rafe buried his head in the paper blizzard on his desk while John slipped out the door. He rode Blaze down to the county's recorder of deeds office and introduced himself to the wizened clerk, an old man with white hair curling over his ears and a neatly trimmed beard. A worn, green eyeshade resting on his head and thick glasses on his nose showed how long he had been a clerk behind a desk, his face buried in books and ledgers.

John explained his reason for the visit. "Mr. Mulway, is it?" he said, glancing at the nameplate on the open door. "I'm interested in making some land purchases around Denver. I would like to see the map of land plots for the local area and a listing of sales in the last year or so."

The old clerk took John to an empty table and brought out the record books and title ledgers. "Here's the last twelve months, Mr. Whyte. Call fer me, if you need anything else." The old clerk shuffled back to his desk, and John went to work, a pad and pencil at hand. The work was tedious and slow, but by noon John had listed the names of four individuals and three named companies that had purchased large amount of real estate in and around Denver. Finishing just as the Episcopal Church bell rang for noon vespers, he took a hasty lunch of rabbit stew at the corner cafe and walked over to Sheriff Gilbert's office, where he met the genial lawman tying his horse to the wooden hitching rail.

"Howdy, Mr. Whyte. I spoke to three different smithies, and none admitted to making your horseshoe any time in the near past." He escorted John into the dim interior of his office and sat at his rolltop desk, resting his feet on its scarred surface.

"Not to worry, Sheriff. I didn't expect it would be fast or easy. I came for another favor, if you don't mind."

"What's that?"

"I would like a short note of introduction from you to each bank president in town. I'd like to talk to them about people who might have made unusually large bank deposits. If I walked in and ask questions like that, I'd be tossed out on my bum."

Gilbert chuckled, reaching in one of the cluttered cubbyholes of his desk for a piece of paper and his pen. "But won't that kill your story about being a visitor to Denver?"

"I didn't expect to keep my business here a secret forever. I didn't want to start out telling everyone in town. I'll ask the bankers for their confidence as it is."

Gilbert hastily scribbled some words and handed John the requested note. The young detective took his leave of the law officer, with the promise to report back with any new information he uncovered. John walked down the street to the first bank he saw, the Denver First Savings Bank. He asked for and was ushered into the office of the president, Silas Appleby. The banker had graying hair and chin whiskers, but the sparkling blue eyes under white eyebrows belied his age. John showed the banker the note from Sheriff Gilbert and saw a definite warmth come over the old banker's face.

"Glad to help Sheriff Gilbert when I can. He's done a fine

job keeping the peace here in town. What can I do for you, sir?"

John explained the purpose for his visit and obtained the banker's promise to keep his inquiry a secret. "I wonder if you could check your records or remember any man or men depositing more money than you might ordinarily expect from them. Men who aren't striking it rich at the diggings or in business here in town."

Silas Appleby scratched his furry chin and called for his deposit ledger from his head cashier. He skimmed through the ledger, front to back, and then looked up at John. "I can't say I've seen a single instance where my depositors were putting in more money than I would think is reasonable. Sorry."

"That's all right, Mr. Appleby. I may be chasing a coon up a tree, to quote a Texas friend of mine." John pulled out his list from the recorder of deed's office. He gave the old banker the list of names. "Any of these people or companies familiar to you?"

Scanning the small list, Appleby nodded his head, making his heavy, white beard wiggle like a waterfall. "I recognize a couple of these. What do you want to know about 'em?" By the time John left, he had scratched two individuals and two company names from his list. Silas Appleby had convinced him of their legitimacy. After three additional stops at local banks, it was time to meet Rafe at his office. By then John had every name save one scratched from his list.

"Foothills Land Company, umm . . ." Rafe tugged at his ear. "Can't say I ever heard of 'em."

"None of the bankers I have talked with so far has," John admitted. "And that makes me all the more interested to find out who owns it. And where the money to buy up numerous sections of prime land around Denver came from."

The two men walked over to the bank owned by Loren Krammer. *Western Bank and Trust* was placed over the doorway in gilded gold script letters, several inches high. *L. Krammer, Pres.* was below that, in letters almost as large. A small sign at the entrance stated that over $50,000 dollars was securely deposited therein.

Loren Krammer ushered the two of them into his office at the rear of the building. It was impressive, with expensive furnishings, including an impressive desk of polished cherry wood. Compared to some of the offices John had visited, it stood in opulent contrast and appeared overly pretentious. Loren did have his son's weak chin, even though his was hidden under an expanse of salt and pepper beard, and his eyes were similar, a very pale blue. The most obvious similarity was in the shape of their bodies, except Loren's showed the wear of thirty extra years in a pronounced potbelly that strained the buttons holding a gray, velvet vest tautly closed.

Loren Krammer gushed his greetings. "A real pleasure to meet you, Lord Whyte. Rafe was over this morning and told me a bit about you. I've read of the famous son of the Duke of Bransworth and his exploits with Grant and Custer during the war. A real honor. Rafe tells me you are a stockholder of Guggenheim's?"

"In a small way, Mr. Krammer."

"You went out and saw Central City? My son works there for Rafe." Krammer laughed, a little smugly. "It was one of the conditions I made before Rafe got his loan from me to set up operations here in Denver."

"That's all right, Loren. Tom's been a good worker. I've got no complaints," Rafe replied.

"Glad to hear it. Now, what can I do for you, Mr., er, Lord Whyte? By gum, how do I address you?"

"Please, Mr. Krammer. Don't bother with this 'Lord' stuff. Call me John. We're all friends, right?"

John could see from the smirk on Loren Krammer's face that

the portly banker was more than pleased at the suggestion. The banker was rubbing shoulders with English nobility and was going to call him by his first name to boot. John imagined that he was deciding how he could flaunt this development in front of the rest of Denver high society.

Krammer reached for a crystal humidor sitting on his massive desk and took out a cigar. "A smoke, gentlemen?" He offered one to John and Rafe. John accepted the offering while suppressing a smile. It was a Cuban El Supremo. He took it but put it into his pocket.

"Not right now, thank you. I'll save it for after supper."

Krammer rolled his in the flame of the match Rafe offered, blowing out a thick stream of smoke, which rose toward the high ceiling.

"Any time's a good time for a fine cigar. Right, Rafe?" He laughed, a deep rumble from his belly.

"I'll say, Loren. And you have some good ones to smoke, I'll be the first to admit. I wish I could enjoy them as often as you do."

"Have 'em shipped to me from New Orleans, every three months." He glanced up at John to gauge if he was impressed by the comment.

John stroked the ego of the pretentious banker. "I say. They must be an expensive habit, this far from New Orleans. But, after trying the local beer, I suppose the local smokes must taste like dried buffalo chips."

Krammer laughed. "You're a regular card, John. Say, how 'bout I have Flo—that's my wife—set up a little party in your honor? Sort of a welcome to Denver kind of thing. I'll invite a few of my friends and introduce you to the cream of Denver society."

"Why, thank you, Loren. You don't have to . . ."

"No problem. Be my pleasure. Say Saturday evening, about

'eight? Rafe, you're invited, too, of course."

"That's only two days. Is that enough time?" John's concern was all sham, but stroked Krammer's inflated ego even more.

"Not in the least. Florence is a party woman. She'll be ecstatic at the prospect and will do it up right, I assure you. It's settled then. Oh, what did you want of me? I almost forgot."

John thought fast. He decided to forgo any questioning of Krammer at this time. "I was just wondering if you had any insight into this gang of villains that is making Rafe's life so miserable. You seen anyone spending or banking more than you think is reasonable for his situation?"

"Nope, can't say that I have. Of course, you know I must respect the confidentiality of my depositors. Still, I haven't seen anything unduly suspicious. You thinking about taking on the sheriff's job?"

"No, I was trying to help Rafe here. He's about at the end of his rope with the scoundrels."

"Can't say that I blame him," Krammer sympathized. "I wish I could do more, but I'm as stumped as anyone."

"One more thing," John interjected. "I was looking at some property, west of town. This place is a good bet to grow even more in the coming years. Anyway, a land speculator I was talking with said it belonged to a company named Foothills Land Company. Know who owns it?"

"I've heard of it. Can't say as I do, though. Still, there's plenty of good land available; please keep your eyes open. And come see me if you find a piece you like. I'll help you set up the loan to aquire it." Krammer nodded his head while he tapped ash from the end of his smoke into an ashtray made from the foot of an elephant.

"Thanks, Loren. I'll look forward to hearing from you if there is to be a gala for Saturday night. Please tell Mrs. Krammer not to go to too much trouble."

John left the bank with Rafe, a beaming Loren Krammer standing in his doorway to watch their exit. The scheming banker mentally started the guest list, knowing Flo would know who to add to it. He had meant to ask if Whyte was married. His Suzanne was approaching prime marrying age. By God, wouldn't that be something? He imperialistically left orders for the cashiers and hurried home. He and his wife had a lot to do and not much time to do it in. As Krammer walked the boardwalk toward his house, he rolled the thought in his mind off his lips, just to hear how it sounded. "Lady Suzanne Whyte. By God, what a fine moniker."

CHAPTER 15
FAVORS FROM BELLE

John arrived at the *Star of India* as Curly Bill and Khan rode in from their day's search. Bill took the horses to the livery to unsaddle, feed, and rub them down, while Khan delivered the bad news.

"Not a single blacksmith admitted to making the horseshoe, Sahib. Several agreed they had done so in the past, but not a man remembered making one in the last year. Were you any more successful in your inquiries?"

John pulled out the cigar given him by Loren Krammer. "I know this cigar band does not constitute absolute proof, but I'm certain the Krammers are connected to the gold robberies. I'm going to request four additional men from the Kansas City office by telegraph. They should be here in three or four days. Then, we'll make a trip to Central City for Rafe's gold stockpile. I have a plan as to how we may thwart the outlaw gang at its own game."

He and Khan finished cleaning up from the day's activities, while listening politely as Curly Bill described in great detail all that Khan had reported in two sentences. For the next hour the three men puzzled over the strange code that Khan had discovered in the letter in Tom Krammer's room.

"You positive fer shore this is what was writ down?" Curly Bill complained. "I jus' can't make heads or tails on what it means. All these here arrows and the numbers by 'em. It jus' don't make no sense."

"That's what makes a code work, William. Believe me, this code is breakable. All we need is a bit of good fortune and we'll have it." John glanced up as the clock on the wall chimed seven times. "I say! I've got to get dressed. I have a dinner engagement at nine. William, I'll write the telegram if you will deliver it to the agent at the train station, please. You will have time before you are due at Miss Claudette's, won't you?"

"Sure, Boss. Happy to. I told her I'd be around 'bout ten or so. Give me a chance to see how my luck is at the faro tables over to the Criterion Saloon first. With any luck, I'll cover my evening expenses. Who's your dinner partner tonight?"

John pursed his lips, treading carefully with his friend, unsure of the mercurial Bill's response. "Miss Flanagan. I asked her yesterday, in hopes of enlisting her aid in our inquiries. She has connections among the working girls I can't tap in to."

"Belle Flanagan? Good idear, Boss. Since I've got all my time scheduled with Claudette, I was worried Miz Flanagan might feel neglected. You've taken me off the hook. I owe ya one, Boss."

"My pleasure, William. I will certainly try and make amends between you and Miss Flanagan. I'll do my best to make her disappointment at your absence a wee bit more bearable."

"Hell, Boss. You're twice the gentleman of anyone I ever seen. You'll do jus' fine. But thanks fer the compliment."

John rolled his eyes at Khan Singh and went to prepare himself for the coming evening. He wore a well-tailored brown suit. He slipped his pistol into a concealed shoulder holster. Kai had re-shined his black boots and brushed the dust from John's broad-brimmed Stetson hat. He stepped out of his room to the good-natured ribbing from Curly Bill and, pulling his long drover's coat on, galloped away from the soft light of the parlor car toward the brighter lights of Front Street and the heart of Denver.

As John rode Blaze toward the Silver Bell, he mentally reviewed his request to the Kansas City office and his blossoming idea for moving the gold shipment safely through the mountains. "If I could think of a way to get past the vigilant Loren Krammer, to see the books of his bank . . ." he grumbled to himself. If the banker was involved in the gold robberies, the money was probably being funneled through the bank. It was a clever scheme and would be hard to prove, unless they uncovered some incriminating evidence that would stand up in court. "We have to find the owner of the dead horse," he exclaimed to Blaze, patting the faithful animal's neck. "A bit of 'persuasion' by Khan Singh and that long, sharp dagger he carries, and we would have the outlaw gang leader's name."

John had never seen the old Sikh warrior fail to obtain the information he was seeking. No sane individual wanted Khan Singh carving him up, piece by piece, even though John knew it was only a threat. Even the toughest confederate guerrilla rider had broken to Khan's efforts during the war.

John arrived at the Silver Bell as the hour struck nine. He entered the foyer and was immediately directed upstairs to Belle Flanagan's suite. She was brushing her hair, Sally curling and tucking stray wisps of the red, silky-fine strands into their proper place.

Upon hearing John's tap on her door, Belle stood. She had on a magnificent, pale-green, velvet evening dress, tucked at the waist by a cream-colored sash. With her imposing height and proud carriage, she was almost as tall as John. He bowed and whistled softly. "My word, Belle Flanagan. You are simply smashing. What a lovely picture you make. You are a vision of loveliness."

"Get on with yer blarney, ye smooth-talkin' English devil. Ya think I don't know me way out of the 'tater patch. But"—her smile dazzled John—"thank ye for the fine compliment. I've been longing for an opportunity to wear this gown since it arrived from Chicago last spring."

"Well, it certainly has found the shape to fit itself around," John replied. His blood was warming at each succeeding second in the presence of the lovely madam. "Are you ready? I have made reservations for us at the Cattleman's Club restaurant."

Belle nodded and appraised her handsome gentleman escort. He intrigued her, far more than any man had in a long time. What a pity the feeling wasn't mutual. She hungered for him and knew she could have sent him back to his railroad home on wheels, blissfully exhausted. She was after all, a skilled professional in the art of love, even if she no longer worked the trade night after night.

"John, I thank you for the invitation, but there will be some diners who believe I don't belong in their refined company and will judge harshly any man who escorts me. Are you sure you wouldn't rather eat here? Sally can whip up something delicious in no time."

John took Belle's hand and caressed the long, slender fingers tenderly. "Miss Flanagan, I wouldn't hear of it. One, as I stated before, I do not hold the view that your profession is immoral. I consider it a legitimate escape from the poverty of birth or misfortune. It should be true here as well, although, unfortunately, it isn't. Two, as the black sheep son of English nobility, I am held to an unusual standard of conduct. And three, I find you very attractive and am proud to be seen in your company. I'll box the jaw of any man who says anything discourteous about you, in or out of your presence. Does that answer your question?"

Belle laughed delightedly, loud and throaty. Grabbing a crocheted shawl and placing her hand on John's offered arm, she accompanied him to the door. "Come on then, me bucko. We're off to eat with the hob-nobs. Won't they choke on their cornbread when we come waltzing in? Shall we walk? It's a lovely evening, and it's only three blocks over."

It was as Belle surmised. The room was crowded with diners, and the racket of their conversation fell substantially quieter as the two of them were escorted to their table by a haughty maître d'. The muted conversation of the diners stayed suspiciously low throughout their meal, while both covetous men and curious women directed numerous glances at them. Bell and John ignored it all and enjoyed the meal and each other's company.

Belle told John a little more about herself, then listened enthralled as John told her of his life. Once, during their conversation, she leaned over and whispered to John. "There's the territorial governor over there. Would you like me to introduce you? I have had the pleasure of his company at my place several times."

John glanced at the table. The distinguished politician, with an oddly matched gray beard on his face and dark hair in stark contrast on his head, avoided eye contact with John and Belle, his every body movement revealing how tense he was. "No, it would be too cruel, my dear. Look at the poor man. He's about to faint, he's so afraid you will greet him in front of his wife." The two of them chuckled together and enjoyed their dessert, relishing in their devilish impact on the other customers in the restaurant.

After lingering over two cups of excellent coffee, they walked together back to the Silver Bell. Other Denver citizens strolling that evening gave way to the regal pair, whose presence, looks, and joy of the night were evident to the men and the occasional woman they passed. All stared, some even stopping in their tracks to watch the progress of such a handsome couple. At the Silver Bell, Belle first checked with the bartender in front and then led John upstairs to her suite. Firmly shutting the door, effectively barring the outside world, she sighed contentedly and relaxed. Sally bustled about, pouring cool wine into sparkling crystal glasses and making sure there was nothing else she could do for the happy couple.

"That will do, Sally. I won't need you anymore this evening. Good night."

"Yes'm, Good nights to you and Massa Whyte. I'll be a goin'. You jus' hollar iffen you need anything a'tall. Night, Miz Belle."

John watched big, good-hearted Sally ease out the door, then turned back to Belle, his eyes gleaming with anticipation and burning desire. Belle could not clearly read his intentions but shyly smiled, a bit mystified in view of the previous night's rejection, content to let him set the pace.

"It was a grand evenin', John. I don't know when I've had such an enjoyable dinner. Do you have to leave now? Would you care for something stronger to drink?"

John said nothing, lounging in a soft chair. He looked at Belle intensely, causing her to subconsciously pose as she stood by the door to her boudoir and preen her hair in a nervous reaction to his scrutiny. Sensual feelings were awakening, feelings that had lain dormant for many, many months. "Belle." John's voice was soft, yet extremely firm. "Would you do me a favor?"

"If I can, yes, John. What is it?"

"I wonder if you would mind washing the rice powder and rouge off your face. I would very much like to see you without the cosmetics. Would you mind?"

"Why . . . why no, if that's what you prefer. You'll be sorry, once I'm done, I'll wager."

"Never," he answered. "Thank you."

Belle opened the door to her boudoir and smiled coyly at John. "I'll only be a minute." She hurried inside and sat down at her makeup table, looking at her reflection in the tall mirror. Not quite sure what John was doing, she unbuttoned several of the top buttons to her dress, pulling it down to where it barely covered her bosom. Pinning up her long, red hair until it was out of her way, she took the jar of creamy makeup remover, wiping her face and neck clean of the white rice powder. She stripped the rouge from her lips and cheeks. Grimacing at the appearance of the numerous freckles bridging her nose, she wondered if John would laugh when he saw them. Shrugging her shoulders, she took a cinnamon stick from a small cup on the vanity, chewing it into slivers, scrubbing her teeth and sweetening her breath.

As she finished, the door opened, and John walked in. Saying nothing, he approached until he was standing directly behind her, still silent, looking appreciatively at her reflection in the mirror by the light of the twin candles burning on either side of her dressing table. The two stared at one another, the silence growing thunderous. Belle's mouth was dry, and she struggled to speak, but John's sudden movement stopped her.

Still watching her in the mirror, he loosened the pins holding her hair, allowing it to fall about her white shoulders. He placed his hands on either side of her face and slowly, so deliciously sensually, moved them down her cheeks to her neck to the swell of her breasts, where he paused. Belle sat silently, scarcely daring to breathe, so soft and so enjoyable was the sensation. Then, John bent at the waist, sliding his hands farther down under the green gown, to her sensitive, swollen nipples, where he stopped. As he paused, caressing her softly, her breath released in a deep, hissing gasp. John leaned lower and she turned her face toward him until his mouth touched hers. Their kiss was long, deep, wet, and fire-hot. Without removing his mouth from hers, John lifted the woman from her seat and, cradling her in his arms, took her to the edge of the soft bed. Resting his knee on the bedside, he lowered Belle onto it and stood so he could look at her again. Belle's face was flushed, and her lips were pouty and moist, anxious for another kiss.

Without saying a word, John stripped the aroused Belle of her clothing, his lips caressing the skin next bared, yet it was so effortlessly accomplished that she scarcely realized what he was doing. As he finished removing the last of her undergarments, he pulled back and stood at the edge of the bed, looking with desire and appreciation at the unashamed nakedness of the flame-haired beauty lying before him. Belle could stand it no more and, groaning in her desire for him, opened her arms and pulled him into her grasp. Somehow, his clothing joined hers on the floor, and the room was silent, except for the muffled sounds of physical pleasure. In her little room off of Belle's, Sally listened and smiled in the darkness. "Yassir, I surely did know it. That John Whyte is a good man fer my Miz Belle. He is a'givin' as well as a'takin'." Sally rolled her immense bulk into a more comfortable position and drifted into a sound sleep, believing everything was right with the world. It was a long time before the objects of her attention would follow her into slumber. A very long time.

CHAPTER 16
A FAVOR FROM BELLE

The clatter of dishes awakened John from his deep sleep. For an instant he was uncertain where he was, until the soft tickle of curly, red hair against his bare shoulder and the warm touch of Belle curled in his arms refreshed his memory. He grinned and stretched, trying not to wake her. Belle possessed a passion for lovemaking only a few lucky men would ever experience, and, this morning, John felt very fortunate. His recollection of the previous night's activities flooded his brain and brought a broad grin to his face. He snuggled close to Belle for another moment, savoring the memory.

Belle owed Blossom some heartfelt thanks, if her acclamations of pleasure were any indication of how well he had applied the lessons so patiently taught by the beautiful Hindu prostitute many years ago. He thought back, relishing the warm, satisfying feeling the thoughts of her provided him. Nearly ten years had passed since he had said his good-byes to Blossom, her tears spilling onto the shoulder of his dress uniform. Another world, another life ago. He wondered if she were still at the cabaret in Kurdistan, on the northwest frontier of India. He hoped she was well and happy, with enough money saved for a good dowry and a wealthy husband. She deserved some happiness and good luck in her life.

He shifted his thoughts to Belle, lying still and snug in the space beside him. Her life was wretched, in the eyes of "average" people. Yet, she was carving out a place for herself through

136

determination and pluck. He had no qualms that she would ever be beaten down by the social rejection of her unsavory background. He turned his head so he could inhale the delicate bouquet of perfume in her hair and gently caressed her bare back. As she moaned softly in her sleep, he moved his hand lower, sensuously stroking her out of her slumber.

Belle stirred and groaned in his ear. "Um. Oh, oh, John, yes, my darling, yes." The sleepy woman's first recognizable words were whispered to the man who had first surprised, then inspired, and finally overwhelmed her with his passionate lovemaking. She reached with her hand to feel his new need. "Oh, John. You rascal . . ."

It was later still before they sat down to the hearty breakfast skillfully prepared by Sally. Belle contentedly gazed at her most satisfying lover. He was swallowing the last of his first cup of coffee, before cutting into the stack of pancakes on his plate. He caught Belle's glance and grinned back, appearing to her very much like a young boy, his face so sweet and innocent. She smiled at his response to her evaluation.

"What? What?" He put the cup down and brushed his mouth with one of the napkins Sally had placed on the tray. His grin spread until his face was alight with humor. "Why are you smiling so knowingly? Your beguiling smile reminds me of Da Vinci's *Mona Lisa.*"

"Who's she? Some gal of yours, me handsome bucko?" Belle's jaw firmed, and her brows arched dangerously.

John laughed. "No, my dear. She was the subject of a famous Italian artist. Her smile is mystery itself. It's a very famous and treasured painting. You could have posed for it yourself, the way you looked at me. What were you thinking of?"

"None of your business, Johnny lad. You're already too cocksure of yourself as it is."

John winked at her. "Oh, I have some idea. These claw marks

on my back convey some measure of your meaning."

"See what I mean? You men. If we didn't need you around to tote firewood on a winter's night, the devil take you all." Belle's green eyes narrowed in mock seriousness, while John grinned at her teasing. He had no doubt that he had introduced the young whorehouse madam to attentions and sensations she had never experienced before, especially in her professional capacity, where it was strictly business, in and out the door with scarcely a by-your-leave.

John reached over and took Belle's hand in his and gently kissed her fingers. "I do have a more serious subject to discuss, Belle, if you will permit me."

Belle rang a tiny, silver bell, and Sally hurried into the room. "Yes'm', Miz Belle?"

"You may clear this all away, Sally. Mr. Whyte and I enjoyed it very much. Thank you." She smiled again at John. "Shall we sit on the balcony? It is a beautiful morning, and we'll have a lovely view of the eastern prairie and Pike's Peak, to the south."

"By all means," he answered. John followed Belle out onto the small balcony, where twin reed chairs awaited them. A small reed table provided a place to rest their coffee cups.

"More coffee?" Belle inquired, as John took in the view. He could see the white-topped peak of the famous mountain, barely visible through the early morning haze. The view seemed clean and fresh, as there was not yet enough traffic on the dusty streets of Denver. "No, thank you. Not right now."

"Isn't this a lovely place to enjoy the morning?" she asked. "I relax here often, to think without distractions. Look, there's an east bound train to Kansas City on its way." The mournful toot of the train whistle punctuated her observation.

The train faded into the distance. John turned to Belle, his eyes serious. "I wonder if I could impose on you for a favor, Belle?"

Belle gazed steadily at John, wondering where this was all leading. "If I can, of course."

"I should start by frankly telling you what my purpose is for coming to Denver." With that, John told Belle the true reason for his being in Colorado Territory. She listened intently until John was finished, her eyes never leaving his face. As he finished with his vow to find and capture the outlaws involved in the gold robberies, she nodded her understanding.

"I wondered why such a gentleman as you was hanging about a dusty frontier town like this. You said that you wanted something from me. What is it?"

John sought to frame his answer correctly. "I need your help in this investigation, Belle. Nobody has a clue as to who these scoundrels are. One of them has to be spending his ill-gotten gains recklessly. It doesn't stand to reason that an outlaw with money in his pocket will save it for a rainy day. What I want from you, if you wish to help me, is to cast your net around among the girls who work in the cribs, all over town. I can't ask them for help, but maybe you can. Because of your special relationship with them."

Belle sighed. "Because I run a whore-house, you mean. One whore to another, so to speak. Is that why you made love to me? So I'd snoop among the whores of Denver and Auraria for information?"

"Belle, I hope you know better than that. If you refuse, I'm still coming back to call on you. I admit when I met you, the idea of using your special position among the working girls came to mind. However, what I shared with you last night was not a performance. I meant what I said and did. I hope you feel the same way. I only want your help if you are absolutely willing to provide it. Otherwise," he grinned ruefully at the red-haired beauty across the table from him, "tell me to shut up, and I'll not mention it again."

Belle searched his face for any sign of deceit, but his face was open, direct. She relaxed and yielded to her feminine intuition. In truth, she did not stand a chance. He was such a satisfying lover, and so damned handsome, in the warm glow of the morning sunlight, that her hardened whore's heart softened. She warned herself not to expect too much; her experience had taught her several bitter lessons about the fickleness of men. Still, she wanted to believe him, and she would have offered much more had he demanded, so smitten was she with his charms.

"All right, John, dear. I'll talk with the ladies who manage the larger places and send Sally around to the smaller ones and the independent girls. It will take a few days to contact all of them, as it is. What exactly do you want me to find out?"

John beamed at Belle, a soft blush of pleasure rising to her cheeks. "I need to know the name of anyone who is spending more money than might otherwise be expected. A cowboy who's not working but has too much money in his pockets. A miner or teamster spending more that he could ever make honestly. That sort of thing."

"You know, of course, that the women I will be questioning make it their business not to ask too many questions, or to probe the motives or wherewithal of their customers. A sort of unspoken rule of business." She paused for an instant. "Shall I say why I'm asking such questions?"

"I understand, Belle. I hope you don't have to explain too much. Try to convince them to be open with you. I hope to keep my investigation a secret from certain parties. I'm trying to cover all possible paths to a solution. You may find out nothing at all. It's a good gamble, just the same. An outlaw with too much money in his pocket may spend large sums on a woman who has captured his fancy. If we find out anything from your contacts, it will have been worthwhile."

Belle nodded her head, shaking her auburn tresses gently about her sleep-softened face. "You will stop by tonight, to see what progress I've made?"

John nodded and took her hand in his. "If I'm welcome, I'll be most honored to stop around. Say about eleven?"

"Make it midnight. I've got a business to run, you know. I'll have Sally fix us a snack, and we can go over my day's report."

"Thank you, Belle. What we are doing is smart business, as well as the right thing. Denver must have law and order in the gold fields, if the town is to flourish. And, of course, I complete my assignment, making Wallace and the Pinkerton Detective Agency quite pleased." John glanced at his gold pocket watch. "Great Caesar, my dear. Look at the time. I must be about my business. Will you excuse me, until tonight, that is?"

Belle allowed him to pull her chair out and led the way back into her apartment, her hand on his strong left arm. "And for me as well. I'll have to scurry to cover all the houses I need to visit this morning."

John took the lovely redhead in his arms. She molded herself to him and hooked one heel behind his right calf. Squeezing tightly, he lowered his lips to hers, relishing the tangy taste of coffee on her sweet breath. Their farewell kiss gave every promise of what awaited them the coming night. Belle moaned softly against his lips, inspiring a most invigorating sensation in John, and he held the woman tightly to him. "I must go, my dear. If we don't stop now, you know where we'll end up. I'll see you tonight, so farewell until then." He hurried out the door and down the stairs, soundlessly whistling a marching song from his old regiment.

Belle closed the door and leaned against it for a moment, thinking about John, his skill as a lover, and his unusual request. As hard as she tried to resist the thought, she knew deep in her heart that he was using her. To her surprise, she didn't care. At least, he was less a bastard than the other men who had been allowed to get close to her.

"Sally," she called, "draw my bath, and then come here. I've got a special task for you."

CHAPTER 17
THE FIRST BREAK

As John rode Blaze up the muddy street toward the rail yard, he recalled the pleasures of the past night and Belle's irresistible charms. He became aware of the insistent tapping of a finger on a glass pane as he drew abreast of the bank owned by Loren Krammer. The well-dressed, portly banker motioned for him to come inside, beaming in friendly greeting to the horseman outside his window. Suppressing a sigh, John turned Blaze to the hitching post and walked into the bank. Two young men were counting and placing bills of money in the cash trays behind the customer windows in preparation for opening. They could have been cut from the same piece of cloth. Both were young, slight of build, with pale, watery eyes that spoke volumes of their long hours staring at numbers and paper only inches from their nose. Neither gave him a moment's notice, so engrossed were they in their work.

John murmured to himself, "Krammer must deduct every penny they are short at the end of the day." The banker gestured to him from the doorway of his private office, and John entered. Krammer closed the door behind him, after a glance at the two tellers, ensuring that they were hard at work.

"Good morning, Lord Whyte," he welcomed John, a pathetic longing for approval in his exaggerated smile.

"The best of the day to you, sir," John modestly replied. "Don't forget, you agreed to call me John. No need to stand on titles from the old country here in the West."

Krammer positively glowed, thinking he was being granted special status with the young "royal" from England. "Thanks, John. But, my wife will skin my hide if she catches me calling you anything but your formal title in front of her. She is so excited that such an exalted visitor as yourself should be visiting Denver. You remember that I mentioned she would want to throw a party in your honor?" At John's nod, he continued, "Well, she's aflutter at the idea, so here's the plan. It's on for Saturday night. We'll have all the finest citizens in Denver there. Can you make it about eight? The heat of the day will be gone by then, and we can watch the sun set from my back garden while enjoying our drinks. Then, dinner at nine and dancing afterwards, until the wee hours of the morning. Will that be all right, er, John?"

"It would be an honor, Mr. Krammer. I'm anxious to meet with your friends. Colorado is such a magnificent place, I'm certain your friends will be just as interesting."

"I agree completely," Krammer answered enthusiastically. "Colorado is certainly a wonderful place to see the grandeur of God's handiwork. Well, John," Krammer beamed, "till Saturday night then. I'll send over a formal invite for you, but it's all set. My Florence will be beside herself with anticipation. And my daughter, Suzanne, will spend the next two days shopping for the best this ole town has to offer to be sure she's appropriately dressed for the occasion."

"Marvelous," John put out his hand, which was taken by Krammer and pumped forcefully. John forced a wan smile at the effusive banker and turned to leave the office. "I must be off, I'm afraid. Until Saturday night, Mr. Krammer."

"Good morning to you, John." Krammer's pig-like eyes squinted in pleasure as he escorted John to the waist-high wooden partition that separated the working area of the bank from the customers' side. Several customers stared at the two, their gaze initially drawn by the difference in height of the two men. Both noticed the proprietary way Krammer kept John's arm in his grasp. Speaking loud enough for everyone in the bank to hear, he bid John another farewell at the swinging gate of the office partition. "Good day to you, Lord Whyte. I'm looking forward to seeing you at my house on Saturday night." Then, he turned and fairly bounced back into his office, shutting the door against the stares of the mere mortals doing business with his tellers.

John walked out of the bank with an impassive expression, hoping the insufferable banker was the man responsible for the gold robberies. It would be such a pleasure bringing the pompous ass down. He swung back into the saddle and continued on his way to the *Star*. William and Khan Singh would be waiting for him, to discuss the day's assignment in the ongoing investigation.

Their efforts that day were as futile as the day before. John had spent all the time he felt comfortable with trying to find out about the Foothills Land Company, without results. The owner or owners were hidden from public view in layers of other companies and in the secrecy of their charter. A federal judge would have to issue orders to open the territorial ledgers in order to more thoroughly investigate the mysterious company. However, John knew he did not have enough proof to convince a judge to give him the necessary authority.

The night with Belle was even more enjoyable and less urgent, with time to experiment with one another and to enhance their partner's gratification. Belle informed John that she had put the word out through her special sources. Now, it was a matter of patiently waiting for the first break, which John felt was inevitable.

Friday morning, as John arrived at the *Star*, he found Curly Bill about to ride away. "Howdy, Boss," Bill greeted his friend.

"Another long night, I see."

"Don't kid me, you Texican rowdy. I saw you coming out of Claudette's room not thirty minutes ago."

"Who, me? Naw. It musta been some other rowdy, who's got that gal's heart all tangled up in his spurs. Any luck from Belle's inquiries yet?"

"No, but I suspect we'll start hearing something shortly. She's making the rounds again today, as is her maid. How about you?"

"Me and Khan Singh has visited every blacksmith in Denver, and Auraria, plus all them what's south of town. Today we was gonna mosey north. Say, a fancy envelope was hand delivered fer ya, about ten minutes ago. It's inside on the parlor table."

"It must be my invitation to the Krammer's party tomorrow night. I've been expecting it."

"What are you going there fer? Don't you think he's mixed up in the robberies, even if Rafe don't?"

"What better way to look around, than to be invited into a suspect's house? Besides, I could not think of an appropriate excuse not to accept." John swung down off Blaze. "You taking Rajah with you?"

"Yep. He needs the exercise. Well, see ya tonight." Bill nudged the flanks of his white-spotted pinto pony and trotted off toward the barn.

"Good luck, Bill, Khan Singh. I'll be here at the *Star* today, if you need me."

"Good morning, Sahib."

Bill released Rajah from the barn and the three of them turned north, across the tracks. John climbed the metal stairs of the *Star* and walked inside. He went to the desk and took out the cryptic code that Khan Singh had discovered in Tom Krammer's office. He devoted the rest of the day to studying the cryptic message, trying to resolve the code. The message consisted of arrows, pointed up, down, left, or right. A number was on the tail of each arrow. The numbers were always zero through nine, never more.

John mused, perplexed by the code. "This thing can't be that difficult," he groused to himself. "I'm not looking at it right." He stared at the tracing for several long minutes and let his mind drift, seeking any idea as to what was written. He ate Kai's noontime lunch, scarcely aware of what it was, and returned to the code, his brow wrinkled in concentration. The faint wisp of an idea struggled to emerge from the recesses of his mind. He sensed he was closing in on the answer when he heard riders stopping at the corral fence, next to the rear platform of the *Star*.

Heavy footsteps clattered on the metal steps, and Curly Bill burst into the room. "Boss!" he shouted excitedly. "We found the man who made the horseshoe. He told us who the owner was."

John tossed the note aside. "Well done, William. Have a seat and tell me about it." He pushed away from his desk and turned his attention to the beaming Curly Bill, who flopped down on the horsehair couch, a dusty hat in his gnarled hands.

"Khan Singh and me rode north of town, stoppin' at every blacksmith we could find, without any results. Then, at one stop the smithy mentioned his cousin had a small shop nearly over to Boulder Creek, about ten miles north. He said his cousin had jus' come out west from Memphis, after the war. Well, me and Khan rode right over to this fellow's place and showed him the shoe. Shore enough, he made it. Fer a fellow named Franks, whose pinto pony had a cracked hoof. Put the last one on 'bout three weeks ago. The blacksmith, his name was Sidell, weren't it, Khan?"

At Khan Singh's nod, Curly Bill continued. "Anyways, this Sidell said he shoed Franks's horse several times, as well as a bunch of his friends'. Said they came around a lot and always needed new shoes, so he guessed they did a lot of hard riding in the mountains, they wore out shoes so regular like. Said Franks was in to see him 'bout a week ago, with a new, roan pony. Said his pinto fell and broke his laig and had to be shot. Got new shoes and a bridle from Sidell."

John asked, "Did he give you a description of this chap Franks? And where he might be?"

Curly Bill shook his head regretfully. "Yes and nope. He hasn't seen the critter since the last shoeing. This jasper what calls hisself Franks said he was a miner and prospector. Sidell said he always paid in greenbacks and always rode away towards Denver. Also, he said Franks was a pretty sharp dresser fer a mining man, with a likin' fer fancy boots and clean shirts."

"But he did say what he looked like, didn't he?"

"Oh, fer certain. Franks is a bit taller than most, medium weight, dark hair and eyes, with a full moustache. Said he was a good looker, fer a workin' miner. And, he's got a scar on his chin, like he was cut bad with a knife, years ago. Oh, yeah—he's left-handed. Wears his gun butt-forward, on the right side. About them nice boots . . . Sidell asked him once where he got 'em, and this Franks fella said they was made in Mexico, so they probably got 'mule-ears' to pull 'em on of a mornin'."

John frowned at the description. "What do you mean, 'mule-ears'? I don't think I've heard that term before."

"Mexican boots are high-topped. They have loops built in to the top a' the boot at each side to pull on when you put 'em on."

John grinned. "I see. Mule-ears. Quite unique. Well, now we have a lead. Let's walk downtown and start checking out the saloons. We have an outlaw to find."

CHAPTER 18
THE BANKER'S BALL

Their initial attempt at finding the suspect named Franks ran into a stone wall. Many bartenders proclaimed to have never seen or heard of the man, and the three who did admit to knowing him said they had not seen him for several weeks. It was useless to try to strong-arm any information out of them without closing the door to any future cooperation. The three hunters scoured every corner of Denver and Auriara until John was convinced that the man was not in the town. John curbed his disappointment. He knew that Franks would show up, sooner or later. Someone would tell the hunted man that others were looking for him, and the outlaw would make a mistake, either try to run, or perhaps confront that person.

"We'll have the scoundrel if he does," he vowed to Sheriff Gilbert. John settled into the wooden chair offered by the sheriff and crossed his legs at the ankles. "Men like these need to find out what's known about them no matter the risk. If he tries, I'll have the 'bird' I need to sing on his comrades."

"Well"—the older lawman picked at his teeth with a well-used toothpick—"jus' be certain he don't plug ya in the back, outta principle."

"That's what Khan Singh is for." John warmly glanced at the silent Sikh, standing by the doorway, patiently awaiting the completion of the visit. Gilbert also stared at the big Sikh. He was certainly a fearsome bodyguard.

The old warrior's watchful gaze never wavered as he returned

Gilbert's long look, causing the sheriff to pause a second before resuming his warning. "Don't forget. These skunks have killed without mercy and will shoot first, if given the chance."

"Khan Singh, who has served me as a soldier and faithful friend, has protected my back for so long, I would be lost without him."

"Umm! Whatever you say. Jus' watch out. By the way, I have some news from the sheriff up at Ft. Collins. That's why I sent fer ya."

"Excellent. What is it?"

"Seems there's been a lot of land bought up there, in an area where it's rumored to be the next big gold strike. A company called Foothills Land Company. Nobody knows who owns it. The sheriff said a lawyer friend of his handled some of the buyin' and never saw the owner. Everything was handled by mail or telegraph. Sort of curious, ain't it? I mean, tryin' so hard not to be seen. By the way, the telegrams were sent from here in Denver."

"That is interesting. Thank your friend. Oh, I wanted to ask you, still keep digging after this Franks fellow. It's likely that he's away from Denver at the moment and has been for some time, but I suspect he'll return before long."

"Well, I'll keep my eyes and ears open iffen he does show up again." Sheriff Gilbert grinned at John. He liked the affable Pinkerton agent, even if he was from England and talked sort of funny. "Heerd you was a'fixin' to go to the Krammers' big bru-ha-ha tonight. It's the talk of high society in Denver, that's fer sure. About everyone who's someone'll be there."

John's response was a bit sheepish. "You know how it is, Sheriff. It's not the first time I've been paraded about by my hosts. It is one of the hazards of my birth. Will you be there?"

"Naw. I'll try and keep the noise down so's that the genteel folks can hear the fancy music. I'll have a part-time deputy there to keep drunks and riff-raff from trying to crash in, though."

"Pity. I'll miss you. Who will I talk to, over a glass of Champagne, when boredom sets in?"

Gilbert shot John a sly look. "I figgered you'd spend your time with Miz Belle."

John's impression of the crusty lawman went up another notch. Careful as he had been, the sheriff had spotted his late night liaisons with the lovely bawdy-house madam. "Congratulations, you caught me. No, I did not want to subject Belle to the whispers and innuendos from the 'nice' ladies of Denver. She understands. She also will have a late night dinner waiting for me afterwards. I can expect a grilling over the latest fashions worn by the ladies attending the party. The price we men must pay for women's company, what?"

Gilbert surprised John. "I like Belle. She's a fine woman. And she runs a good place. Her girls are well paid and clean. She don't allow rough stuff to get out of control or drunks to raise a ruckus. I'd hate fer anyone to hurt her."

"I agree," John replied. "I have no intention of hurting her. Quite the opposite."

Gilbert stared hard at John, his experienced eyes gauging the younger man. "Maybe so, but you two are a long ways apart on the social ladder. Don't give her the ideer that she can climb up too fast, if you know what I'm a'sayin'."

"Right you are, Sheriff. I'll be sensitive to her situation. Now, I must be off. I want to look my best for the fine ladies of Denver."

John exited the office and stepped off the wooden walkway. He paused for an instant and then swung on his horse's back. He did like Belle. A lot, to say it like a Yankee. Still, was she the one he wanted in Oakview, as his life's companion? When he thought about it in the clear light of day, the answer was painfully obvious. Generations of social breeding and mores stood between them. He shook his head and spoke softly to the quiet horse carrying him toward the rail yards. "I had better play my cards a bit closer to the vest, what, old horse? Things have been progressing at a too rapid pace between us."

John arrived at the home of Loren Krammer promptly at eight. He had ordered Curly Bill to rent him a comfortable carriage, pulled by matched sorrel horses. He was driven by young Kai, with old Khan Singh sitting beside his young son, proudly observing his performance. John grinned at the pair of them, so much alike you would have thought them more like twin brothers.

As they reached the front drive, John spoke up. "Khan Singh, do you wish to come for me at midnight, or shall I walk back?"

"No, Sahib. I will be here promptly at twelve. Do not leave without me. Enjoy your party with the sahib banker and his friends."

"That's easy for you to say. You don't have to endure listening to pampered wives gabbing about items that are of no interest to any man."

Khan Singh chuckled. "It is the burden of your birth, Sahib. You will handle it with your usual dispatch."

"Smashing. Your words inspire me. Well, here we are. Luck to me, and I'll see you about midnight, if all goes as planned."

A formally dressed man, performing his best imitation of a proper butler, answered John's knock immediately. "Welcome, sir. May I ask who is arriving?"

John suppressed a laugh. "I do believe I am the guest of honor. I am Lord John Whyte, of Bransworth, England, late colonel of cavalry, army of the Potomac. I dare say Mr. Krammer is expecting me?"

"Oh, yes, Lord Whyte. I am to escort you to Mr. and Mrs.

Krammer immediately. They are in the garden with some of the early arrivals. Please follow me, sir."

John rolled his eyes at the back of the man leading him out to the rear garden. The pretentious butler was as pathetic as his employer, the well-fed banker and gold robber, Loren Krammer. John paused at the doorway, as the butler announced him.

"Ladies and gentlemen. Lord Whyte."

"Ah, Lord Whyte. So glad you could come." Loren Krammer moved to shake John's hand, making certain everyone saw him. "May I present my wife, Florence? She's all aglow you could honor us this evening."

John took the plump woman's hand, bowing low and gallantly kissing her knuckles. "My pleasure. Delighted, Mrs. Krammer. Thank you so much for the kind invitation."

Florence Krammer almost stuttered she was so thrilled at the presence of shirt-tailed royalty in her house. "Lord Whyte. I'm simply honored to have you grace our presence. Please, allow me to introduce you to my daughter, Suzanne."

John dutifully fawned over the daughter, grazing his lips against her offered hand. He critically noted that while she had golden curls framing a very pleasant face with peaches and cream complexion, she already showed signs of the same pear-shaped bottom that her mother had in excess. Both women were stuffed into lavish ball gowns. Their bosoms were pushed up so high the first sneeze would threaten to reveal all to any on-looker, and corsets bound their waists so tightly that John doubted either could swallow a spoonful of food at the dinner table.

With Suzanne and Mrs. Krammer on each arm, he made the rounds, meeting the others in the garden. The men were obviously wealthy, with well-dressed wives to prove it. Some of the men were direct and straightforward, while others were brimming with self importance. Their discussions revolved around the money they made off the sweat of the miners down in their mines or the clerks in their stores.

John accepted a glass of champagne and conversed with the women and men whom Krammer deemed worthy to be guests in his house. The spectacular view of the setting sun behind the deep purple and black mountains set the tone of the party. As the burning red orb dipped behind the mountain tops, the guests filed inside for dinner, led by John and Mrs. Krammer, followed by Loren Krammer and Suzanne.

Because of the great number of guests, a sumptuous buffet was set up in the main dining room. After filling their plates, the guests were escorted to the ballroom to eat at small tables. John sat at the center table with the Krammers, the president of the Denver and Rio Grand Railroad, and his wife. He saw Rafe, eating at another table with some people he seemed to know, but all the two men could do was wave at one another. The women with John maintained the conversation, peppering John with questions about London society and any news John had of the social circuits in St. Louis or New York.

To John's delight, the food was excellent. The main course was buffalo roast or beef tips in Beaujolais sauce for the main dishes, along with baked brook trout with rice. Mint carrots, as well as fried cabbage and sausage, were side dishes. A steaming dish of bread and corn layered with fresh cream butter complemented the meat. Both raised and flat breads were in plentiful supply. Fresh cherries and cool, beaten cream were followed by steaming cups of fresh coffee. Only the wine failed to live up to the standards of the rest of the food, and John appreciated how difficult it was to obtain quality wine this far from New York.

As a continuous stream of waiters cleared the tables, Loren Krammer invited the men into his study for brandy and cigars, while the women repaired upstairs to ready themselves for the coming ball. Most of the men clustered around John and questioned him about his service during the war or what he knew of the financial markets back east. Meanwhile, Loren Krammer took every opportunity to ensure that his guests were aware of his favored status with John, enjoying what he thought was a bond of friendship between himself and the young, undercover Pinkerton detective.

Mr. Andrews, one of the other bankers John had met previously, inquired about John's search for answers regarding the owner of Foothills Land Company. Loren Krammer's face squeezed into such a frown of consternation that John almost laughed. "No, sir. Unfortunately, I have not found out who owns Foothills Land, but I will, rest assured."

Krammer's face became agitated, and he questioned John. "Why on earth should you care about that, John?" In his haste to ask the question, his feigned indifference dissolved.

"I am certain that whoever owns Foothills Land can answer some questions I have about land investing here in Colorado. The company seems to own half the available property sold in the last year."

One of the other men broke in. "What's that to you, your lordship?"

"I wonder what is one company doing with so much property? It's a question every honest man in Denver should want to find the answer to: one company owning so much property. Why, I wonder?" John looked around. "I'm especially interested in ensuring that any land purchased is legally obtained. For this territory to grow and prosper, lawlessness must be stamped out."

"Hear, hear." Rafe Wallace had joined the group and now spoke enthusiastically. "And we can start with the varmints that are robbin' my gold shipments."

The butler, announcing that the ballroom was clear and the

dancing was about to commence, interrupted their conversation. John led the men from the study, a disturbed and very agitated Loren Krammer trailing far behind. John's comments did not make much sense to the portly banker, but the tone was decidedly ominous.

A string sextet was earnestly trying to do justice to a Strauss waltz as the men entered the ballroom to find the women awaiting them. In moments, the room was filled with the swirling colors of brightly dressed women swinging in the arms of their escorts. John danced first with his hostess and then with Suzanne Krammer and then with nearly every woman in attendance. He only skipped one number to sip a glass of punch with Rafe Wallace and to observe the twirling clusters of color flowing past.

"Looks like the gals got their hooks out fer you, John," Rafe chuckled. "You're the talk of the party, fer certain. Every mother here is trying to figger out some way to introduce ya to her daughter."

"They are very charming, for the most part, Rafe. They think I'm something special because of my birth, but these people have nothing to apologize for. They are the aristocrats of America, if they only knew it. You know what astounds me the most?" His gaze wandered over the gaily dressed women, all of them in silk or satin-luster dresses, with crinoline petticoats crinkling underneath. Tight corsets and pushed-up bosoms accented their hourglass figures. Colorful leather and satin shoes peeked out from underneath the mounds of fabric.

"What's that?"

"I was in New York not six months ago for the queen's birthday ball at the British legation. The dresses I saw there, reflecting the very latest in Paris fashions, I see here tonight. In only six months, the latest fashions have crossed two thousand miles to Denver. I find that most fascinating."

Wallace muffled his hearty guffaw. "Hell, son. Fashion is like sin. It follows money like a fox after a hare, and don't you forget it. There's money here in the west. Mountains of it. Speakin' of such, any word on the arrival of your extra guards? There's nearly a hundred thousand stacked up in Central City."

"They will arrive on tomorrow evening's train. I'll take them to Central City Monday. Your gold will be here in Denver by a week from today."

Rafe smiled. "Praise be, it can't be soon enough. Say, looks like someone is a-comin' to gather you up fer some more dancin'." Both men grew silent as Suzanne Krammer glided up to them. "Evenin', Miz Suzanne. That's shore a mighty pretty dress you're a'wearin'."

"Thank you, Mr. Wallace. Your Lordship, isn't this my dance?" She tried her best to look like the sophisticated young lady she wanted to be. Her young face was flushed from the dancing and the status of the man she had so boldly approached. Her golden locks were tightly curled, piled high on her head, and she carried a small, ivory fan in her left hand. An expensive brooch, possibly her mother's, graced the smooth, white fabric of her gown, drawing the viewer's eyes to the silky skin of her bosom.

John bowed in surrender. He returned her infectious grin and held out his hand to the young woman. She was aglow with the night and the fashionable dress she had received from New York, which accented her youthful charm to the fullest. "I believe it is. See you later, Rafe. Duty and pleasure call me."

Rafe smiled as the two young people twirled away, in step with the music. His eyes were already visualizing the piles of gold that would soon arrive from his office in Central City. Rafe hummed to himself as he reviewed the chores he needed to complete before John left for Central City. Alert young Tom tomorrow to begin packing the accumulated gold purchases for shipment. Rent six—no, eight good mules with harness to carry the gold as pack animals. It was the news he had been waiting for.

CHAPTER 19
DEADLY DECISION

The outlaw who called himself J. B. Franks led Spots Taylor and Injun Lopez into Denver as the Catholic mission at the south end of town rang the ten o'clock evening chimes. He had peered down at the bright lights of Denver and Auraria from the top of Cold Springs Pass over an hour ago and was anxious to feel the cool relief of a beer sliding down his throat. Nearly two hours earlier, he had bet Spots that he could swallow an entire over-sized mug from Frenchie's Saloon without taking a breath, and he meant to collect the four bits Spots had so thoughtlessly wagered. J.B. grinned to himself. He had done the trick several times and was confident he could again. The money would cover the cost of the beer, so it would be like a free drink.

"Yes, sir, Spots," he smirked to his disreputable riding companion. "That there beer'll taste mighty good, knowin' yew're a-buyin' it fer me."

"First ya gotta drink it like ya said without no pausin' fer a breath." Spots shifted in his saddle. "Dammit all. After layin' around the hideout fer two weeks, my butt's sorer than a broke tooth. How long we been in the saddle? Ten hours?"

"Only about six, I reckon," J.B. agreed. "Still, it beats ridin' in from the gold camps. That takes more'n twice as long."

"I should ride some instead of jus' layin' around," Spots grumbled. "I wish there was some way we could wait fer the signal here in Denver, instead of at that damned cabin. Them Adams boys don't keep it fit fer a hog, much less a man. It's gonna be a pure pleasure to stand at a bar fer a spell." Spots scratched the birthmark on his cheek, the source of his unusual nickname. His dirty finger rasped against the red, roughed skin of his birth affliction, caused, it was believed, by his ma having being scared by a demon while carrying him in her womb. The taunts from his youth contributed significantly to his early descent into criminal behavior. His greasy, brown hair hung down so far that it nearly masked the offending area, which was how the surly outlaw liked it. He glanced over at J.B., tall and lean, with nary an imperfection on him, from his curly, blond hair to the well-formed and handsome face, blessed with dark-blue eyes that seemed to melt the hearts of every whore that J.B. took up with.

Spots glanced behind him at their fellow rider, silently following the two of them. Injun Joe Lopez had scarcely spoken since they rode out of the hideout, hours earlier. A half-breed Mexican and Navajo, Injun was not the sort of traveling companion one would choose if conversation was expected. The stocky, tawny, half-breed was the ideal sidekick for an outlaw, though. Taciturn, remorseless, and deadly with a gun or knife. The amoral breed was fearless, seemed to enjoy hurting people, and never complained about the hard times all criminals endured. "How 'bout you, Joe? Ready fer a cool glass of beer?"

Injun Joe grunted. "And a bottle of tequila, *por favor*. I will drink until I sleep like a *niño* in his *madre*'s arms."

Spots nodded his agreement. "Fer sure somethin' harder, as soon as I win my bet with J.B. here." He scratched again at his "curse." Rubbing his hand against his dusty pants, he cussed softly. "It's damn pitafull the way we gotta spend two weeks over to the hideout between visits to town. Three days ain't enough to make up fer the time we waste there."

J.B. spoke up. "You knew the deal afore ya signed on. Every three days three men get off. With fifteen men, we gotta wait fer

everyone to have his turn. Quit yer bitchin'. Ain't ya got more
money than ya ever did afore?"

"Aw, I ain't complainin', J.B.. Not really. It's just that I get
damned thirsty a ridin' the trail in from the hideout."

"Well, we're almost there. There's the banker Krammer's
spread. Looks like he's a'throwin' a shin-gig. Wish I was a goin'.
Ya ever see his daughter? She's some peach, fer a fact. I'd like
to pin her down on the hay, with her dress up and her legs
spread." J.B. wondered again if Krammer was the unknown
boss Squint Harrison, who was the acknowledged leader of the
outlaws, was always talking about. Signs pointed to that conclu-
sion, but Squint never said and J.B. dared not ask. He was
content with his lot. He had nearly five thousand dollars in
Krammer's bank and was certain more would be there before
he had to quit these parts for safer pastures.

"Yeah, me, too." Spots Taylor's scarred face brightened at the
thought. He had to settle for the cribs, where the oldest whores
worked, to have his fun. The classier girls shunned him because
of his face. At least he felt that way, not realizing his filthy body
and rotting teeth were more to blame for his cool reception.

The three men rode on into the heart of Denver. J.B. decided
he would wait until the next morning to check in at the hotel,
where an unsigned message addressed to Squint, who remained
back at the cabin, usually awaited him. His thirst was more
important at the moment. The three outlaws rode to their
favorite saloon, Frenchy's Place, located across the bridge, in
Auraria. The rough and tumble town was more to their liking
than the classier Denver. They swung down from their tired
horses and looped the reins over the dried branch of the hitching post before clumping up the steps and into the busy saloon.

Pausing at the entrance, they checked for any sign of danger,
then shouldered their way to the bar. They rudely shoved their
way to the scarred, polished surface, beside the row of drinkers

already there. "Three steins, Louie," J.B. called out to the potbellied, baldheaded bartender serving the thirsty customers, a soiled, white apron tied around his ample waist.

The bartender barely looked up and swiftly had the ordered drinks in front of the three. "Well, Spots. Here goes," J.B. announced. He tilted the filled glass mug and gulped, draining the golden brew without pause until it was empty. Slamming the empty glass down and wiping the foam moustache from his own blond one, he chortled. "Drinks on you, Spots. Another round, Louie."

Cursing his bad luck, Spots threw down a five-dollar greenback. "Damn your hide, J.B. You done that afore. I was set up."

J.B. laughed. Even Injun Joe let a shadow of a smile cross his dark face. "Serves ya right, Spots. Don't jump afore ya look in the future."

Louie delivered the second order and leaned over until he could speak so only J.B. could hear him. "Need to talk with ya, J.B. Park yerself over at one of the tables until I can get a break."

"Whatever ya say, Louie. Bring us a bottle of tequila when ya come." J.B. led the others to an empty table, where they sipped their second beer and watched the activity around the saloon.

"I think I'll try my luck at the Chuck-a-luck wheel," Spots announced. "I need to get back the money you swindled me outta." He moved off, ambling toward the gaming tables along the back wall, leaving the silent Lopez and a musing J.B. alone.

J.B. was intently staring at a particularly attractive bar girl working her way toward him, when Louie slid a bottle of golden tequila in front of him and sat down, groaning at the relief of his tired feet. "Whew. Busier than a fox in a hen house tonight."

"Well, take a load off, then, and have a drink of head-buster with me." J.B. filled the glasses Louie had delivered and settled back, leaning close to Louie so they could talk undisturbed.

"What's happenin'?"

Louie sipped his drink, glanced around conspiratorially, then whispered in a coarse voice. "Someone's lookin' for ya, J.B. Lookin' hard. I spoke to some other barkeeps. This guy's been all over town asking about you. By name."

"You don't say? Is he claimin' to be a particular friend o'mine?" J.B. jerked around, a little uneasy.

Louie shook his head. "Not likely. This fella's been hangin' around with Rafe Wallace, over to Guggenheim's."

J.B. was more than uneasy. "Askin' fer me, ya say?" He fingered the heavy Colt at his side. "What else?"

"Just that. Oh, and askin' about yer horse."

"My horse? What the hell would he want to know about my hor—" J.B. suddenly remembered Ju-ju, the easy-riding paint filly he once owned. Dead and pushed off the Georgetown road. "What about my horse?"

"I'm not sure. I jus' overheard a couple of smithies talkin' at the bar about a horseshoe and a dead pinto. At least it sounded like your horse. You still ride that pinto filly?"

"Naw, dammit. She broke her laig a while back. Had to kill her. Shame, too. She had a fine gait." He looked intently at Louie. "Ya didn't say anything, did ya?"

"Of course not, J.B. I was a waitin' fer you to get back so's I could tell ya about it. From what I can tell, nobody's said nuttin', so far. The jasper's still scratchin' around though."

"Well, what do ya know about this fella what's lookin' fer me? You have a name?"

Louie shook his head. "Don't know much. He's some sort of British fella. Named Lord Somethin' or other. Like I say, he's been hangin' out with Wallace, the manager over to Guggenheim's Refinery. Lives in a fancy railroad car over to the switchyard. That's all I know, honest. I gotta get back to work."

"Much obliged fer the warnin', Louie. Here's a gold eagle fer your troubles. I'll look into this here information right off."

The attractive bar girl eventually reached J.B.'s table. "Hi, cowboy. Havin' a good time? My name's Carla. How 'bout you and me have a little drink and you tell me what you've been up to since I saw you last."

Louie got up, his mission accomplished, and moved back behind the bar. J.B. shook his head regretfully at the woman. "Sorry, sweetcakes. I'm afraid ya caught me at a bad time. Maybe later." He motioned her away and stood. "Injun Joe, get Spots and meet me at our horses. We got a problem."

As soon as his two henchmen had joined him outside the saloon, J.B. relayed what Louie had told him. "I don't like it. We better amble up to the switchyard and have a look at this jasper. He's too damn close to turnin' over the right rock. Maybe a rattler might jus' spring out and bite his big nose fer 'em."

Injun Joe grinned like a wolf eying a broke-legged deer. "Good. Make the rest of the night even better."

Spots gulped and hesitated. He preferred a safer advantage when he did his killing. "Maybe we oughta get some more of the guys from the cabin?"

"Naw," J.B. decided. "We need to resolve this thing right now, afore others start asking too many questions. We shut this yahoo up real sudden like, it sends the message to everyone else. Mind yer own business or get hurt, bad."

"Well, where do we find this fella?" Spot's eyes swept the dark street, as if their quarry was nearby, waiting for the first shot.

J.B. climbed into his saddle and swung the nose of his horse toward the rail yards to the north of Denver. "I reckon our first stop should be his fancy railroad car. Come on, and don't attract nobody's attention."

John's parlor car was not hard to find, and the three outlaws eased into the shadow of the barn where John had stabled the horses. Curly Bill was already at Belle's Place, and although Rajah growled at the intruders from inside the barn, nobody paid any attention to his warning.

"Joe, slip up there. Be quiet. Look inside, and see if our man's home. Spots and me will wait here fer ya. Don't start nothin' yet. Jus' take a look-see."

Injun Joe glided off, and J.B. eased his gun out of its holster. If the man was there, he would lead the others in a silent rush, shoot the man through the windows, and disappear in the darkness before anybody arrived to see what was going on.

J.B. watched as Injun Joe slipped back through the night shadows to where he was waiting with Spots.

"Well, was he there?" J.B.'s harsh question demanded an immediate answer, but Lopez seemed uncertain.

"I don't think so. A man, *sí*. But he was strange looking, with a rag around his head. He was cleaning boots, like a peon does for his master. No gringo, no one who seemed to be the *patron*."

"What'll we do, J.B.?" As usual, Spots was unsure what to do next, which was why J.B. always came to town with him.

J.B. thought for a moment. "Louie said he was a hangin' 'round with Wallace, over to Guggenheim's. We'll drop in and see iffen he knows."

J.B. led his deadly duo back into Denver and to the office of Guggenheim's Metal and Refining Company. "Wait here fer me," he commanded and went up to the door with iron bars over the glass front. He knocked until a guard with a sawed-off shotgun came into view.

"Whatta ya want?" The guard held the gun so the huge openings were pointed right at J.B.. "If you have dust to drop off, come back tomorrow."

"Oh, hell. Well, all right then. Say, where's Mr. Wallace? I need to speak to him real bad."

"He's over to the bash at the banker Krammer's. He'll be

back tomorrow, 'round nine o'clock."

J.B. nodded and started to turn away, then spun back as if he had an afterthought. "Is the English fella—what's his name—with him?"

The guard nodded, happy to talk to someone during the boring hours of his shift. "Yep. Nearly all the swells in Denver are there, I reckon. Lord Whyte, that's his moniker. He's the guest of honor."

"Thanks, pard. See ya tomorrow."

"Not me, fellow. I'm off at twelve, and it's payday. I'll be in bed all day tomorrow, nursin' the hangover I'm gonna get afore the saloons throw me out with the mornin' trash."

J.B. mounted his horse and started up the street. "Our man's at Krammer's place enjoyin' a special party in his honor. Let's mosey up there and see if we can make this night the last one he's ever gonna enjoy in this world."

Chapter 20
A Nefarious Scheme

"Hold my reins, Injun. I'm gonna ease on up to that fella at the door and see what I can about spottin' the nosey Limey. Spots, you stay here, too. No need to spook the guy." J.B. passed his horse's reins to the swarthy half-breed and casually walked out of the shadows. He crossed the empty street over toward the hired doorman at the Krammers' house, who sat cooling his heels in a rocking chair outside the closed doors. J.B. could hear the faint sounds of music from within the house but could not see inside. Every lamp in the place must be lit, he decided to himself, watching the dark blur of his shadow matching his every move.

"Howdy, partner," he greeted the startled doorman. "Looks like some shindig a'goin' on inside."

"Howdy." The doorman surveyed J.B. as he immediately stood, demonstrating the massive physique that was the first prerequisite for his job. Sheriff Gilbert did not want any gate-crashers or drunken riffraff ruining the evening's festivities. "You can't go in unless you have a invite."

"No, I figgered as much. I was a'hopin' I could catch sight of the Englishman. I ain't never seen a real English lord afore."

"Well, I'm shore sorry, pard, but I got my orders from Sheriff Gilbert. Nobody inside except with a invite. Period." He smiled resignedly at J.B. "Ya know how these here society dames are about their parties."

"I follow ya. I shore woulda liked to catch sight of the

167

Englishman, though." J.B. paused as if a thought had just stuck him. "Say, I tell ya what. I'll wait over there, across the street. When the grand man comes out, if you'll tell him good night right loud like, so's I could hear it, I'd give him the once-over, and he'd not even be bothered with me. I'd give ya this here five-dollar gold piece fer the favor."

The burly doorman did not take long to decide. The gold coin disappeared from sight, and he bobbed his shaggy head up and down. "Fair enough. I'll make sure you know when the limey dandy steps out. You look to your heart's content."

J.B. grunted in satisfaction. Giving the man a hearty handshake and profuse thanks, he ambled across the street to where Injun Joe and Spots awaited in the shadows. Gathering his friends around him, he outlined his plan to the complacent pair, who nodded in eager anticipation as the nefarious scheme unfolded.

"Spots, you and Injun Joe go down to the corner of Main and this street, whatever it is. Put out the gas street lamp and hide on each side of the street. Stay alert. When our snoopy Englishman comes out, I'll follow along behind him and give a prairie hen whistle afore we get to the corner. When you have him in your sights, open up. I'll come up fast from the rear and finish the job. Watch out ya don't plug me. Got it? All right then. Get going. Get good and hid, and wait fer my signal."

The two drifted back into the shadows. J.B. hunkered down, his back against a large cottonwood tree, in the darkness, to await the end of the party. He had learned a long time ago to be patient while waiting out the tense moments until the action started. A good outlaw knows how to remain silent when he has to, and J.B. was a good outlaw. He knew Spots and Injun Joe would be where he told them. They did not have enough brains to think of anything else and would follow his orders.

Inside the Krammer house, the party proceeded, with John

living up to his hosts' expectation. He danced nearly every dance. He charmed the old and young women of Denver, and, between dances, he met and stroked the egos of the rich and powerful men of Denver. He paid particular attention to Suzanne Krammer. It pleased his hostess, and she spent most of the time while John and Suzanne twirled around the floor looking to see who was looking at her daughter. To John's keen interest, Suzanne happened to mention in an early dance that she was allowed to work in her father's bank twice a week, as assistant teller and bookkeeper.

"You surprise me, Miss Suzanne." John smiled at the young woman in his arms as they spun to a Strauss waltz. "I never would have thought a young woman would even consider banking, much less be responsible for so much money. I am impressed."

Suzanne Krammer gazed into the dark eyes of her dancing partner, her innocent heart aflame with forbidden thoughts and dreams. "Why, thank you, your Lordship." Not calling him "Your Lordship," was impossible for her, even though he had asked her to use his first name. "It's not so unusual. Women have brains, you know. I have a head for figures, my father says. I enjoy working there, and I'm learning a lot. I plan to work in the bank full time, once I return from finishing school in New York next year."

"Why not, if it's what you want. However"—John's boyish grin stoked a fire in Suzanne—"I'll wager that some fine young man will come along and grab your attention soon, and then all you will think of is a home and children."

"La-te-da, my lord. Women are capable of so much more than that. We can still be a mother and homemaker and hold an outside job. You wait and see." Her blue eyes flashed with the fire of youth and undaunted self-confidence.

"It would be a pleasure to hear more of this, Miss Suzanne,"

John replied as their dance reached its end. "Would you care to show me around tomorrow afternoon? Say about two? I'll rent a rig, and you could bring a picnic. We'll thrash this thing out then, without the demands of Mrs. Gordon, whom I owe the next dance."

"Oh, my." Suzanne almost squealed in delight. "I'd be happy to. I'll be ready, and I'll bake my famous apple pie for you."

Suzanne rushed off to tell her mother the news, while John escorted Mrs. Gordon out onto the dance floor, hiding his satisfaction. The matronly Mrs. Gordon congratulated herself the rest of the evening on the good impression she must have made on the dashing Englishman, he seemed so happy as they danced.

As the clock neared midnight, John was finally able to bid his farewells and depart the Krammer home. In his most gracious manner, he praised his host and hostess for a delightful time and confirmed their approval for his ride with their daughter for the following day.

John stepped outside, and the doorman tipped his dusty hat and bellowed out loudly, "Lord Whyte's carriage, please."

J. B. Franks jerked to attention and peered at the doorway of the Krammer house. An open carriage pulled up, and the man he was stalking climbed inside. There was only the driver, a large man wearing a rag on his head. It must be the same one that Injun saw at the railroad car. The carriage pulled out of the circular drive in front of the house and rolled down the street, toward the corner at Main Street, as J.B. expected. He waited until the carriage was a couple of hundred feet ahead, then followed, keeping his horse in the murky center of the street. As the carriage reached the inky pool left by the extinguished gas lamp at the corner of Main Street, J.B. puckered his lips to whistle. He did not bother to suppress the grin on his face at the surprise coming to the nosey rider ahead.

"How was the party, Sahib?" Khan Singh turned his head so he could see John, sitting below and behind him. As John started to answer, J.B. gave his whistle. Khan heard the sound and glimpsed the shadowy figure trailing them. He held up his hand as John started to speak. "Sahib," he whispered, "someone is following the carriage. He whistled as a bird, but one that does not fly at night."

John twisted in his seat to peer over the folded-down top of the carriage. He caught sight of the man following them illuminated by the light of an open window from one of the homes facing the street. John glanced around. The carriage was entering the shadowy intersection of Main Street, with the tall buildings making the blackness even more complete. John dropped to one knee, in the space between the seat and the front of the carriage. He grabbed the little .41 caliber two-shot derringer that he had carried in his coat pocket. It was almost useless, unless fired within twenty feet of the target.

"Khan Singh. Do you have a gun I can use?"

"Yes, Sahib. Do you want a pistol or rifle?" The old Sikh pulled a rifle from between his legs and laid it in his lap.

"Give me the pistol. You keep the rifle. Angle toward the water trough, there, to the left. It will give us some cover if we're ambushed." Khan passed his pistol back to the crouching John. He aimed the carriage toward the side of the street where the full trough of water stood, next to a long hitching rail in front of the building, a feed store.

Spots groaned softly. The carriage was moving across the street from him. He had lost a clear shot at the passenger and now had only the bulk of the carriage for a target. He hoped Injun Joe could see the Englishman. He would wait for the breed to make the first shot, before adding his fire to the attack.

Injun Joe Lopez had almost waited too long, assuming Spots would fire first. Then, the carriage turned abruptly toward his side of the street, and he dared wait no longer, or he would not have a shot from his location in the recessed doorway of the building next to the feed store. He pulled out his Army .44 and fired twice into the back of the carriage. He aimed at the location of the passenger he had seen as the carriage had passed him before entering the murky shadow of the intersection. Spots fired a second later, and J.B. spurred his horse, riding hard for the carriage, six-gun in hand.

Injun Joe's first bullet would have killed John Whyte had he been sitting with his back against the seat support of the carriage. However, as John was kneeling on the floor of the carriage, the bullet simply passed by his head, close enough to make John's bowels chill with the icy realization of passing death. Joe's second shot hit a metal coil in the seat and split in two. One fragment slammed into the wooden back support of the driver's bench, jarring Khan Singh but not injuring him, while the second fragment passed over the seat and grazed the rump of the off horse, cutting a bloody, six-inch gash.

The startled animal, surprised by the pain and shock, screamed and jerked hard away from the pain, causing the carriage to swerve and overturn, unceremoniously spilling John and Khan Singh exactly where they wanted to be—on the ground next to the water trough. Spots fired twice more, but the sudden movement of the target caused him to miss with both shots. J. B. Franks put three shots into the back of the carriage, lying on its side, and galloped past, pulling up his horse and dismounting next to the alley where Spots was hidden. For an instant all was quiet, except for the pitiful whinnying of the wounded horse and the scrape of the carriage as the frightened animals dragged it away, toward the livery that the two horses called home. In another moment, they were far down the street and out of sight.

J.B. whispered to Spots, whom he could see across the alley

from him, crouched behind a half-empty water barrel under a downspout.

"Didya git 'em?"

"I ain't sure. Joe fired first. I think I missed when the team bolted. I don't see either of 'em. Do ya?"

John and Khan crouched behind the water trough, squinting into the inky darkness. "How many?" John whispered. "Three?"

"I think so," Khan Singh answered. "One on this side and two over there, in the alley." Khan Singh surveyed his surroundings. The wooden sidewalk had three steps down to his left. He touched John's arm. "I will hide behind those steps. You stay here. Watch the two across the street. I will watch the one on this side." Without waiting for an answer, Kahn Singh squirmed on his belly to the wooden steps, then peeked over the top step toward the doorway where Lopez was hiding, pointing his rifle in that direction.

J.B. spotted the movement and hissed at Spots. "There he is. To the right of the water trough. Let him have it." J.B. and Spots both fired at Khan Singh, and John immediately fired at their muzzle flashes, driving both back under cover. One bullet slammed into the wood of the building next to J.B.'s face, showering him with splinters and causing him to drop to a knee, cursing in frustration. The noise would bring help soon, so they had to end it now. The man over there was too good a shot to rush. J.B. fired a couple of rounds in anger in the general direction of the trough.

Lopez had not seen Khan Singh move and thought John was the only armed target. He eased out of the cover of the recessed doorway and tiptoed toward the water trough, his gun ready.

Khan Singh detected the dark silhouette of the outlaw moving against the lighter wood of the building and aimed his rifle. He paused for another instant, to ensure the approaching mass was a target. As soon as he saw the silver flash of reflected light off a gun barrel, Khan squeezed the trigger. The sharp *crack!* of the Winchester rifle jerked John's head around, and he witnessed Injun Joe stagger forward, firing one shot into the dirt at John's feet, then collapsing in an awkward heap, his legs on the boardwalk and his face in the dust of the street.

"Jesus," J.B. snarled. "The bastard got Injun Joe." He blasted away, hitting the trough, scattering wood chips and water splashes, but otherwise accomplishing nothing. Spots rose up and wildly fired two shots, hitting nothing but the dirt of the street, before crouching back behind the barrel, where several return shots peppered the area around the scared outlaw.

"Come on, J.B. Let's get the hell outta here," Spots whispered desperately, cursing while he reloaded his empty pistol. "Someone's bound to hear them shots and are a-comin' on the run to see what's up. We gotta git and right now."

"Damn, damn." J.B. fired three more times across the street before slipping down the alley toward the rear of the building, Spots racing after him. The two outlaws peeked around the corner of the building. Across the street was a large barn, and they both turned for it. Horses and freedom beckoned if they were lucky. They weren't.

"Sahib. Two men running away. Down the alley." Khan Singh moved back to John's side. "Are you hit, Sahib?"

"No. Thank you, old friend. I'm out of cartridges, however. Do you have any more?"

Khan Singh handed John six more gleaming brass rounds of .44 ammunition. "This is all, Sahib. Make them count."

John swiftly thumbed them into the chamber of his pistol, dropping the spent brass in the dirt at his feet. As soon as he finished, he jogged across the street, Khan Singh right behind him, and peered down the dark alley.

Inside the horse barn, J.B. and the scared Spots found six stabled horses and one small burro in their stalls. Overhead a loft was filled with stacked hay. J.B. ran to the rear door and peeked through a convenient knothole in the dried wood. He could see several men, standing outside their homes across the street from the barn, some with guns in hand. If he and Spots ran toward the houses, it would be straight for trouble.

The walkway was ominously quiet. Swallowing the lump in his throat, John led the way down the menacing pathway, hugging the wooden side of the building with his back. To his relief, they reached the far end without incident. Both looked across the yard at the horse barn, standing stark and silent to their front.

"Spots," J.B. hissed, as he puffed up behind him. "Get back! Too many people out there. We'll have to go out the front." He ran back to the closed front door and pulled it open a few inches, peering out, hoping to catch sight of his opponents.

The front door opened, and the silvery barrel of a six-gun poked out. Khan Singh fired his rifle, and the barrel jerked back. The old warrior whispered in John's ear. "They are in the barn, Sahib." He fired the rifle at the open gap of the barn door.

The bullet slammed into the door frame, not two inches from J.B.'s head. He ducked back and cursed again. "Damn, they're outside already. We're trapped in here."

CHAPTER 21
DUSTY DARKNESS AND DEATH

WHAM! Sheriff Gilbert did not know if the sound of his feet hitting the floor from their accustomed resting place on his cluttered desk, or the all-too-familiar sound of gunfire, had awakened him from his little cat-nap. "Damn," he grumbled to the empty office. "Those were gunshots and lots of 'em." Cursing at the interruption, he jammed his hat on his tangled, gray hair and hurried outside his office, swinging his head in both directions.

There it was again. Up to the north, toward the rich side of town. He paused for a moment, his hand rubbing against the handle of his holstered pistol. The banker Krammer was having a hoo-raw up at his house. Could that be the source of the ruckus? "If that damned, no-good Harvey let some drunk get inside, I'll have his hide," he vowed to the deserted street as he hurried toward the sound of the guns. In a dead run, he pulled the pistol from his holster and spun the cylinder, checking the loads.

"Dammit to hell. Where are those deputies when I need 'em?" he grumbled again to himself. Another clatter of gunfire turned him toward the north. "Pistols and a rifle. Nope, it's not some fool hoo-rawin'. There's serious gunplay goin' on." Gilbert slowed to a hasty trot over the empty sidewalk, checking the dark doorways and empty alleys as he went.

He saw the huddled form lying motionless ahead of him. For an instant, the grim whisper of death chilled his brain, and then, like the good lawman he was, he cautiously moved toward the crumpled shape, swallowing the lump of fear in his throat. The lawman reached the spot where Injun Joe Lopez lay crumpled in death and looked around, his eyes desperately trying to pierce the blackness. Some slight sound from the alley across the street drew his eye, and he advanced toward the unknown, gun out and ready to fire. As he reached the far end, he saw the two men crouched behind the corner of the building, facing toward the Reynoldses' barn, guns drawn. Cocking his old army .44, he spoke in his sternest lawman's voice.

"Hold it right there. This is Sheriff Gilbert. I got you boys covered. Don't move, and lower them guns. Now, what the hell is goin' on?"

John flinched at the sudden command from his rear. He relaxed as he recognized the firm voice of Sheriff Gilbert. For an instant, he feared another outlaw had slipped in behind him. "Sheriff Gilbert," he loudly whispered, "it's me, John Whyte, and my servant, Khan Singh. We've been ambushed by three men on the way back from Loren Krammer's party. One of them is still out there in the street."

"I saw 'im. He's dead. Where are the others?" Sheriff Gilbert moved on down to the end of the alley, where he could see around the edge of the building, alongside John and Khan Singh.

"Khan Singh saw them over there, in the barn," John whispered softly. "We were about to rush them when you showed up."

Gilbert peered around the corner, careful not to expose himself to anyone inside. "They may have scooted on out the back by now," he observed.

"I don't think so," John answered. "Observe the men over there, on the next street. Anyone leaving the barn would be seen by them."

Sheriff Gilbert paused for a second. "Fred Albright lives over there." He cupped his hand at his mouth. "Fred. Fred Albright. This is Sheriff Gilbert. You over there?"

A man answered from beyond the quiet corral, across the street from the barn. "Yeah, Sheriff. I'm here. So's Jim Herkmann and Bob Wells, too."

"Anybody come outta the barn, there?"

"Nope, nary a soul."

"You fellows armed?"

"Yep."

"Then you boys watch the back door there. There's two bushwhackers inside the barn. Anybody comes out, you give 'em one chance to lay down their irons and then blast 'em to pieces iffen they don't. Got it?"

"You betcha, Sheriff."

"And stay outta the light. I can see y'all plain as day." The last warning was followed by their immediate withdrawal into the shadows. Sheriff Gilbert turned his attention to the barn. "Hello the barn. You men in there. Can ya hear me?" Silence was the only reply. "Listen, you two in the barn. I got both doors covered. Ya can't git out. Surrender and nobody gits hurt. Otherwise, we're gonna smoke ya out. Ya got one minute to make up yer minds."

J.B. and Spots cracked open the barn door and strained to see the men hidden behind the corner of the building across the barnyard.

"Can you see 'em?" Spots whispered to J.B.

"Naw, damn the luck. They're hid up in the alley." J. B. Franks poked his pistol barrel out until he was lined up with the darker silhouette of the alley's entrance. If he could only get a glimpse of his pursuers, he'd cut them down like cordwood.

"What'll we do, J.B.?" Spots shifted nervously, looking wildly in all directions. "They got us trapped in here like skunks under a porch."

"Quiet. I'm tryin' to think. Fer shore, we ain't givin' up. Not yet anyways. If I could jus' get a shot at 'em."

"Why not give up? I ain't ready to push up daisies, yet. Maybe the boss'll go our bail." Spots worried his droopy moustache with his lower lip.

"Not much luck of that. You know the rule about stayin' outta trouble when we come to town. You remember Ray Hobson, don't ya? Shot dead in his cell after cuttin' that whore fer liftin' his poke whilst he was asleep."

"Yeah," Spots whined. "But maybe it was one of her friends, not our boys, what done it."

"No, I think the boss had it done. If we have to quit, we'll have to talk fast and don't fergit. There's been a dozen men kilt durin' the holdups of the gold shipments. We'll hang fer certain if we spill our guts. Our best bet is to make a break outta here."

J.B. warily eyed the alleyway. "You cover the door down here whilst I get up in the hayloft. We might get 'em in a crossfire and have a chance to make a break for it. As soon as the sheriff hollers at us agin, pop a couple of rounds in his direction, and then take cover in the back. When they come in, I'll try and catch 'em betwixt us." J.B. hurried up the ladder to the loft, without awaiting Spots's reply. He slipped between the stacks of bagged feed and piles of hay, positioning himself so he could see out the open loading door at the front of the hayloft.

J.B. had a clear view of the ground between the alley and the barn door below him. Nobody would be able to run across the yard before he got off a shot at them. Settling into his position, he took a cautious look around. To his rear was another loft opening, over the rear exit of the barn, where the neighborhood men were on guard. The rest of the loft was bounded by the slanting roof of the barn. A dim break in the darkness showed where some shingles had come off at the south intersection of the roof and the second-story loft. That might be a way out, he figured. He would break through the weakened roof and drop to the ground outside the south wall of the barn. If he did not break his leg when he landed, he could scoot over the fence of the attached corral before the men inside could run out and around to the side of the building.

First, he had to lure them into the barn, not out where he would be spotted making his escape. Spots might have to be sacrificed, but that was the breaks of the game. J.B. looked back at the ladder. From where it was located, anyone climbing up to the loft could not see the hole in the roof because of several fifty-pound sacks of feed. He grinned to himself. Things were looking up; he had a way out.

Sheriff Gilbert steeled himself. "Time's up in the barn. Are ya comin' out?" He glanced around the corner of the wall. Spots's shot slammed into the wood, not six inches from his face, causing him to jerk back in surprise and anger. "Damn that owlhoot. That was too close." He fired a couple of shots at the door of the barn, hoping for the best.

"Seems like we have to go drive out the swine." John spoke softly. "Too bad. I wanted to ask them some very pointed questions."

"Well, it can't be helped," Gilbert answered. "You two cover me."

"Wait, Sheriff. Khan Singh and I will go. You cover us from here."

"Thanks, but it ain't your job. I'll go." Gilbert fired twice at the door of the barn, hoping for a hit.

John put his hand on the brave sheriff's arm. "Let us, Sheriff. Don't forget, I'm a sworn US marshal. It is my job. You've done it alone too many times. We'll do it; you cover us. Don't forget: these ruffians started this party with us and now have to pay the piper for their dance."

"Fine by me, but watch yourselves. Those boys mean business. I'll do what I can from here. Say when you're ready, and I'll put some rounds into the door until you reach the barn." Gilbert took up a good firing position and waited John's move.

"Khan Singh and I will each head to a side of the doorway. You lay down covering fire. Also, watch that opening over the door. One of them might have climbed up in the loft."

"Got it." Gilbert grunted in acknowledgement.

John turned to Khan Singh. "Ready, old friend? Be careful. Here we go, Sheriff."

Gilbert fired twice at the closed barn door and then shifted his aim to the dark square of the access door to the hayloft above. From his peripheral vision he saw the running forms of John and Khan Singh dashing toward the shelter of the barn walls, next to the double doorway into the huge barn.

J.B. caught the movement of the two men running toward the barn door and leaned forward to get a good shot. The speed of the runners and the darkness of the barnyard made his aim difficult. Momentarily he forgot about Sheriff Gilbert. J.B. pushed his pistol out of the opening to obtain a better aim. The movement allowed a faint reflection from the light of the quarter moon on the barrel. That was enough to catch Gilbert's eye. Swiftly the old lawman thumbed off four shots at the dark square opening, driving J.B. back under cover and spoiling his shot. As he peered out the loft opening, it was too late; his intended targets had reached the barn wall. Now, he would have to lean out of the loft to get off a shot, exposing himself to the hidden gun in the alley.

John checked Khan Singh. The Sikh warrior was ready, the rifle cocked and loaded. John motioned with his hand. He would enter and go left of the door; Khan Singh would go to the right. "Now!" he whispered loudly, and the two men ducked inside. Gilbert watched them disappear and wished them luck. He knew they needed it, fighting inside the unlit barn against desperate killers.

John fought to control his breathing. The barn was a series of stalls on both sides, with a wide passage in the middle. Some of the stalls were made of board rails and some of solid board walls. Motioning with his hand for Khan Singh to start down one side, John ducked into the first stall on his side. A startled horse uttered a snort and moved to the end of the small stall, away from the threat to its sleep. The noise alerted any foe that John was coming his way, and the determined English lawman groaned softly in disappointment.

Meanwhile Khan Singh crawled between two wooden boards of the stall he was clearing and ducked into the second stall. It, too, had a surprised horse and also a fresh pile of droppings, which caused Kahn Singh to slip. He struggled to regain his balance, lurching against the wooden gate. The noise and move-ment gave his position away to Spots, hidden behind a large, foot-thick roof support beam near the back door. The scared outlaw's shot echoed in the inky blackness. The sudden bright flash highlighted the dust motes drifting lazily in the air, stirred up by the movement of the four men in the barn. The bullet whistled over Khan's head, slamming with a loud *THUNK!* into the wall behind him. Then, once again, there was silence.

In the gloomy blackness, John could barely make out what the wily, old warrior was doing. Khan Singh pointed to his eyes and then in the direction of the fired shot, nodding his turbaned head. He had seen the place where Spots was hiding. He waved his hand, up and down. He wanted John to draw the hidden outlaw's fire. John nodded and moved to the rear of the stall, by the horse's head. He stood and fired a shot in the darkness, dropping back down and moving to the front of the stall. Spots answered, splintering the wood at the top of the stall where John had fired his shot.

Khan Singh fired his rifle, showering Spots with splinters

from a near miss and driving him away from the post to a position behind a pile of feed sacks. John glimpsed the movement and put a .44 bullet next to Spots's head. This forced him away from the sacks, back across the aisle of the barn to a dark corner in the end stall, where he gasped for breath and tried to see the two hunters who so relentlessly stalked him. "J.B.!" he screamed. "They got me pinned. Get 'em off me."

John and Khan stopped abruptly, waiting for J.B. to respond with new gunfire, but the barn remained silent, except for the nervous shuffling of the animals forced to share this unwelcome experience with the human intruders.

John motioned for Khan Singh to stop and quietly climbed between two boards that separated his stall from the next one in line. At the front of the stall was one of the large support posts like the one Spots had first hidden behind. John knelt behind the post and eased his head out, seeking the outlaw. Khan Singh made a noisy commotion and fired his rifle toward the rear door. Spots raised up to see if he had a shot, and John caught his movement in the momentary flash. He swiftly put two bullets into the thin wood of the stall wall and was rewarded with a groan of pain. Khan Singh fired two more at the sound. Both men heard the sound of a body slamming up against the back wall of the barn, and, again, there was silence in the barn.

Moving with practiced care, the two slipped from cover to cover until they were at the rear stall. John pointed to the body of Spots sprawled limply in the corner, the shine of fresh blood on the front of his light shirt. Both men looked around. Where was the second outlaw? As if in answer to their unspoken question, the floor above them squeaked softly, as a fine stream of dust drifted down, adding its coat to the layers below. The second man was above them, and on the move.

"Boys," Sheriff Gilbert shouted. "Ya all okay in there?"

"Fine, Sheriff. One down, one to go. He's in the loft. Don't let him jump out."

"Ya got it. Hey, Fred, watch the loft," Gilbert shouted to the men at the rear of the barn.

"Got it, Sheriff."

John searched for a ladder, and Khan's pointed finger showed him the wooden ladder leaning against the opening on the second floor. He darted for it, Khan Singh right behind. As they arrived, the Sikh stopped John.

"Sahib. Let me go first." The whisper was so soft it was barely perceptible.

John shook his head and whispered back, "You cover me with your rifle. I'll go." Testing each step, John started up the rickety ladder, Khan Singh standing where he could fire past John into the inky void of the opening to the upper floor. Meanwhile, during the lull in the fighting, Sheriff Gilbert ran to the entrance of the barn, where he could cover the interior better. He waited there, his pistol gripped tightly in his gnarled hand, awaiting the next phase in the gunfight.

John cursed his extravagant use of bullets against the first gunman. His pistol had only two shots left. He reminded himself to get his little derringer out as soon as he reached the loft, to use as backup, pitiful as it was. His eyes level with the loft floor, he peeked out of the square-cut hole, his pistol ready. The floor was covered with straw, bags of feed, and the dust of many years. John scanned all directions, trying to pierce the gloom, hoping to spot the hidden outlaw. Screwing up his courage, he drew up his legs to the last rung and then sprang into the loft, rolling away from the opening and toward a nearby stack of feed bags, each filled with fifty pounds of oats.

J.B. was waiting for John to clear the opening and expose his whole body for his shot. It was a mistake. The sudden rolling scramble to the piled grain sacks spoiled his aim, and his hasty shot only gouged wood from the floor next to John's foot. John crouched behind his cover, bobbing up to fire at the pile where J.B. was hiding, while Khan Singh, below the two of them, blasted away through the floor with his rifle at where he sensed J.B. was hiding. The higher power of the Winchester bullets punched through the hard, wooden floor of the loft as if it were paper. J.B. was fairly dancing about, trying to avoid getting a .44-40 lead bullet where his pants met the saddle.

The crossfire was too much for the outlaw, and he slammed his body against the weakened shingles of the roof. His second effort broke through. He rolled off the roof onto an eight-foot pile of stable swamping, straw mixed with horse and cow manure, moistened by foul-smelling animal urine. Cursing like an alley cat with its tail in a rattrap, he scrambled off the mess and ran for the far fence across the corral yard, toward the welcome freedom beyond. He climbed over the three-pole fence and jumped to his escape.

John shouted down to Khan Singh. "He's out on the roof!" The old warrior ran for the exit but had no chance. Sheriff Gilbert, on the other hand, was exactly in the right spot. Hearing the commotion, he moved to the corner of the barn in time to see J.B.'s shadowy figure climbing over the fence. Sheriff Gilbert fired at the legs of the fleeing man, but, as he did, J.B. jumped to the ground, and the bullet hit him dead center, two inches to the left of his spine, square through his outlaw's heart.

Sheriff Gilbert was bending over J.B. when John and Khan Singh arrived. "Sorry, boys. I was tryin' to hit him in the laig, but he jumped right smack into my bullet." He handed John a bankbook, with a name on it. By the dim light of a nearby window, John could read it plainly. "Account of Mr. J. B. Franks," written in the flowery script of a woman. "Looks like ya found the gent who owned the horseshoe."

John stared at the dead man crumpled in the dust, his soul

already on the long, dark, trail to hell, and shrugged. "Looks like Mr. Franks found the devil. Not a bad trade, all things considered."

Chapter 22
Belle Comes Through

"Well, bucko," Belle teased the awakening John, who was snuggled in close beside her. "What got into you? You roar in here an hour late, randy as a stallion in heat, and the next thing I know we're here and my late-night supper still sits untouched in the living room. What happened? You get all worked up dancing with the female swells up at Krammer's?" She drew in closer to her partner's warm body, rubbing his muscular arm with her fingertips.

John nuzzled her sweet-smelling auburn hair for a moment as he climbed out of the depths of heavy sleep his intense lovemaking had provided for him. As the memory of last night's gunplay flooded back into his consciousness, he chuckled. Good thing Belle had some experience as a girl on the line. Anyone else would have run in terror from the room before he finished what his adrenaline-charged body delivered.

"Sorry, my dear. I had a rather enlightening experience on how much one should appreciate life with a beautiful and desirable woman such as yourself."

Belle sat up, her back against the satin-covered headboard and shook out her tangled, red locks as she rang her little, silver bell for Sally. "Sally, darling, bring us some coffee and some of those molasses cookies you made yesterday. John and I will have breakfast on the balcony in thirty minutes. Is that agreeable, John?"

John nodded, yawning and stretching. From the rear of Belle's balcony, she had an unobstructed view of the high plains to the east and the mountains to the southwest of Denver. On a warm, sunny Sunday morning like today, their view would be spectacular. "Fine. A capital idea, my dear."

"Now," Belle announced—wrapping the silk sheet about her like a comforter—"what happened last night that set you off?"

John hesitated, but only briefly. He had already confided in Belle when he needed her help. No reason to hold back now. Without going into the bloodier details, he told his attentive companion about the ambush on himself and Khan Singh. "I'm disappointed we did not capture one alive to question at our leisure, but I did find something of interest when we searched their bodies."

"What was that?" Belle asked, mesmerized by John's account of the exciting battle.

John sipped the coffee delivered by the rotund, smiling Sally and reached for his pants, thrown on the floor next to the bed. He pulled two bank books from a pocket and passed them to Belle, who wiped the cookie crumbs off her mouth with the back of her hand and opened them, a questioning expression on her face.

"Notice the bankbooks. They're both issued by Krammer's bank. And both have about the same amount in them. Eight robberies and nearly eight thousand dollars in deposits in each man's account. We know that Franks was at one of the holdups, because he lost his pinto there. It seems very probable that the Taylor fellow was there as well. Look at the owner's name on the cover, Belle. Wouldn't you agree that the writing is very likely a woman's?"

Belle nodded. "If not, some poor dude will never hear the end of it, the first time he signs his name in the presence of real men."

John told Belle about his invitation to ride with Suzanne

Krammer. "You can bet I'll find some way to talk to her about the account books. If she works in the bank, she may very well be the person who set up these accounts."

Belle lightly punched him in the arm. "Don't forget why you are there, bucko. I'll bet young Miss Suzanne has a whole lot more on her mind than talking about banking."

John grinned at his lovely companion. "Compose yourself, Belle. She's a child, barely seventeen, I'd wager." He pulled his pants on and moved to the water pitcher and bowl on Belle's dresser, where he proceeded to wash his face.

"Old enough in Colorado Territory, me handsome bucko. And delivered up to you ripe for the pluckin', as badly as her Momma wants to climb the social ladder of Denver."

John grinned at Belle's reflection in the mirror, enjoying the flash of pink-tipped breasts as she rose from her bed. "With all you put me through last night, how would I have the strength to swoop a little gold digger like her off her feet?"

Belle glanced up to catch John spying on her and threw a pillow at him. Suddenly, she snapped her fingers, causing John to turn and look at her. "Hell, I almost forgot. One of my gals, Opal Shirk, and I cracked your coded message yesterday."

"You did? I say, well done. What was the message? How did you two darlings do it?"

Belle pulled a satin shift of gossamer pink, trimmed with ostrich feathers, about her freckled-kissed shoulders and walked over to her secretary, where she rummaged through a drawer until she found the piece of paper with the strange code written on it. Smiling triumphantly, she spread it on the small table by the bed and motioned for John.

"Opal gave me the clue. She likes to do word puzzles, to pass the slow times." Belle pointed to the arrows, pointing in different directions, with numbers from one to nine at their tails. "Opal said if you broke the alphabet into three segments of

189

nine, nine, and eight, you would have a number and arrow
direction for each letter. "Watch."

She wrote *A, B, C,* and on through the alphabet, until she
reached the letter *I.* Underneath, she put an arrow, its tip pointing toward the top of the page, and then numbered them 1
through 9 below the shaft. "Now," Belle said, "we do the same
with *J* through *R* with the arrows pointing to the right side of
the paper. And, finally, the eight remaining letters, *O* through *Z,*
where the arrows are pointing down."

"But look here, Belle. Here's an arrow pointing down
numbered 9. In fact, there are a large number of them."

"Right. Look, a down arrow numbered nine after three other
arrows. Then after four, then four more, and then nine. Opal
guessed it was the space sign, between the words, and she was
right. Here, let me show you what the message says." Belle
pulled out another sheet of paper. On it was the coded message,
broken from code to English.

Son,

*Good work. Your information correct Operation successful Your
share deposited in our bank I bought more land in Fountain
Springs One or two more shipment and we will own all we will
ever need Stay alert*

Father

"Belle," John kissed her lustily. "You are brilliant. A smashing
good piece of detective work. We about have enough now to
slam the jail door on Mr. Loren Krammer and his gang of villains. Well done, indeed. And to your friend, Opal, my sincere
appreciation."

Belle blushed, truly happy to receive praise for something so
unrelated to her profession. Grabbing his arm, she steered him
toward the open doors of the rear balcony. "Come eat, then go
make yourself presentable for the little Krammer filly. I'm jeal-

ous. I would like to picnic with you today, myself."

"Tonight, my red-headed beauty. First business, then pleasure." His kiss was a promise of what lay ahead that night. After a satisfying breakfast, John rode back to the *Star*, paying no attention to the street where he and Khan Singh had so nearly met disaster the night before.

Curly Bill, having received John's directive from Khan Singh, had rented the best matched pair of buggy ponies in town— twin grays, with a cozy, two-person carriage. "Very nice, William. Do they respond well to the reins?"

"You betcha, Boss. I drove them around a while to make sure they was used to the bit in their teeth. Now, don't you git in trouble today. I'm plumb put out that you and Khan Singh had all the fun last night. You keep on your toes, hear? Them boys ya drilled last night may have some more friends about, lookin' to even up the score fer their friends' sudden demise."

"I don't expect it, but thank you for the warning. I asked Sheriff Gilbert if he would circulate a story that he caught them trying to rob the freight office and that he and his deputies were involved in the shootout. That will keep certain people from becoming too nervous while I inquire around."

"You don't think Krammer told them three jackals to waylay ya?" Curly Bill fingered his six-gun, eager to add his efforts to any more fighting.

"I think not, William. It happened too close to his home. He would never want any suspicion cast upon him this late in the game. Those three took it upon themselves to ambush us and without thinking it through."

"Yeah, and damn well paid fer their sins, too," Bill airily concluded. "I'll be around, if ya need me, just the same."

"If I'm not back, please meet the five o'clock train from Kansas City, William. I sent for four men from the Pinkerton office there to help us transport the next gold shipment. Treat them to a dinner. I have rooms reserved for them at the hotel. Get them settled and then have them wait for me in the parlor car about seven. Stop by Rafe's office, and make sure he is ready for us to leave tomorrow for Central City."

John pulled the carriage into the circular drive of the Krammer mansion at two o'clock sharp. Suzanne did not keep him waiting. She bounced down the stairs as soon as he was admitted to the house by Loren Krammer, at ease in smoking jacket and worn slippers. Suzanne was impeccably dressed in a pale-blue dress with a white knit shawl for her shoulders and baby-blue, leather slippers on her feet.

"You take care with my little gal, John." Krammer was warm and friendly, his polished manners reflecting the impression he wanted to give the English visitor. To John, it appeared that Krammer did not know about John's involvement in the gunfight the previous night.

"Yes, sir," John promised. "We'll ride a bit, see some of the beauty surrounding Denver, and I'll have her back here before sundown." He greeted Suzanne and her mother, then escorted the radiant young lady to the carriage.

As they drove out the road toward Apex Pass, Suzanne excitedly recounted the tidbits of gossip she had heard the night before. She tried very hard to be a proper young lady, one the enticing man beside her would find an enjoyable companion. At a remote intersection she directed him to turn south, away from the main road. The sun was shining, and the warm summer day set the horses to prancing as they trotted along, enjoying the fresh, crisp air.

"These hills are called the Hogbacks." Suzanne acted as tour guide. "Up ahead, there are some odd footprints, right in the stone itself. Can you imagine?" She showed John where to stop, and they walked among the fossilized prints, in size from a silver dollar to a large pancake, that tracked up the sheer side of a bare rock cliff.

John bent over and crumbled some of the reddish sandstone in his hands. "Look here, Suzanne. A piece of a fossilized seashell. This area must have been under water at one time, many millions of years ago."

"La-te-da, John. We're thousands of feet above the sea. You know that." She held his find in her hand, struggling to comprehend its origin.

"Nevertheless, it's a seashell. According to my geology class back at Sandhurst, mountains rose up from the sea, pushed up by the hot lava of volcanoes, many centuries ago. That rock where the footprints are was once a flat, muddy shore, I'll wager."

Suzanne clung even tighter to John's arm. "I'll swear, John Whyte. What you know would make a poor girl's head ache. Come on. We're only a little ways from my special picnic site." She pulled him back to the carriage, and they passed over the low slab of hills into a valley, its far boundary defined by high mounds of red and brown sandstone and sharp spires of gray granite rock.

"Here we are," she announced. "I come out here whenever I can. Isn't it the grandest sight you ever did see?"

John stopped the buggy in the field where green grass and yellow snow daises competed with the blazing red of the fire-weed plant and a pale blue flower he did not recognize.

"What is that beautiful blue flower, Suzanne? Look, it grows up the hill, as far as I can see."

"We call it the blue columbine. Wherever there are aspens, you'll find it. Its color ranges from dark blue to almost white, with a touch of green in it. Aren't they lovely? Come on. I want to show you something else."

She led John into a red, rocky, semi-circular natural amphitheater. She motioned for him to stop, then ran a distance away from him, holding up her dress high enough to make certain he had a clear view of her ankles and calves. Whispering softly, she called his name. It sounded as if she were standing right beside him. The rock amplified her voice in an astounding manner.

"My word," he blurted. "I can hear you easily. That is astounding."

"Isn't that the grandest thing?" she bubbled when they grew tired of whispering at one another. "I love this place. I'm so happy Papa owns it. Someday I would like to build a house right up there, where I can overlook this place every morning as the sun comes up."

John surmised this land was part of that which the territory records would show was owned by Foothills Land Company, the organization Loren Krammer claimed he had never heard of.

The picnic lunch was excellent, and the dried apple pie that Suzanne offered for dessert was even better. The two talked, joked, laughed, and thoroughly enjoyed the afternoon. John skillfully directed their conversation around to the bank. He pulled out the bank book he was carrying and showed it to Suzanne.

"I found this on the street this morning. It's from your papa's bank. Look at the cover. Did you write the customer's name on the front?"

"Why, yes, I did. Do you want me to turn it in to Papa?"

"No, that's all right. I'll give it to the sheriff. The man who lost it may have reported it to him." John casually flipped through the book. "This fellow seems to be doing rather well for himself. Eight thousand dollars in deposits over the last year."

"Oh, yes. Many men are doing very well out in the gold fields. You should see Tom. He's saving his money and has developed a fine nest egg for the future."

"Is your brother mining on the side?"

"No, I asked him once how he got so much cash, and he said he won it gambling with the prospectors. They run through money something awful. But, I guess there's nothing else to do."

"Funny,"—John probed, being careful not to seem too inquisitive—"I don't think I would wait until I earned one or two thousand dollars before putting it in the bank, would you?"

Suzanne fawned over her partner, completely mesmerized by his company and their leisurely discussion after their meal. "Oh, I'll bet I could name a dozen men who do it that way. Even Tom. Must be some sort of man thing about having a wad of money in his pocket, out in the diggings." She smiled brightly at John, desperately trying to figure out some way to let him kiss her.

John had been in this kind of maneuver before. Smiling at Suzanne, he rose to his feet and held out his hand to her. "Come on, sweet Suzanne. The day grows short, and I promised your father I would return you before sunset. It's been a grand time, and I look forward to our next ride together."

He kept up a meaningless chatter all the way to her house, without ever saying when the next time would be. After kissing her hand in the most continental fashion, John left the slightly perplexed vixen at her doorstep and hurried back to the *Star of India*. The men from Kansas City would be in by now and plans had to be made. Another bar had been added to Loren Krammer's future jail cell.

Chapter 23
Back to Central City

Curly Bill and four other men rose as John opened the rear door of the *Star* and entered the parlor of his private car. As John was introduced to each man in turn, he evaluated them with interest. He was soon satisfied that the Kansas City office had sent him their best. Although different in height, complexion, and physical appearances, they all bore the same recognizable stamp of strength, character, determination, and honesty expected of detectives working for the greatest investigative agency in the world.

Curly Bill made the introductions. "John, here are the men ya asked fer. Just got in from the KC office. This here is Walt Pate, Joe Richardson, Vernon Vane, and Will Jeries. Gents, this here is the boss, John Whyte."

John stepped forward to greet each man and shake their hands. The firm handshake and calm resolve in each man's eyes brought a smile to the young English detective's face. "A pleasure to meet each of you." He saw Khan Singh standing silently at the far end of the room. "Did William introduce Khan Singh to you?" At their nods, he continued. "I look forward to completing our mission here with your help. I hope William explained what I have in mind for us all?"

The shortest man, the husky, full-bearded Walt Pate, stepped a half step forward. "Yessir, he was startin' to. We're to accompany you into the mountains to pick up a gold shipment and escort it back here to Denver."

"That and more, I fear. I expect that the same outlaw gang that has been robbing our client will ambush us before we get out of the mountains. We are likely to hear the elephant roar, to quote an amusing metaphor I heard more than once during the war."

Vernon, Jeries, and Walt Pate smiled. "I see that you three were in the army of the Potomac as well," John remarked, grinning back at them, another bond binding the new acquaintances together.

"Yes, sir," Vernon answered. "Me and Will here were in the 8th Illinois, while both Walt and Joe was in President Lincoln's security protection detail. I think we've all heard lead whistle before."

"The president's security detail. That must have been interesting duty."

Walt paused, a look of melancholy crossing his face. "Yeah, but, unfortunately, we were off that night at Ford's Theater. I always wonder what if . . ." He left the sentence unfinished.

John nodded in sympathy. "It must have been devastating to you and your men. However, who was to know?"

Joe Richardson spoke up, his voice surprisingly deep for his slender build. "Those of us on the detail were heartbroken, for a fact. President Lincoln was so danged determined to go around without us, it made it hard to protect him."

"I can imagine," John answered. "However, to the business at hand. We'll leave tomorrow morning for Central City, about forty miles to the west of Denver." John led the way to his desk and unrolled a map of the territory. Curly Bill held one side, while John placed his silver pen and ink set to hold the other end. John pointed with his finger for the four detectives gathered around him. "This is the Georgetown Road, the only viable way back to Denver from Central City. Somewhere in between the town and here"—he pointed at the spot on the map described as "Eight-Mile Gulch," tapping to emphasize the importance of the place—"we should be ambushed."

Joe Richardson stroked his brown, flowing moustache. "Interesting they never try anything past the gulch, ain't it? I wonder why? There's bound to be some good spots further on, before they get too close to Denver."

"Good point." John praised the observation. "I believe the outlaws leave the road somewhere beyond the gulch and don't return to Denver after a raid. The outlaws have been seen riding over the gulch on two occasions but never seen riding into town."

Walt Pate drew his bushy eyebrows together in a studied frown. "Are you planning to fight your way through the ambush?"

John shook his head emphatically. "No. It's been tried before, and all that happened was some good men were hurt and killed. I do have an alternative plan, though."

The four men gazed at John, calmly waiting for him to outline his plan. Walt Pate, the oldest of the four, his wrinkled face and thinning hair showing his age, glanced at the three men with him. "We're game to whatever you have in mind, Mr. Whyte."

"Please, Walt, call me John. Well, here it is. William, Kahn Singh, and I have been to Central City and believe we have uncovered the gang's contact. This cur signals the outlaws when a gold shipment leaves the town, and the outlaws hurry to set up the ambush. What I have in mind is to tell him that our plan is to ride only at night until past the danger area, camping and guarding the gold during the daylight hours."

"And?" Vernon Vane, tall, blond, and raw-boned, with innocent, blue eyes that seemed to proclaim his youth, asked the obvious question. His face was clean-shaven, and he appeared years younger than his three companions.

"And," John continued, "we'll let the contact know where we

are going to camp for the day. Assuming we can make twelve to fifteen miles a night, the only time the outlaws can strike is during the middle day's stop. If I am there with Khan Singh early,"—John motioned at the silent Sikh, standing at the rear of the car—"we may trap the outlaws in a cross fire between us."

Bill Jeries spoke for the first time. He resembled the older Pate, but with a lighter complexion and younger by several years. He traced the red line marking the trail on the map. "Why won't the outlaws try to stop us before then, even if it is dark?"

"You haven't seen the Georgetown Road. It's more of a goat path than a road. Steep drop-offs and winding about like a drunk donkey. You'll have to have oil lamps to see enough to pick your way along after the sun goes down. I don't see how the outlaws would dare try anything at night. Too much chance of missing us in the dark and losing the gold, or being shot by their friends."

Walt stroked his beard. "You plan to leave early and be waitin' on them?"

John nodded. "Correct. Khan Singh and I will leave ahead of you and be in position above where you stop for the day. If they don't strike the first morning as you stop, it is my belief they will try on the second. If they wait until the third morning, you will be far past Eight-Mile Gulch."

Vernon spoke up, concern in his voice. "Can you two keep up with us if they pass makin' their move on the second day? Off the trail ought to be mighty rough ridin.'"

"Khan Singh and I have a great deal of experience in the mountains. We will move faster than you, believe me. We'll also approach from high ground and travel in the daylight. Any outlaws we cross will have their attention down, toward the road, not above them."

Joe spoke again. "And the outlaws' contact will find out what we want him to know about the plan?"

John nodded. "I'll make sure of it. Any more questions? No? Good. Walt, William will escort you fellows back to the hotel. We'll leave for the mountains tomorrow morning, about ten. That will put us at Eight-Mile Gulch at sundown. I want to look the area over before we continue on to Central City. Oh, William?"

"Yeah, Boss?"

"Make sure everyone has a rifle. And one of you take a 12-gauge 'Greener' along in case we have some close work."

Curly Bill nodded. "Sure thing, Boss. A twin dose of double-aught buck-shot will discourage anybody who has any sense a'tall."

"We'll have Will here carry it. He's the worst danged shot with a pistol I ever saw," Walt announced. "Right, Will?"

Will Jeries was a shy young man. He stammered a soft, "Now, Walt. It ain't that bad. It's only that you fellows seem to hit what you're aimin' at every time. I'm all right."

Joe Richardson laughed. "That's the point, partner. We have to hit 'em, or they fill our gullets with hot lead." He grinned at John and Curly Bill. "Ole Will, here, is still the best man among us iffen it comes to fists or rasslin'. Any fool what goes up agin him is like raw meat in front of a hungry bear."

John smiled at the shy man, noting his blush at Joe's vivid description of his prowess. "You'll have to take on Khan Singh some evening. He's some wrestler in his own right. Well, let's get the preparations started, shall we?"

John shook each man's hand again and turned to Khan Singh as they exited the door. "Off we go again, old friend. Be sure and pack the moccasins. We're going to need them when we run the mountains. That is"—he goaded in good humor at the older man—"if you think you can stay up with me in the rocks and hills of this wild country."

"Speak for yourself, Sahib. We will see who pants for air first and who falls asleep over his food at night."

John laughed. "And now, I think I shall wander down to the Silver Bell. I'll be back around eight tomorrow." John caught the look Khan Singh gave him. "What? What?"

"Nothing, Sahib. It seems you are spending a great deal of time there."

"Why, Khan Singh, you old rascal. Don't forget you're the man who first took me to the 'Gardens of Earthly Delights,' back in Kashimir."

"That was only to relieve the tensions of a scared youth. Now, you behave as if you cannot spend a night alone without the one whose favors you seek so regularly."

John shrugged. "She is really something, old friend. It will be hard to leave her when our work is done."

He stepped out onto the rear transom and shut the door behind him, not hearing the older man's reply, "As long as you do leave her, Sahib."

His night with Belle was all he hoped for and more. John's sleep was sound and refreshing, what little he managed to get. After a tender and satisfying good-bye from Belle, who made the moment most memorable, John returned to his parlor car to find the others patiently awaiting him, their goods packed in their bedrolls or on the pack mule carrying their extra gear.

Curly Bill had the extra mules that were going to carry the gold back to Denver roped together and John's horse, Blaze, already saddled for him. Rajah was scampering about, sniffing and barking, knowing he was off again on a grand adventure away from the confines of the barn. The four detectives were mounted on solid animals and seemed ready for the ride. Kai Singh stood outside the *Star*, awaiting John's final instructions. Within moments of John's arriving, the seven men were on their horses and, followed by eight mules and one noisy dog, rode up the steep slope of the road toward the stark spires of the mountains to the west.

Loren Krammer was at his desk, the door to his office closed, and a worried frown on his face. He had heard about the shoot-out on Saturday night from Harry Simpson, a nervous employee of the bank. Three men, killed by Sheriff Gilbert while trying to break into the freight office. Injun Joe Lopez, J. B. Franks, and Spots Taylor. Members of his gang. Krammer squirmed in his leather-covered chair. "I don't like it one damn bit," he mumbled to himself. He looked up at his cowed employee. "Harry, take a stroll down to Auroria and drop in to some of the saloons, and see if you can find Seamus O'Flynn. Tell him I need to see him right away. He'll understand. Tell him to hurry."

Krammer was still fuming when O'Flynn shuffled in. His unkempt, uncut hair and greasy moustache told the story of a drunkard and ne'er-do-well, anxious to make a few dollars any way possible, honest or not. "Yes, sir, Mr. Krammer. Harry said ya wanted to see me right away?"

"Yes. Ride out to the Adams cabin. Tell Luke that the livery owner told me Rafe Wallace rented eight pack mules this morning. Tell him to keep a watch on the mountaintop. Repeat that back to me."

O'Flynn recited the message and licked his lips. He contemplated asking the scowling banker for an advance on his ten-dollar wage for the message, only one of many he had delivered, but decided against it. Instead, as soon as he was given permission to leave, he would stop by Mickey's Saloon and ask if he could have one on the tab. As much as he bought from the fat, Irish tavern owner, he should be good for one drink.

Krammer kept his eyes on the saloon bum as he shuffled

202

across the street, straight for the stable where he kept a decrepit old mare. The knowledge that a shipment of gold was about to come his way soothed the aggravation he felt over the needless deaths of three of his men. Briefly, he wondered if a dozen men would be enough for the job. Then, shrugging the negative thought from his mind, he pulled out a map of the area where he wanted to buy more land. Soon, a smirk covered his porcine face.

John and his party reached the haphazard collection of buildings and tent homes that was Central City without incident. Even though they had stopped at Eight-Mile Gulch and inspected the ground, nothing was found that gave any indication of where the outlaws escaped after their robberies. They camped overnight at the spring down the road from the gulch.

The four men bonded with John, Khan Singh, Curly Bill, and even Rajah. "These boys will do to ride the trail with," Bill announced, as he and John rode together on the second day. "They all got sand in their craw, as far as I can see."

"I agree, William. Of course, when the bullets fly . . . But, I would agree whole-heartedly from what I've seen so far."

Curly Bill shifted in his saddle. "Boss, I aim to be a part of any action where the bullets do fly. Ya unnerstand that, don't ya? I don't wanna be left out of the action."

"Of course." John smiled at the loyal friend riding effortlessly beside him. "You'll be in charge of the gold convoy, and I suspect will be up to your suspenders in any gunplay. Hopefully, we'll have the scoundrels trapped between us, and they'll surrender. We need their testimony to convict Loren Krammer and his son, anyway."

"These are bad folks, Boss. I wouldn't count on any of them quittin' too easy. I figger we'll have to ventilate most of 'em afore any even think about quittin'. Right, Raj?"

The happy dog frolicked among the horses, deliriously happy at being free to romp again, and he barked a joyous response to the question from one of the two men he loved most in the world.

"See what I mean, Boss? I can smell a fight a'comin'. Jus' like when I was a'scoutin fer General Talbot, back in Red River country. We're gonna smell gun smoke a'fore this little shiveree is done dancin'."

CHAPTER 24
A TRAP IS LAID

Central City was as filthy, disorganized, and frantically paced as when John first saw the grubby mining town. "Not much changed in the last week," he remarked to Curly Bill. Main Street was a muddy ruin, as if recently doused by a thunderstorm, yet no rain had fallen in several days. Miners and prospectors jostled up and down the sloppy thoroughfare or jousted among one another as they used the single, soiled, wooden sidewalk that fronted the row of buildings clustered along the west side of the main street.

"Looks like a new saloon's opened since I was here last," Curly Bill observed as the seven tired men rode toward the only decent hotel in the town.

"You keep count of those things?" Joe Richardson queried with a grin creasing his lean face, the ends of his flowing moustache bobbing with the movement.

"Damn tootin'," Curly Bill replied. "I always like to know where the nearest waterhole is, when I'm out and about. 'Cides, the boss gave me the very important duty of goin' around to every saloon in town the last time we was here, checkin' on any suspicious happenin's."

Walt Pate chuckled. "I don't think John could have tasked a better man for the job, Curly Bill. It 'peers to me like you would put your heart and soul into doin' it right."

"You're dag-gummed certain'," Curly Bill shot back, trading barbs right back at Walt. "The boss knows who he can count on to do the tough jobs right. Why, I suspect I'll have to make a round tonight, to see if anything new has come up since I checked last. Right, Boss?"

"Perhaps, my friend. However, I'll ask Vernon or Will, or even both to accompany you, since I want you clear-headed tomorrow when we plan the gold shipment."

Curly Bill flashed a knowing grin. "Why, Boss, there ain't no need fer that. There ain't no coffin-juice made that can put me off my feed the next day. I reckon these here children will only slow me down, oncest I get to goin'. I'm not fer sure that Will even drinks a'tall. How 'bout it, son?"

"I imagine I'd better stay sober, to drag your mangy butt home after a few swallows of the rotgut served about these parts." Will's remarks were the most he had spoken since they left Denver two days earlier.

Everyone laughed. Even stern Khan Singh smiled at the good humor of the youngest detective. The four detectives from Kansas City had taken to their new companions with gusto and had already cataloged Bill as the party's clown prince. Rajah added his joyous barks until they arrived at the hotel and swung down from their saddles in front of the long hitching post. Stretching and stamping the flow of blood back to their legs, the trail-stiff men climbed the wooden steps to the hotel veranda. The azure-blue sky was filled with long, thin stringers of white clouds. "Appears tomorrow will be a nice day. William, will you be so kind as to take care of the horses? As for the rest of us, let's refresh ourselves and meet in an hour for dinner, here in the hotel dining room. Agreed?"

With no dissension, the weary travelers trooped inside and checked into their rooms, eagerly anticipating washing the trail grime off their faces and necks. Curly Bill took the horses, mules, and Rajah to the nearby stable and, after leaving detailed instructions on the care and feeding of the animals, hurried back toward the hotel and the prospect of a cool beer at the bar.

As he hurried down the wooden sidewalk, he nearly bumped into Tom Krammer, who was walking in the opposite direction, his head lowered as if in deep thought. "Howdy, Tom. It's Curly Bill Williams. I met ya when I was up here last with Mr. Wallace and John Whyte. Remember?"

"Oh, yes, I do. How are you, sir? Sorry, I was thinking about something else. I did not mean to crowd you off the sidewalk. You and Mr. Wallace up here again, so soon?"

"Nope. Only me and John Whyte, this time. We brung some Pinkerton detectives along. We're gonna slip the gold ya got stacked up in yur office past the owlhoots tomorry, iffin everthing goes right."

Tom Krammer was all ears. "Wonderful. How many guards did you say you brought along?"

"Four. That oughtta be plenty, with me and John Whyte along. I 'spect we'll not even see hide nor hair of anyone, as it is. Ya see, me and John Whyte has got us a plan."

"Well, that's good news. I suppose you will be in tomorrow morning to pick up the shipment. I'll have everything ready to go. Please, tell Mr. Whyte I'll need a release from Mr. Wallace before I can sign over the gold to you. Now, if you will excuse me, I have an appointment, and I'm very late. Nice seeing you, Mr. Williams. See you tomorrow."

Tom Krammer hurried away, not noticing that Curly Bill watched him blend into the crowd, a sardonic smile on his normally cherubic face. "Yep, young Master Krammer, I suspect we will see ya tomorry, fer a fact."

Tom Krammer walked even faster to meet the gang member who had sent him word to rendezvous at their usual spot, outside the main business area in a dingy saloon next to the partially constructed opera house. The young outlaw assumed it was to relay a message from his father that the gold was being shipped soon. Tom smiled to himself. With the information that the gabby Williams had given him, he had vital news to pass on to the outlaws. The whole gang would be waiting at the Adams cabin about ten miles north of Central City, close to the secret trail leading back to the Georgetown Road. The Adamses supposedly were two unsuccessful prospectors, working a no-account claim off one of the many streams feeding into the rushing waters of Fraser Creek.

Frank Adams and his younger brother, Luke, had discovered the secret passage out of the mountains, which followed a dry creek bed up a desolate canyon to the road, cutting eight hours off the normal time from Central City. The outlaws waited there between robberies, well out of sight and away from the hazards of saloons and flesh-pots of Denver. It was from here that Spots, Injun, and J. B. Franks had departed only five days ago. None of the outlaws at the cabin knew their three chums were now planted in boot hill.

Young Krammer entered the dim interior of the sour-smelling saloon. He spotted "Squint" Harrison sitting by himself at a far table, his back to the wall. The one-eyed outlaw, who had the sallow face of a man who had spent a lot of time in prison, was moodily sipping a whiskey while picking at a sliver in the unpainted tabletop.

Tom looked around. He did not want to chance upon someone he knew, especially talking to one so obviously on the wrong side of the law as Squint. He eased on over to the table and took a chair. "Howdy, Squint. You wanted to see me?"

Squint jerked up, startled at the intrusion. "Oh! Howdy, kid. I didn't see ya come in. Yeah. The boss sent the word that there's gonna be a gold shipment soon. Said to keep yur eyes opened."

"I know," Tom smugly answered. "I met one of the men who

will be guarding it a while ago. Should be six men for this run, I gather."

"Six? That don't seem like enough, especially since the last time."

"Apparently four are Pinkerton agents. The blowhard I spoke with thought it would be plenty. He said they have a plan. As soon as I can find out what it is, I'll signal you with the heliograph from the top of Bear Mountain. Keep a sharp eye on it all day tomorrow."

"Don't fret. We will. I wish J.B. and his pals hadn't got themselves kilt in Denver." Squint worried the sliver, and his good eye took on a crafty sheen. "How much gold we talkin' about this trip?"

Tom shrugged. He could care less about the problems of the outlaws who did his father's dirty work. He was much too important to worry about them. He certainly never wanted the outlaws to know too much. "I don't know. About one hundred thousand, I suppose. It will take eight mules to carry it all."

"Hot damn. That should mean a good bonus fer us all, I reckon. Well, I'll mosey on back. We'll be waitin' fer yur signal."

Tom Krammer tarried until he was sure that Squint was well away from the saloon before he returned to his room behind the assay office. He immediately put the two men hired as night guards to work packing the dust and nuggets into fifty-pound leather sacks in preparation for the coming day. His stomach fluttered and growled like it did every time a robbery was set in motion.

Tom Krammer wondered what plan the Pinkerton men had up their sleeve. He'd find out tomorrow and then flash the message to the men at the cabin. Without a doubt the convoy would not leave until the day after tomorrow, at the earliest. He tunelessly whistled a refrain while he worked. The last message he had received from his father said this would be the final holdup.

If it was, then he was off to San Francisco to enjoy his hard-earned wealth.

John was silent as Curly Bill finished his account of the meeting with Tom Krammer. He thought about it momentarily, then shrugged.

"Very well, William. Hopefully he'll inform his colleagues about our plan to move the gold immediately." John chewed on a piece of his seared elk steak and turned to the four new men. "I'm fairly certain that the man in question is the gang's contact here in Central City."

Will Jeries spoke. "And he works at the assay office. Mighty handy job for an outlaw, isn't it?"

John agreed. "His father got him the job. I'm just as positive that Loren Krammer is the real leader of the gang. When we finish with our work here, I hope to have enough evidence to arrest him." He chewed the tough meat. "Meanwhile, let's finish and retire back to my room. I want to review my plan with you and hear your questions."

John led the others into the assay office late the next morning. Tom Krammer was all business and inspected the signed authorization from Rafe Wallace to release the gold to John's care. He presented the filled bags of gold and stood aside as Curly Bill and Vernon Vane loaded the pack mules with their precious cargo. As soon as the mule train was loaded, John brought Curly Bill and Walt into the office of Tom Krammer. He opened a map he was carrying and pointed to it. The sun was already past its zenith and starting its slide down the day into evening.

The men gathered around the opened map spread on Krammer's desktop. "My plan is simple, gentlemen. We shall travel at night and lay over during the day at an easily defended camp site. The outlaws can't attack at night, and, if they show up during the daylight hours, we'll hear them coming and have cover and concealment to resist them."

"G-G-Good idea," Tom Krammer stammered, hiding his disappointment. "Any idea where you are going to hole up during the daylight hours?"

"That's why I wanted to show you our plan," John smoothly answered. "I assume you know the road as well as anyone. What do you think? I was thinking that the first stop would be here, where Soda Creek cuts the Georgetown Road. The second day, we camp here at Beaver Brook. The next day, we're so close to Denver we ride on in and sleep in a hotel. What do you think?"

Tom Krammer thought furiously. He had to put these men in a location where his outlaw buddies could ambush them without too much risk. Otherwise the bandits might give up and not attack the gold escort. Pointing at the map, he indicated a different spot for the second day's layover. "Here, Mr. Whyte. The intersection of Georgetown Road and the Creswell Stage Road. It's only a six- to eight-hour ride in the dark and has good water and forage for the horses."

"Very well, at the Creswell Stage Road intersection."

Young Tom suppressed a shiver of anticipation. What he had not said was that the intersection did not have as good a cover as the other location, while the high ground to the south would be an ideal spot to hide and wait for the convoy and riders to arrive. Then, as soon as most were asleep, the outlaws could open up and subdue the guards before they were fully awake.

"That's it then," John announced. "Walt, will you go with William to the store and buy a dozen oil lanterns and a gallon of coal oil? We leave as soon as the sun starts to set."

Tom Krammer was nearly dancing a jig, he was so anxious to get to the top of the mountain and send his message to the waiting men at the Adamses' cabin. He puttered about as John and the others made their final preparations for departure and then announced, "If you will excuse me, Mr. Whyte. Now that you're moving my backlog of gold, I need to get out and urge the miners to start depositing some more. Have a safe and successful trip." He shook John's hand and dashed out the door, up the street toward the livery.

"Shouldn't we arrest him, John? As soon as he sends his message, I mean," Walt Pate questioned, fingering the holstered .44 Colt on his hip.

"No, I think not," John replied. "If for some reason we don't achieve success this time, I will want him here for our next effort. We can always pick him up after the gang is taken."

The seven men lead the mules out of town as the sun touched the top of the highest mountain behind them. John gazed at the peak of Bear Mountain, where he was certain Tom Krammer was about to heliograph the convoy information to his outlaw companions. He saw nothing, but that was exactly what was happening.

Squint Harrison looked at the message from Krammer, painfully written on a piece of paper by Luke Adams, who was the best copier of Morse code. "So, they think they'll outsmart us by riding nights and holing up days. We'll see about that." He started his planning. The outlaws would leave before noon tomorrow and be at the ambush site suggested by Tom Krammer before sundown. They would hide out under good cover and wait for the convoy to arrive the next morning. As soon as everyone was bedded down and asleep, the dozen riders he would take with him would open up and clean out the guards before they knew what had happened. Squint chuckled as he started his motley crew to cleaning their weapons, filling canteens, and getting ready for the trail. The plan appeared to be solid to the hardened outlaw.

"Frank, you come with us. Luke, you stay here and watch the

place. We'll have the guards outnumbered thirteen to six. Easy pickin's, I would suspect."

"Damn, Squint," Luke Adams griped. "I want to come, too. I'm tired of missin' all the fun."

"Naw, I got enough men fer the job. 'Cides, ya gotta watch the place, in case someone unexpected shows up."

"Thirteen is a unlucky number," Frank Adams pointed out, hoping to help his brother. But nobody was listening.

Chapter 25
A Trap Is Sprung

The sun was a red-gold sliver on the mountaintops to the west when John led his small party out of Central City. "Here we go, William. I certainly hope I am right about Tom Krammer. I would hate to have targeted the wrong man."

"Nary a chance, Boss. Our young Tom has got some serious explainin' to do, once we finish up with his pards." Curly Bill spit a brown stream of tobacco juice onto the muddy street. "I jus' hope they don't get anxious and hit us tonight or tomorrow mornin' afore we're expectin' 'em to."

John turned in his saddle, seeking a glimpse of Tom Krammer outside the assay office, but the sidewalk was empty. The two guards had already gone inside, and there was no sign of young Tom. "I doubt it, William. He deliberately chose the location for our second day's camp, and I suspect he's instructed the gang to be there by tomorrow afternoon. So, Khan Singh and I will ride hard and be there well before that."

"You be careful, John," Walt Pate chimed in. "This trail is damned treacherous in daylight. I shudder to think what it'll be like in the dark."

"Khan Singh and I have covered many a dangerous trail by moonlight. This old warrior can see like a cat in the dark, so don't worry. We'll be fine. You chaps have the harder job, herding these mules along and still finding the stopping point in the dark." John's face grew serious. "If for some reason we don't trap the outlaws where I have planned, I'm counting on you

214

gentlemen to escort this gold through to Denver, no matter what."

"Don't fret about us, Boss. Jus' you and Khan Singh git there in one piece. Me and the boys will be there the day after tomorrow mornin', sure as the sun rises." Curly Bill glared around, as if daring some outlaw to dispute his claim.

"Be on full alert as you near the intersection. The outlaws may decide to hit earlier or immediately as you arrive there." John tried to think of any other possible instructions but realized he was prolonging the inevitable. They were crossing the first hill out of Central City, away from any prying eyes. In the dusk of early evening, among the fir trees along the trail, it was almost impossible to see anything. "We're off. Rajah, stay with William. Stay, now." John spurred Blaze, and he and Khan Singh galloped ahead, leaving Curly Bill and the others far behind.

The half moon provided some light to the riders. Once John and Khan Singh's night vision adjusted to the dim moonlight, they made fairly good time. "Seems like the night we led the 12th up the road to the castle of the Maharaja of Kirkistan, doesn't it, old friend?"

"A long night, Sahib."

It was about ten the next morning before they trotted their tired animals into the flat meadow where the Creswell Stage Road twisted its way out of the mountains from the south of Denver. They dismounted at the intersection and searched for any sign that they were under observation.

"Good," John announced, stamping his legs. "I think we beat the highwaymen here, if this is indeed where they plan to spring their ambush." He shaded his eyes against the sun, angling down the steep slopes of the high mountains and asked Khan Singh, "Where would you set up an ambush, if you wanted to do the most harm with the most safety?"

Khan Singh paced around, staring up at the steep walls of

dirt and rock covered with scrub juniper brush and small pine trees. He pointed to the side of the high mountain to the south and east of the meadow. "There, Sahib. Good cover, a clear shot at our men when they camp." He pointed to a small stand of trees. "And, over there, next to the stream. From up there, they have easy access to the trail ahead." Khan Singh then pointed up the Georgetown Road. "See, the road goes over the hill up there, so the outlaws can be away from any gunfire once they are over the top of the trail. Yes," he firmly declared, "up there, in the rocks. About forty yards off the trail. Far enough to make it hard to be hit by a man with a pistol, but close for a rifle."

John shaded his eyes and gazed at the likely ambush position Khan Singh had pointed out. "When do you think they will strike?"

"If it were the evil Afghanistans from the Kashiker Pass, they would wait until their unfortunate victims unsaddled their horses before attacking. The sun will be in the eyes of William and the others, and when it is time to escape, the unsaddled horses will make pursuit that much harder."

John voiced his agreement. "Makes sense to me, old friend. The question is, now where do we position ourselves to best ambush the ambushers?"

"If you would, Sahib, take the horses to where William will camp. I will climb up above and look around. I wish to ensure that what I have suggested is the best location for the outlaws. Then I can find a satisfactory location above them."

John walked Blaze and Khan Singh's big roan down the road to the intersection. At Khan Singh's wave, he took them on back into the woods until he found a location where they had plenty of water and grass, yet were well hidden from anyone at the intersection. He walked back carrying their bedrolls, dried jerky for their supper, and freshly-filled canteens. When he returned to the intersection, he spotted Khan Singh high above, working his way along the steep side of the mountain, pulling a large log from a long-dead tree around to construct a natural barrier. John scrambled up the slope, his feet slipping and sliding in the loose dirt and shale of the hillside. "What are you doing, old friend?"

Khan Singh finished pushing the log into position. It was at the edge of a shallow, flat spot on the hill and, with the log barrier, provided good cover. "I have made this place look like an attractive choice for the outlaws to set up their ambush. Now we can go above them, to that ledge about forty yards up the hill. See it?"

John looked where the old Sikh warrior was pointing. "Yes. We'll have to climb it with ropes, but I think we can get there."

Khan Singh nodded. "From there, we will be above any ambushers hiding here, with good cover. They will never be able to reach us, and we'll have a good field of fire down at the outlaws."

"I agree, old friend. Well, let's climb on up. We have a long afternoon and night ahead of us." Easily visible was the small grove of trees where Curly Bill would be leading the convoy in the morning. "We have to be right. There's not much cover down there. Unless we stop them before they start, I'm afraid William is in for serious trouble." He started to pick his way up the sheer side of the cliff to the ledge his trusted friend had discovered.

As he reached the ledge and pulled himself over the top, his breath coming in ragged spurts, he agreed with Khan Singh. It was a prime location to spring a surprise on the outlaws below. The hollowed cut in the mountainside was twenty feet long and ten feet deep. At the back, a shallow depression had been carved into the rock by the wind and rain of countless centuries. He and Khan Singh could wrap up in their bedrolls and find some shelter from the elements. There were plenty of small boulders scattered about to build a barricade to hide behind, and their position was not visible from directly below. He peered over the side at Khan Singh, who was busy below, erasing any sign that someone might have been near the fallen log. John threw an end of the rope he had carried up with him and called down to his friend.

"Tie the bedrolls and canteens to the rope, and I'll pull them up. Then, I'll drop it back down for you." Khan Singh waved and finished scattering dirt and brush on their footprints before going to where the end of the long rope dangled. He attached the bedrolls and canteens to the dangling end of the rope, and John pulled them up. After placing the gear in the small cave, he returned to the side of the ledge and once again dropped the rope to the waiting Sikh. With John pulling, Khan Singh was soon standing beside him. The two men rolled several small boulders to the edge until they had constructed concealed fighting positions with clear shots to the rim below.

When their fighting positions were completed, they returned to the cover of the tiny cave, where they ate and drank sparingly from their canteens. John chewed on his jerky, patiently softening the hard meat until he could swallow. The two men would be able to cover any ambush spot chosen by the outlaws as long as they did not go to the other side of the road. If they did, he decided he would open fire immediately, driving them away before Curly Bill and the convoy rode too close to the outlaws. He would not risk their lives unless the odds favored him. He sat moodily, worrying that maybe he had been too careless in putting both him and Khan Singh on the same side of the road.

About the same time John decided to send the old Sikh over to the other side of the road, he felt Khan Singh nudge his arm. "Sahib. Men come over the pass."

John swung his eyes to the crest of the road, several hundred feet to the east. "Ten, eleven, twelve, thirteen." He counted softly. "Thirteen men. They aren't taking any chances, are they?" he grumbled. They watched in silence as the party rode to the intersection below before stopping to dismount. Some order must have been given, because four men separated from the others and started climbing along either side of the road, struggling to gain a foothold among the rocks and trees, looking over the ground. John held his breath, praying the two on the far side did not find anything suitable.

"Hey, Squint," one of the searchers shouted back to the men still at the intersection. He was standing at the fallen log, precisely where John wanted him.

"Ya find somethin', Soapy?" one of the men below shouted back. The two men across the road slid and stumbled up the steep hillside to the roadway. They had found nothing promising on that side.

"Yeah. Here's a good spot. Good cover, a log fer protection, and a clear shot to where you're standing."

"Hold on, I'll be right there." The leader worked his way up the steep slope and inspected the small flat protrusion before announcing, "This here'll do." He called to the men waiting below. "You men git up here. Frank, you take the horses back up the road and hide 'em over the rise. Stay with 'em tonight. We'll camp out here, in case them Pinkertons get here early. If any of 'em git past us tomorrey, ya'all pick 'em off. Don't let none git past ya. Fires out as soon as it's dark, unnerstan'? Anybody comes down the road from Denver, give a whistle."

He looked down from his perch on the ledge and shouted to the waiting men below. "The rest of ya fellas grab the bedrolls and chow and climb up here. I wanna be all located a'fore the sun sets."

John and Khan Singh lay flat behind their boulders, listening to the men below. Squint personally took each man around, assigning a fighting position. John crawled between two large rocks where he could peer over the edge while he listened to the men below.

As soon as every man had fixed up his individual fighting location, the eleven outlaws gathered around the one called Squint, who squatted down at the rear of the flat protrusion, against the sheer rock face that John and Khan Singh had climbed earlier. In a low voice that John could not distinguish, he gave some further orders to the men. A small fire was started. The outlaws cooked a hot meal and made coffee. From where John hid, the pungent aroma of the coffee was powerfully appealing.

John motioned to Khan Singh to scoot back into the small cave, where they could whisper without being heard by the noisy men below. "Can you see them all from where you are?" he quizzed Khan Singh softly.

"All but the three farthest away from me, Sahib. Can you see them from where you will fire?"

"No, curse the luck. But, if we make it hot enough for their comrades, they may panic and run for it, exposing themselves to us or William below."

Khan Singh glanced up at the setting sun. "Sahib, it is nearly sundown. Why don't you rest while I watch. You can replace me later."

The two men spent the night alternating watch, but the waiting men below them never thought of looking upward and never discovered the deadly peril they were in. John and his trusted companion monitored the men below while they ate, drank from whiskey bottles stored in their bedrolls, and eventually bedded down for the night. Two men stayed on guard throughout the night. John and Khan Singh debated when to announce themselves to the men in ambush below. They decided to declare themselves as soon as the outlaws made any incriminating move.

The noise of the men below woke John, as Khan Singh

touched his shoulder. "Sahib, the sun will be up shortly."

John rolled out of his thin bedroll and crawled over to the edge of the bluff. "Any sign of William yet?"

"I do not see him," the old Sikh whispered. "It is still dark on the trail. The men below have taken their places and are waiting for him."

John and Khan anxiously waited. The morning sun had not yet peeked over the ragged points of rock. John yawned, and, almost immediately, Khan Singh pointed back down the road. "William comes, Sahib."

John squinted through the dim light at the road, far below. Sure enough, Curly Bill was guiding his horse off the downward slope onto the flat expanse of the mountain meadow toward where the two roads intersected. John glanced up. The sun was barely visible over his shoulder. He stepped back until he was hidden from the hiding men below and took a small, polished mirror from his bedroll. Swiftly he flashed at Bill, nearly half a mile away. The distant rider suddenly stopped and got off his horse, as if inspecting the animal's hoof. John flashed the short warning, "Be ready," three times. He saw Curly Bill swing back on his horse and lead the convoy of four men and eight mules forward, toward the grove of trees that marked the intersection.

"Do you think he saw me?" he whispered to Khan Singh.

"Assuredly, Sahib. Assuredly."

Curly Bill led his procession into the trees and swung off his horse. From where John lay, he could hear him call out. "Nap time, men. Let's get these animals taken care of and grab some shuteye."

John glanced at Khan Singh. The old warrior had his rifle poked around his pile of rock, aimed at one of the outlaws below. John did the same, choosing the outline of Squint, who was the outlaw in charge. He saw Squint suddenly rise up, his rifle pointed down at Curly Bill, deadly intent in his action. The cur was going to start the action by killing without warning. "So be it," John murmured through clenched teeth. His shot took Squint in the back of his head and blew out the only good eye the outlaw had. If he had not been dead when he hit the ground, the unfortunate Squint surely would have been blind.

Khan Singh fired an instant later, and the ambush of the ambushers was under way in murderous efficiency. Four men were dead before the outlaws could figure out what had happened. Their first shots were down, toward Bill and the others, who had seen the warning and taken cover at the first shot. Six were dead before anyone turned and fired up at the deadly threat decimating their ranks from above. Three outlaws jumped from their cover and returned John's fire with rapid shots of their own.

To their misfortune, this exposed them to the fire of Curly Bill and the detectives below, and they were disposed of. Two men ran toward their waiting horses and safety, but Khan Singh and Walt Pate fired as one, dropping the trailing outlaw in the dust of the road. The second ran over the top the hill, bullets aimed at him by every man in John's party, whining off into the distance.

The ambush was a spectacular success. In the deafening silence following the gun battle, John and Khan Singh stood and waved to their friends. Curly Bill was whooping in glee. "Way to go, Boss. We cut these buzzards into dog meat."

Rajah barked loudly, adding his approval.

CHAPTER 26
THE HIDDEN TRAIL

"William," John shouted down from his position to Curly Bill, still on the trail, celebrating their victory over the outlaw ambush. "Two men are with their horses, escaping over the hill." He pointed. "Catch them. We need to question them."

"Gotcha, Boss," Curly Bill shouted back. He bounded into his saddle and galloped up the stony road after the fleeing outlaws. Will Jeries and Rajah were right behind him, the excited dog howling like a wolf.

John and Khan Singh threw their ropes over the ledge and inched their way down the sheer cliff to the bandits' ill-chosen ambush. It was a place of carnage. Eleven men lay sprawled in awkward positions, their life's blood soaking the rocky soil. John went from man to man, seeking any still alive.

"Bloody, hell, Khan Singh," he groused to his Sikh friend. "We're too damn keen a shot for our own good; only two still alive. Walter," he called down to the stocky detective standing below, staring up at him, "is everyone all right?"

Walt Pate moved over to Vernon Vane and looked at the kneeling detective. "Vern was grazed in the short ribs by a bullet. He'll be fine, as soon as he catches his breath. Barely broke skin." The assessment was as much for Vernon's sake as for John's.

"Take good care of him, Walt. Joe, get some water up here, straight away. Two of these outlaws can still talk, if we hurry."

Joe Richardson gathered several canteens and clawed his way

up the rock-strewn slope toward them. John turned his attention back to the two outlaws; both gasped for breath, fighting the grim reaper. One was already unconscious, shot through the throat and bleeding heavily, the shallow rise and fall of his chest announcing the inevitable. His dying companion, shot through the lungs, lay pale and still with his back against the fallen log. A bloody froth bubbled out of his mouth and nose with every breath. He watched with fear and shock as John approached, too wounded to even move toward the rifle lying beside him.

As Joe reached the ledge, he handed John a full canteen. The young English detective knelt down beside the wounded outlaw and sprinkled some cool water on the bloody lips. He could see Khan Singh and Joe Richardson working on the other outlaw, trying to staunch his bleeding. The outlaw at John's feet licked the cool fluid and swallowed, before coughing up more scarlet froth. His eyes cleared, and he blinked in appreciation.

"Thanks, pard. I'm hit bad."

John slid the kerchief off the outlaw's neck and moistened it, wiping the dust and blood from the dying man's face. "You are, most certainly. What's your name? Do you have family I can contact for you?"

"Sleepy Settles. Naw, my kin all died durin' the war." He coughed again, re-staining his lips and chin. "Thanks fer the water, I 'preciate it. Put Luther Settles on my marker, will ya, please?"

"I promise, if you'll do something for me. You don't have long now, Mr. Settles. Who is your boss? Where is your hideout? Any more in your gang? Don't face your maker with sin on your breast. Speak to me, man, before it's too late." John shook the dying outlaw's arm, emphasizing his urgency.

The wounded Sleepy looked up at John and grabbed the young detective's arm. He opened his mouth, but only a fresh gout of frothy blood issued. With a shudder, his eyes rolled back in his head, and he was gone. John dropped the head, which hit the hard log with an audible *thump!* and looked over at Khan Singh.

"This one is done for. Any luck with yours?"

Khan Singh shook his head. "This one will not awake until he reaches the next world, wrapped in the burning fires of damnation."

"Damn. I can't believe we have killed all of these villains, with not a single one left to answer my questions." He glanced toward the sound of many horses riding over the hill. It was Curly Bill, leading eleven horses, obviously belonging to the men lying at his feet. John turned to Joe, standing beside the dead outlaw. "Joe, you and the others run these fellows down to the road. I'm going to talk with William. Come on, Khan Singh."

John and the old Sikh reached the road as Curly Bill rode up with the string of horses, followed by a downcast Will Jeries and Rajah.

"Sorry, Boss. Them two fellas lit out as we came over the hill, like scared jackrabbits. Me and Will's horses was too tired after ridin' all night. I was a'feered to let Rajah go after 'em. They might a shot him afore we caught up with 'em."

"Bad luck. Were they still on the Georgetown Road, the last you saw of them?"

"Yep. Ridin' like the hounds of Hades was after 'em."

John glanced at the top of the hill and then back to Walt Pate, who patiently awaited his orders. "Walt, lash these outlaws to their horses and dispose of them somewhere. Then, continue on to Denver. Take your men with you. I suspect you can make Apex Pass before mid-afternoon. Lay over there until it is dark, and then go on in to Denver. Deliver the gold to Rafe Wallace, and give Sheriff Gilbert the bodies."

John turned to Curly Bill, watching and listening. "William, if you are going with Khan Singh and me, you had better switch your horse with one of these fresh ones. Khan Singh, would you bring our horses up, please."

"Might as well," Curly Bill answered. "The previous owner won't object, I reckon. That there dun looks like a nice ridin' animal. I jus' hate to make my poor ole pony tote some worthless carcass on his back all the way to Denver. Why, I might never hear the end of it."

"It can't be helped, if you plan to ride with Khan Singh and me. I plan to track those fleeing outlaws, even if it's clear back to Missouri. I suppose you do want to accompany us?"

Curly Bill hitched up his gunbelt in a defiant manner. "You're damned tootin', Boss. I ain't about to let ya git into any more gun scrapes without me there to cover your back. Lemme change my saddle, and I'll be ready to ride."

John turned back to Walt Pate. The stocky detective was quietly giving instructions to Will Jeries about the disposition of the dead outlaws' bodies. "Walt, we'll leave you now. Don't let anyone know what has happened here. Report to Sheriff Gilbert, and ask him to keep it quiet. Tell Rafe Wallace to say nothing about the gold being delivered, until I return to Denver. Tell him I'm positive Loren Krammer and young Tom are in it up to their necks, so don't mention anything about the gold to Krammer. Keep your weapons visible, and don't take any chances with those you meet on the road. Don't allow anyone to surprise you. I know I can count on you and the others. Good luck."

"Luck to you, John. Me and the boys'll be waitin' on you in Denver. We'll take care of these jaspers," he pointed his thumb toward Joe and Vernon, dragging a limp body down the rocky slope. "We'll hide 'em out so's nobody can find them and put the gold in Rafe's safe." A toothy grin parted his moustache and beard. "Then, we'll lay low at your car till you fellas arrive."

John took the reins of Blaze from Khan Singh and climbed aboard. "We'll be along shortly, Walt. Grab our excess gear out of the cave, and pack it back to Denver, if you will. See you then." He spurred the stallion, and it trotted up the trail, Curly Bill, Khan Singh, and Rajah right behind. The four Pinkerton detectives were left to complete their grizzly task, before they could ride on to Denver. Eight mules carrying gold and eleven horses with cadavers were enough of a burden for convoy, no matter how disciplined they were.

Rajah loped ahead, his big snout sniffing the ground as he ran, while John motioned for Curly Bill to ride up beside him. "Where did you lose sight of them, William?"

Curly Bill pointed to the top of another rise, about a half mile directly ahead. "We got to the top a' that hill and seen they was already at the top of another, about a mile away. Ya can see what I mean, when we git up there."

John nodded, eyeing the rocky road bed. "It will be hell trailing anyone on this," he announced. "Let's hope Rajah will let us know when they get off the trail. That is, if they don't decide to ride all the way into Denver this time."

For nearly six miles the three men rode east, following the twisting Georgetown Road without seeing any sign that their quarry had left the relatively easier route of the rocky trail. They rode in silence, their eyes glued to the rocky path, looking for the tracks of recent horsemen among the rocks and dirt on the road.

As they trotted across the wooden bed of a bridge built over a swift-flowing stream, Rajah suddenly stopped and started circling around, seeking the scent he had been following so easily until then. John held up his hand, and the three men stopped and dismounted.

"Hello. They've left the trail. William, ride on ahead and look for any sign that they are back on the road. Khan Singh and I will search here." He called to the scurrying dog. "Rajah, come here, boy. Follow me."

John took Rajah and retraced their steps for a hundred feet. Khan Singh carefully guided his horse close to the edge of the road, hoping to find a sign of where the fleeing men had exited. John patted the massive head of the hound. "Now, Raj, find the horses. Go on, find them. Good boy."

The Great Dane started again, sniffing and working his way toward the bridge. Before he reached the end of the wooden trestle bridge, Rajah stopped and circled, losing the scent yet again. John hurried to the end of the bridge; the near side was a steep drop-off. He slowly walked across the wooded timbers of the bridge. Eyes down, he saw a fresh gouge on the muddy lumber of the crosswalk. He called to Khan Singh, walking along the edge of the road ahead.

"It's very near here, I think. Rajah loses the scent as he comes off the wood crossties." Rajah nosed around a large rock sitting at the end of the bridge, as if placed there to mark the beginning of the bridge. John thought of the trail up the mountain where the heliograph was hidden. He remembered the boulder, which had been rolled over the path. "Khan Singh. Help me move this rock."

The two men put their shoulder to the large rock, straining to move it. To John's delight, it moved with very little effort, exposing a narrow pathway off the road down toward the rushing waters of the stream below. "By thunder, I think we've found it!" John exclaimed. As if to ratify his statement, Rajah darted down the narrow path, right for the white-foaming waters, apparently inches away from falling off the narrow pathway. The Great Dane barked joyously, his wet nose back to the ground, on the trail of the scent. At the bottom, standing by the foaming waters on slick, wet stones, he impatiently barked and whined for John to follow him.

"You think the scoundrels went down there?" John asked Khan Singh. "It doesn't appear wide enough for a mountain goat." About then, Curly Bill came galloping up.

"I found a wet spot in the trail, 'bout half a mile ahead. No hoof prints a'tall. The bastards got off 'round here somewhere's." He looked over the edge of the road at Rajah, barking, below them. "Down there?"

John nodded. "It has to be. Come on, let's make our way down that goat path. If thieving outlaws can do it, so can we." He cautiously led Blaze down the rock-strewn path, while Curly Bill and Khan Singh monitored from above. The rushing waters drowned out all other sounds, but, as he descended the level of the road bed, the path widened, undercut back into the rock wall, and the trail grew more accessible. As John reached the bottom of the path, he shouted up for the others to follow him. They, too, safely traversed the treacherous path. Then John led the way as they followed the wet, rocky streambed, cut by ten thousand years of spring thaw runoff.

Ahead was the silvery spume of a small waterfall. The path cut behind the wet spray, hidden from view from the road above. John spotted several small rocks, freshly scratched by metal horseshoes, proof the outlaws had passed this way. He motioned for the others to join him and rode Blaze behind the splashing waterfall. The horse initially resisted the experience, but with clear ground on the far side, he hurried through the shower of cold water. On the far side, John wiped the moisture from his face with the sleeve of his shirt and awaited his comrades. Curly Bill was the last and spit a wad of tobacco juice at the cold drops as he exited from behind the falls.

"Didn't expect to shower so soon to Saturday, dag-gummit. I shore hope we don't have to go through many of them natural shower baths afore we catch up with them varmints. The skin on my gun hand will get so puckered I won't be able to shoot straight."

"You mean you think you can shoot straight as a matter of

course, you Texas hay-burner?"

"Hell," Curly Bill snorted. "When the time comes, you jus' count the holes in the front pocket of my target, Boss. Then we'll talk."

CHAPTER 27
GUN FIGHT AT THE CABIN

Khan Singh took the lead along the rocky sides of the mountain stream. The path wove back and forth across the rocky streambed while continuing away from the road. The steep walls of the towering mountains on either side enclosed the small stream. For an hour they picked their way along, noting occasional signs of a prior passage and assured by Rajah's actions that he was still on the scent of the outlaws.

As the rushing water dove into a rocky gorge that sliced through the sheer walls, muddy prints marked the way up a steep, but accessible, path to a more passable trail. Their speed increased, and soon they saw fresh tracks. Khan Singh climbed off his horse and knelt by the muddy swath caused by a narrow mountain stream across the trail. "Look, Sahib. The tracks in the mud are still filling with seepage. We cannot be thirty minutes behind them." Khan Singh leaped back into his saddle and led the way. The winding trail gradually cut back to the west, until they were riding toward Central City.

Curly Bill raised himself in his saddle as high as he could and stated, "Danged if I don't think Central City's over that there mountain ahead of us. Hell's fire, we done cut twenty or more miles offa the regular road, I s'pect."

"That means we should be catching up with our friends soon, wouldn't you say?" John asked.

"Yep. I reckon so." Curly Bill pulled his army .44 from its

holster and spun the cylinder against his forearm, checking his ammunition. "I'm ready fer a fact."

Jesse Lawton and Frank Adams galloped into the clearing where the run-down log cabin was built, the noise of their arrival bringing Luke Adams outside, cradling his .44 Henry repeater in his arms. "Howdy, Frank, Jesse. Where's the others?"

"Deader than Sunday fried chicken, I reckon," Jesse gasped, swinging off his panting horse and opening the gate of the corral. He herded his and Frank's sweaty horses inside, while Luke bombarded Frank with questions. Rusty tied his to a corral post and headed for the outhouse, needing immediate relief for his bursting bladder. The three men entered the cabin and shut the door, Jesse anxiously peering out of the small firing hole cut into the front wall.

"Who were these fellows?" Luke asked. "How come they knew where you was gonna put your ambush? Has somebody give up on us and spilled his guts?"

"I don't know," Jesse grumbled. He continued to look nervously out of the small window opening at their back trail. "I thought at first it might have been Spots, or J.B., got picked up in Denver and spilled the beans, but they don't even know what we had planned. It hadda be Tom Krammer. He's the only one 'ceptin' us that knew where we was gonna hide out fer the gold convoy."

"Why would Tom Krammer give up on us? He's got the most to gain of any of us?" Luke was nearly hysterical, he was so upset.

"Damned iffen I know," Jesse answered. "All I do know is we're finished, and now's the time to cut and run while we still can."

"Maybe we should lay low here fer a while," Frank offered hopefully. "Nobody can find us back here. Luke," he snarled, irritation evident in his voice, "why the hell are you lookin' out there? You think those fellows are gonna track us back here, when nobody else has?"

"Fire and hell right I know it," Luke answered softly. "I know it, 'cause there they are." His eyes locked onto the trail into the dark woods that they had emerged from. Jesse and Frankie rushed to look out the hole, muffled curses filling the air. Rusty rushed inside, adding confirmation to the bad news.

"What'll we do?" Luke almost wailed.

"Get your rifles, and be ready. If those jaspers ride out where we can get a shot, we'll blast 'em. Otherwise, we'll hold them off till dark and make a run fer it, back to Central City."

"What if we give up now?" Luke asked.

"Don't be an idjet," Jesse snarled. "We've kilt a dozen men robbing their gold. I don't want to be the main guest at a rope necktie party, do you?" The three outlaws clutched their rifles in sweaty palms, anxiously waiting for the unknown men hiding in the dark shadows of the forest to make their move.

John, Curly Bill, and Khan Singh sat on their horses, staring through the trees at the cabin, set serenely in the small glade.

"Ya think they're in there?" Curly Bill whispered.

John patted his horse's damp neck. "Yes. There's sweat on two of the horses in the corral I can see from here. Look at Raj. He knows. They're inside, all right. The question is, what are we to do about it?"

Curly Bill calculated the choices. "Well, we could sneak up among the trees here and blast 'em out."

"The cabin appears substantial, William. They would be at an advantage, as far as protection from our fire. What do you think, Khan Singh?"

The wily Sikh surveyed the cabin and the surrounding area. Then he spoke. "Sahib, the roof is made of wood shingles. If I were to work my way around back while you and Sahib William draw their attention here in front, I might be able to sneak close enough to throw a burning branch on the roof. Once the outlaws inside realize their cabin is aflame, they should come out without delay."

"A capital idea, my friend. Come on, let us spread out a bit and give it a go. Rajah, stay with me, now. Good dog." John retreated deeper into the cover of the trees and tied his horse to a branch. Taking his rifle, he looked up at the old Sikh warrior. "Go on. We'll wait five minutes and then offer those inside a chance to surrender. If they refuse, give them the torch. You have matches and . . . ?"

Khan Singh nodded. "I have a small bottle of rifle oil in my saddlebags. It will do to light the torch." He rode away from the cabin until he cut off the trail into the woods, around to the rear.

"Come on, William. We'd best position ourselves. I'll go to the left of the trail, you go right. Raj, stay with me and be quiet." John angled into the woods and was soon out of sight. Curly Bill did the same, finding a place where he could both see and fire at the cabin and the outlaws trapped inside.

Luke whispered to the two men at the front of the cabin from his spot at the rear window. "What's happening? I can't see nobody from here."

"Shut up and keep yer eyes open," Frank whispered back, his voice harsh with tension. "They're back in the woods, so's they may be splittin' up to circle around us. You keep yer eyes on the woods back there and let us worry about what's up here."

John eased his head around the large stump he had spent several minutes crawling to. He had a clear shot at the front of the cabin and could cover any attempt to run to the corral from the front doorway. He figured five minutes had passed since Khan Singh had left for the woods behind the cabin. He glanced to his right. He did not see Curly Bill but had to assume the Texan was ready. John ducked down until he was peeking through some spiky weeds, further hiding himself. "Hello the cabin," he shouted. "This is Marshal Whyte. You men inside. Come out with your hands in the air. You are under arrest. You have one minute."

All was silent inside the cabin. John pointed his rifle at the wooden door and cocked the hammer back. John sensed the presence of Rajah, lying behind him, where John had ordered the dog to stay. His eye caught a rifle barrel poking out of a firing port by the door and firing at some target off to his right. John spotted the smoke from Curly Bill's Spencer repeater returning the fire. John aimed at the hole and pulled the trigger on his Winchester rifle. Wood chips flew from the edge of the small hole, causing the rifle barrel to pull back. John fired as rapidly as he could aim, and, when his rifle was empty, he pulled his .44 pistol and emptied it at the door. By the time he had reloaded both weapons, he saw smoke rising from the roof and could hear Khan Singh firing from somewhere at the rear of the cabin. Curly Bill kept up a steady stream of bullets from his location off to John's right.

Inside the smoke-filled cabin, a coughing Jesse wiped tears from his eyes and peered through his firing slot. "Frank, they's one of them over there, by that old fall-downed tree. Crack the door and see if you can get a shot at him." He fired at the spot where another of the hidden lawmen might be. "Luke, see anything back there?"

The younger Adams shouted over the crack of rifle fire, his voice broken by a hacking cough. "Not since that strange lookin' one threw the burnin' branch on the roof. He's back in the woods. Damn near got me twice, and I ain't even had one good shot."

Frank Adams fired twice and shut the heavy wooden door,

wiping his stinging eyes with the back of his hand. "We gotta get outta here soon, Jesse. The roof's on fire fer certain, and it won't be long till it burns through." He cracked the door and peeked out, flinching back when a heavy rifle bullet slammed into the wooden jamb next to his face. "Them bastards got us pinned down, but good." He slammed the door shut and sat with his back against the log wall, coughing and looking up at Jesse, still trying to get a good shot at the place where Curly Bill was peppering the wood around his firing slot with rapid and well aimed rifle-fire.

Jesse was cursing the fickle fate of an outlaw with every breath. "Luke, any chance of gettin' out that window?"

"No way, Jesse. That fella has us plum' covered like a squaw's blanket. Every time I raise up, he puts a round through the window." Luke raised up and slammed three shots wildly out of the window, before ducking back. The answer was two rounds from Khan Singh's Winchester through the window, scattering glass and wood chips around the room. "See what I mean?"

"Oh, Lordy," Frank moaned from his seat on the dirt floor of the cabin. Jesse followed the sitting man's gaze upward. A tiny flicker of red flame could be seen lapping around the junctures of several of the wooden slats that covered the roof. "It's burning through, fer sure."

Jesse fired again and levered another round into his .44 Henry. He coughed until his lungs hurt. "We gotta make a run fer it. You and Luke get ready, and when I go, give me cover. Luke, get over here, and be ready. When I get to the corral, I'll use the horses fer cover and keep their heads down while you two run over."

Luke rose up to give the hidden tormentor in the back one last shot, but the wily Khan Singh had been waiting for him to make that move, and he fired a bullet into the young man's shoulder, breaking Luke's collarbone. "Sweet Jesus," the young outlaw cried out. "He got me. Frank, Frank. I'm hit. Oh, shit, it hurts. Frank, I'm hit." Luke slipped to the floor, holding his arm tightly to his chest. At that same instant, a bullet hit Rusty square between the eyes, killing him instantly.

Frank scooted over to Luke, cradling his younger brother's head on his lap. "Here, let me see. Hell, it ain't too bad. Looks like it busted your collarbone. You'll be all right. Let me put your kerchief on the hole so's you don't bleed too much." He applied a crude compress to the wound and tied Luke's arm against his body with a torn piece of blanket. He helped the wounded man to the front door, where Jesse was putting out a continuous stream of poorly aimed fire at both targets in the trees to the front of the cabin.

Fred crawled through the thickening smoke inside the cabin to Jesse's side. "Luke can't shoot his rifle," Frank announced in Jesse's ear. "What do ya want to do now?"

"He can still use his pistol." Jesse coughed, struggling to take a breath in the thickening smoke. "Nothin's changed. Luke, see the large pine tree? Your man's hid out behind it, I think. When I say, you let him have it with your six-gun. Frank, draw down on that bastard by the stump. As soon as I get to the horses, come a-runnin'. I'll open up on them from the corral." Jesse had already decided he was hightailing it as soon as he reached the horses but figured the two brothers coming out the door at the same time would better his odds.

Jesse fired the last of his bullets and threw open the door. "Let 'em have it!" he screamed. Running in a zigzag manner, he darted for the corral. Frank and Luke both fired their weapons to cover him, causing John to duck back under cover. Curly Bill caught the running shape of Jesse in his sights and squeezed off a hasty shot, but John did not have time to react before Jesse made the partial safety of the corral. He saw Jesse stagger, as one of Curly Bill's bullets struck the fleeing outlaw, but all that happened was the wounded outlaw dropped his pistol. John knew if the man got on a horse, he stood a good chance of getting away. John turned and shouted at Rajah, still crouched behind him. "Get him, Rajah. Attack."

That was all the eager dog needed. He streaked across the ground like a wild catamount, leaped between two rails of the corral and slammed into Jesse, who never saw the animal coming, he was so busy trying to get on one of the skittish horses. Dog and man rolled into a ball of struggling mass, and then it was over, Rajah straddling Jesse, a fierce snarl baring his toothy jaws. Jesse lay petrified, afraid to move.

John saw that Rajah had control of the outlaw, so he switched his attention back to the cabin. He spotted movement inside through the swirling smoke and hammered several shots into the opening of the doorway. Curly Bill added his fire to the onslaught, and the two men inside gave it up, completely whipped.

"Hold yer fire. We quit. Hold on. We give up. Here's our rifles. Don't shoot no more. We're a-comin' out. The roof's on fire." Frank stepped through the doorway, supporting Luke like a half-filled sack of flour, both men coughing uncontrollably.

"Watch them, William," John shouted, and ran toward the corral, his rifle ready. He might as well have walked. Rajah was still poised over a terrified Jesse, growling softly at every breath of the beaten outlaw.

"Oh, God almighty. Get him off me. I quit, I quit. Get him off me." Jesse's right shirt sleeve was torn in shreds. Blood from several bite wounds trickled on the dust of the corral. Another wet stain on his right hip indicated where Curly Bill's round had nicked him.

"Good boy, Rajah. Hold him right there. You, sir. I suggest you lay very quiet and make no loud sounds. You might scare my dog into thinking you want even more of his attention." He glared at the frightened outlaw and went to where Frank and Luke were sitting, hands raised, unhappy expressions on both their faces. "Khan Singh, we have them. William, come on down."

Almost instantly, both men were at John's side, rifles trained on the two captives. Curly Bill checked both outlaws for concealed weapons before going to gather up the limping and defeated Jesse. Rajah trotted along behind, growling in fierce satisfaction. Wrapping his kerchief around his nose, John dashed inside the cabin, its roof now thoroughly ablaze, retrieving items of personal belongings scattered on the shell-strewn floor. He and Khan Singh then inspected each for meaningful clues. Among the debris they found a bank account book from Krammer's bank and one of the cryptic notes with arrows instead of letters. John did not even bother to decode it now; he had more important things to accomplish.

"You may as well confess," John admonished the trio. "Krammer's your boss, isn't he? Young Tom sends you information about shipments by way of the heliograph, and you take the gold to Krammer's bank after you steal it."

"How'd you know all that?" Fred exclaimed.

"Shut up," Jesse snarled, but too late. "Don't say nuthin' to these bastards."

"Any more from you, hardcase, and I'll sic Rajah back on ya. Savvy?" Curly Bill's curt admonition shut Jesse's mouth.

John placed his hat firmly on his head. "I thought as much. Well, it's down the trail to Central City for you three, arrest young Tom, and then back to Denver for the final accounting. Loren Krammer has a scupper-load of sins to answer for."

"Oh, God," Luke moaned in stark fear. "That means a miner's court. You know what that means. A necktie party fer sure. Can't you take us on in to Denver?"

John shook his head, fixing the dejected outlaw with a steely glare that caused Luke to drop his eyes in defeat. "Your fate was carved on your tombstone the day you became a highwayman. You've just been a while catching up with it."

Chapter 28
Justice and Retribution

John rode at the head of the posse of riders, Rajah trotting proudly beside him, as they entered Central City along the back route from the Adamses cabin. The sight of three men tied to their horses drew a slew of onlookers along as they traversed the main street of the town. John stopped in front of the assay office. He swung down from Blaze and spoke to Khan Singh.

"Go around and cover the rear door, old friend. William, stay here with our prisoners. I'll gather up young Mr. Krammer myself."

John stepped inside the office and spoke to a man he did not recognize, barely out of his teens. He was dressed in clean but worn pants and a faded shirt of indeterminate color. The young man had recently shaved for the first time in some weeks, to judge by the pale skin below the nose, plus two small nicks patched with plaster on his chin and cheek. He sat beside the counter where the gold dust was weighed. In front of him lay a blank book of receipts and several pens in an inkwell. The receipts were to be given to the lucky prospector who first discovered and turned in their dust to Guggenheim's. At John's entrance, his eyes lit up expectantly.

"Howdy, sir. You have some gold dust for me?"

John shook his head and looked around. "Where's Tom Krammer? That's who I am seeking."

"He ain't here, sir. Tom hired me two days ago and around noon today left fer Denver. Said he was most likely not coming

241

back. You're the first customer I had since, and here it is almost dark. Dang, and you ain't got any gold for me to weigh in. I'm afraid I'll forget how iffen I don't get some soon."

John could not hide his disappointment. He choked back bitter words, smacking his fist into his other palm. "Bad luck, bad luck." Briefly, he wondered if the younger Krammer had discovered his plan, but then shook his head. It did not seem possible. It was old-fashioned bad luck, nothing else. "Don't worry, my good man. You'll have plenty of business in the near future. By the by, do you know who is the head of the local miners' committee?"

The young man brushed back his mop of brown hair with a work-hardened hand and stood up. "Sure do. His name is Sam Berg. Works a small claim south of town."

"Well, Mr. . . . ?

"Sean MacQuinn, sir. But call me Mac. Everybody does."

"Well, Mac. Would you do me the favor of fetching Mr. Berg. Tell him John Whyte, of Pinkerton's Detective Agency, has some prisoners here and wishes to discuss their disposition."

Mac frowned. "What's that mean?"

"What are we to do with the gold robbers that I have captured?"

"Oh, I gotcha. Sure, be happy to, Mr. Whyte. I'll be back directly with Mr. Berg."

John followed him outside. "William, please put our captives inside and keep a close eye on them until I return."

"Gotcha, Boss."

After the three outlaws were pulled from their mounts and ushered inside, John turned to the crowd of curious onlookers. "These men were part of the gang that was holding up your gold shipments. We sent eleven into Denver, slung over the backs of their horses."

"Yay!" one of the mud-spattered mined shouted. "I thought

you was one of them what rode outta here with the gold shipment. Did ya git 'em all?"

John jerked his head toward the office. "All but Tom Krammer, who worked here at the assay office and rode out ahead of my arrival. I'll gather him up in Denver with the leader of the gang, as soon as I get there."

"Who's that?" several voices demanded.

John held up his hand and spoke so all could hear. "I'd best not say, in case there are prying ears who might pass the word. I've sent for your miners' committee chairman, Mr. Berg. He'll decide what we are to do with the three inside. A couple need medical help. Anyone here willing?"

One of the men held up his hand. He was tall and lean, with a ragged hat that covered his shaggy hair and with mud splattered up to the hip pockets of his worn coveralls. "I was a medical aide durin' the war. I set bones and what-not fer the soldiers. I'll take a look at 'em."

John passed the man through and followed him inside, leaving Khan Singh and Rajah outside the door, barring the inquisitive onlookers. Luke and Jesse's wounds were swabbed with drinking whiskey and wrapped with clean bandages. The three outlaws were hog-tied and set down on the floor in the corner of the office, where a stern-eyed Curly Bill watched their every move. His fierce glare cowed the three, and they sat sullen and morose, contemplating their grim fate. John poked around the back room where Tom Krammer had lived, but it was cleaned out, and he found nothing of interest.

"Any luck, Boss?" Curly Bill asked without taking his eyes from the three dejected outlaws glumly sitting with their backs to the green-timber wall.

"Nothing, William. Cursed bad luck. But, we'll catch up with him in Denver and close the book on him and his crooked father."

They were interrupted by the arrival of the clerk, Mac, escorting a short, husky, and bald but thickly bearded miner, his boots and pants still wet from working on his claim. He clomped into the assay office and surveyed the scene with calm interest.

"Mac says ye have some of the highway robbers fer us. This them?" He walked over to the hog-tied trio and gazed intently at them. "Why, Frank Adams. You involved in this sorry endeavor?" He looked at the others. "Ain't this your brother, Luke? Goddamn, Frank. You know what you've done here? You're facin' a good chance of gettin' your fool neck stretched afore the sun crosses the mountains tomorry."

"Mr. Berg. You know me and Luke. Ya gotta give us a chance. Let us go, and I'll tell ya all I know. Me and Luke will be long gone this time tomorrow iffen you will, I promise."

"Ain't up to jus' me no more, son. You'll have to take your chance with a miners' court. Once you crossed the line and took gold from another man's diggin's, you sealed yer fate. I'm shore sorry, son." Berg turned and appraised John. "You the detective what sent fer me?"

"Yes, sir. John Whyte, of Pinkerton's Detective Agency. These are my associates, William Williams, and Khan Singh." He produced his US marshal's badge for Berg's inspection.

Berg shook hands all around. His grip was strong enough to bend a fresh horseshoe, and his blue eyes were wise and calm. "You sure about what ya say, Marshal? I shore hate findin' out these here boys are involved in this mess. I've known 'em both fer the last two years."

"I'm certain, Mr. Berg. We trailed two of them from where they tried to ambush the gold shipment that left town. This one"—he pointed at Luke—"told me enough to implicate him at their cabin. I'm afraid your friends are involved, clear to their eyeteeth."

"Well, I'm afraid they ain't my friends no longer. Jus' some owlhoots who have to stand accountable for their actions."

"May I turn them over to you now?" John asked. "I must get back to Denver and apprehend the leader and Tom Krammer, who also is involved. He's the accomplice who alerted the outlaws when a shipment was leaving town."

Sam Berg's jaw dropped. "Ya don't say. Tom Krammer. Well, I reckon I know who's the boss you're a'talkin' about then." He shook his head, almost sorrowfully. "Think of that. Tom Krammer. Shore seemed like a nice boy, too."

"Yes, sir. That is why I am so anxious to return to Denver."

Berg smiled grimly. "Not so fast, Mr. Detective. We've gotta have your testimony at the trial, afore you depart."

"When will that be? I must get back to Denver before the word leaks out about the capture of the gang."

"I'll convene one tonight. You boys be here at eight, sharp. I'll send a deputy to gather you to the place of judgment. Probably be Mel's Saloon. It has the most room. Iffen we clear out the gamin' tables, there oughtta be plenty of room. Wait a minute whilst I git some of the boys to take over guarding these fellas, and I'll relieve you of the responsibility fer them."

In no time, three serious miners armed with shotguns were stationed in the room, with two more standing outside the door. John and the others trooped over to the hotel, where they cleaned up, had a meal, and enjoyed a cool beer before returning to the assay office. When they arrived, only young Mac was there, busy sweeping the bare wooden floor of the mud carried in by the numerous visitors.

"Howdy, gents," he cheerfully greeted John and his friends. "Mr. Berg has things all arranged. He said come on down to Mel's before eight and take a seat in front. I'll be happy to show you the way if you'd like."

"Certainly," John agreed. He knew where the saloon was but saw no need to disappoint the eager young MacQuinn. The four of them leisurely walked to the far end of town and entered the large saloon. The interior was packed with miners shoulder to shoulder at the bar, talking and drinking. Around the balcony lining the second story, numerous whores sat upon chairs pulled from their rooms, watching the activity and gaily jabbering away, careful to show leg and half-bared bosom to the men below. An armed guard stood at the bottom of the stairs, discouraging any amorous miner from trying to slip upstairs before the trial was completed.

Numerous smoky oil lamps had been added to the standard lighting. The room was brightly lit for the occasion. At the far end, opposite the bar, a table with five chairs faced the room, now empty except for a large Bible placed in the middle of the unpolished wooden surface. Three chairs backed against the far wall, the one without windows. Numerous chairs were positioned in rows facing the table, and already some more experienced miners had grabbed a seat, where they could witness the coming trial from a preferred vantage point.

John, Curly Bill, and Khan Singh were escorted to the front row by an armed miner, one of the guards who had relieved them at the assay office. They had barely taken their seats when five solemn men filed out of a back room and sat down at the table, Sam Berg in the middle chair. Their arrival was the signal for the drinkers to put down their glasses and scramble for the remaining seats.

Sam Berg hammered on the table with the butt of his six-gun, the loud noise causing an immediate hush from the ladies upstairs and the miners below.

"The bar's closed till this here miners' court is adjourned. No loud talkin' or cussin'. Any disturbance will mean immediate ejection from these here proceedin's. I hereby convene the Central City miners' court. Bring out the prisoners."

One of the shotgun-toting guards walked to a closed door

and rapped on it. Within seconds, the three prisoners were escorted to the three empty chairs, each with his hands tied to a long rope, held by one of the guards. Luke Adams was half supported by his guard, looking much the worse for wear from his wound. His young face was pasty white, in fear or pain, or both. Jesse Lewis glared about, still the tough guy as he limped to his assigned chair, while Frank Adams shuffled along in the rear, his head down as if ashamed to look his fellow miners in the eye. All three were directed to their chairs, and the grim-faced guards stood on either side, shotguns cradled in their beefy arms.

John scanned the room. Everyone was silent. The faces of the work-hardened miners were not friendly toward the prisoners, by any means. He glanced upward. The ladies of the night were focused on the proceedings, slouched in their chairs, legs crossed or splayed apart, as the mood struck them. An expression of spiteful cruelty was evident on every painted face. The women certainly had very little regard for men in general. Now they were going to see three of them get themselves hanged, most likely. John imagined the women who witnessed the guillotining of French royalty during the French Revolution a hundred years earlier must have had the same expression of righteous vengeance on their faces.

Sam Berg hammered the table again. He stated the charges against the three and called for John as the first prosecution witness. "You say you arrested these three men at their cabin after trailin' 'em from where they tried to hold up the gold shipment?"

John confirmed the statement and proceeded to explain his plan, its execution, and the results. He described in detail the gunfight at the ambush, the tracking of the fleeing outlaws, and the fight at the cabin.

One of the other judges spoke up. "Did you give these boys a chance to surrender afore you opened up on 'em?"

"Absolutely," John answered. He then repeated the statements made by Luke and Frank while in his custody. He answered several more questions concerning how the robberies were conceived and carried out and then surrendered the stand to Curly Bill, who added his supporting statements to John's testimony.

The five judges didn't ask Khan Singh to take the stand but conferred among themselves after Curly Bill had finished. Then they called two men who had ridden on earlier convoys as guards. From them they heard how the earlier holdups had occurred and about the death or wounding of the guards. The final witness was one of the assay office guards, who revealed how Jesse had promised him a gold bribe if he would help the outlaw to escape.

The improvised courtroom was as silent as a winter snowfall. All eyes were on the three men. The five judges conferred again, then Sam Berg addressed the crowd. "Any man out there wants to talk fer these boys?" He waited for a tense moment, but not a man rose. He addressed the three outlaws. "Any of you boys got anything to say in your own behalf?"

Frank Adams stood. "Me, Mr. Berg. I wanna ask you to go easy on Luke, here. He's only nineteen. I reckon I drug him into this and I'm a'hopin' you'll see fit to cut him some slack."

Sam Berg looked at Frank Adams with sad eyes. "You admit what has been said about you and the others, Frank?"

"Yup, Mr. Berg. Me and Jesse and the others done what was said. But Luke here—hell, he only went on one holdup, and there weren't nobody kilt on that one, honest."

Sam Berg cleared his throat. "Fair enough, Frank. But you know miners' law. You steal gold from a miner, and it's a hangin' offense. We'll certainly take your words to heart, though, afore we decide. Sit on back down now." He looked at Jesse. "You have anything to say, Jesse Lewis?" Jesse glared at the old miner and said nothing. After a moment's silence, Sam looked at Luke, slumped in his chair, apparently barely conscious. "Luke Adams. You got anything to say, son?"

Luke gulped twice, his throat rippled, but only a croak came out, so he shook his head and slumped further in his seat.

John stood. "Mr. Berg, if the court decides it wants me to, I'll escort Luke Adams back to Denver for trial."

Sam looked at John and nodded. "Thank you, Mr. Whyte. We'll take that under advisement when we deliberate." He faced the crowd. "You miners have heard the evidence. Is there any motion to find any of these men innocent?" Not a sound was heard. "Are these men guilty?"

An overwhelming chorus of "Yes" was the reply from the crowd.

Sam Berg stamped his pistol on the wooden top. "The miners' committee will adjourn to the storeroom to decide punishment. No drinkin' while we're out." He smacked the gun butt again and stood, leading the other four out of the main room to a small storeroom, where they shut the door to deliberate in private.

John and the rest of the crowd remained where they were, a low murmur of voices building as the miners waited and the time dragged on. The room grew quiet as the door opened and the five men re-entered the room. The silence was electric. As soon as the five men were seated, Sam Berg thumped the table and called out. "Jesse Lewis, stand forward."

One of the guards escorted the limping Jesse to the front of the table, where he stood glaring defiantly at the five judges. Sam met the outlaw's glare and delivered the sentence. "You have been found guilty of robbery and murder of miners. By a vote of five to nothing, you are sentenced to hang by the neck until dead tomorrow morning, at sunrise." Sam stamped the table with the butt of his pistol, and Jesse was dragged away, sputtering and cursing at the judgment. As soon as he was shut in the detention room, Sam spoke again. "Fred Adams, stand forward." The verdict was the same. "Death by hanging, at sunrise, five to nothing in favor." With a much less strident voice, Sam called again. "Luke Adams. Stand forward." Luke was helped by his guard, barely ably to stagger to the table. "Guilty, son, of robbery and aiding of murders and outlaws. Death by hanging, at sunrise, by a vote of three to two."

Luke's face drained of color, and he nearly collapsed in the arms of his guard. He was taken to join his comrades. Sam Berg stamped the tabletop for the last time. "This court is closed, and the bar is open. I need a drink of whiskey, right now."

With a whoop, the miners rushed for some liquid refreshments, while several of the more impatient ones started up the now unguarded stairs to the waiting whores above.

John, Bill, Khan, and Mac worked their way through the crowd, accepting the back slaps and commendations of gratitude from numerous miners before they reached the doors. Mac was chattering excitedly about the coming hanging, but none of the others paid him any heed.

As they exited the saloon, John glanced back. He saw Sam Berg standing alone, with a tiny, but noticeable, space between him and the rest of the packed bodies at the bar, sipping from a glass of amber fluid. On the weather-beaten face was a look of immense sadness and remorse. Curly Bill caught John's glance and gazed at the old miner.

"Shore wouldn't want to be in his shoes tonight," he murmured. "He'll not have much sleep afore dawn, I'll reckon."

"No, I suppose not," John agreed. "I imagine he was one of the two who voted for Luke Adams's life. Heavy hangs the burden of justice on those who have to carry out its ministrations. Let us find our beds, gentlemen. I want to be on the road tomorrow morning as soon as possible."

"You mean you ain't gonna stay fer the hangin'?" Mac asked, astounded at the statement.

"You ever see a necktie party?" Curly Bill asked.

"Nope," the young man answered. "Not yet."

"Believe me, pilgrim, once is enough," was Curly Bill's caustic reply, as he pointed the young man toward the assay office.

As John and the others rode out of Central City the next morning, they passed Sam Berg and the rest of the town surging toward a huge cottonwood tree at the north end of town. Three looped ropes already hung limply over a large limb, awaiting the condemned outlaws. Riding in the back of an otherwise empty wagon, the condemned men sat glumly, fear and uncertainty etched on their faces. Sam simply nodded his good-bye as John and the two parties moved away from one another. As John reached the top of the first hill out of town, he heard the roar of the crowd and knew its significance. He paused for an instant, collecting his thoughts and patting the neck of his horse, as if to reassure himself that all was as it should be.

"The final retribution has been rendered. I hope it means peace for the town now." He gently spurred Blaze on either flank. "Come on, let's hurry to Denver. Our work isn't quite done. We've got some outlaws to arrest."

CHAPTER 29
DENVER SHOWDOWN

For the last time, John, Curly Bill, and Khan Singh rode down the hill from Apex Pass into the booming gold rush town of Denver. As usual, Rajah led the way, with an animal's instinct turning toward the railroad yard and John's personal railroad car. The sun had dropped behind the western mountaintops before their arrival, ensuring very few people even saw the three tired men. John felt confident neither Loren nor Tom Krammer were aware of the fate that had befallen their henchmen in crime.

John climbed off of Blaze at the rear of the *Star of India*, greeting the burly Walter Pate, who was sitting on the bottom step, smoking a cigar and watching their arrival. "Evening, Walter," John greeted the detective. "All quiet here in Denver?"

"Yep, quiet as a rabbit in a fox's den," Walt answered. "We delivered the gold to Mr. Wallace and took the bodies to the undertaker's, like Sheriff Gilbert wanted. We slipped into town real quiet-like. It was well before sunrise when we arrived. I don't think anyone saw us." Walt walked over to where John stood, pushing hard against his weary back, working the kinks out of it. He shook hands with everyone and continued. "Rafe Wallace was as tickled as a new papa with the gold and promised to keep his yap shut till you got back." Walt's eyes crinkled as he made the next statement. "You boys must have found your crooks, else you wouldn't be here yet."

"You betcha," Curly Bill answered, while Khan Singh hurried

252

inside the *Star* to find his son. "There was three more, hid out in a cabin. We tracked 'em, flushed 'em out, and turned 'em over to the miners' committee in Central City afore the day was out. Tried 'em that night and hung 'em afore the sun was up the next day."

Walt Pate nodded. "Swift justice, for a fact. I've got Vernon and Joe watching Krammer. His boy showed up this morning. You know that?"

John nodded. "We missed him in Central City. He departed four hours before we arrived. I thought we would catch him here with his father. By the by, how's Joe?"

"Jus' fine. He hardly even knows he was nicked." Walt asked John and Curly Bill, "You wanna go after the Krammers tonight? Will Jeries is sleepin' inside the car. We was gonna trade off with Joe and Vernon at midnight. We can go with ya now, iffen ya want."

John shook his head. "Loren Krammer doesn't act like he's scared, does he?" At Walt's shake of his head, he continued. "I think I'd rather arrest him tomorrow, with Sheriff Gilbert along. Keep him under observation tonight. I'm going to bring the sheriff up to date and then stop by the Silver Bell. If you need me, I'll be there. You don't need William or me to stand watch tonight, do you?"

"Lands no," Walt announced. "Me and the boys'll handle things jus' fine. You and Curly Bill relax and get some rest. We'll all follow Krammer to his bank tomorrow morning and wait for ya there. You can make your play anytime ya want."

John wiped the dust from his lips. "That's agreeable, I guess. What say, William? Care to accompany me to the Bell, with a short stop at Sheriff Gilbert's?"

"Lead the way, Boss. Hell, I'm even gonna take a bath, 'though it ain't even Saturday, to celebrate my homecoming with Claudette. Walt, let's get two fresh horses, whatta ya say?

These poor nags are about wore out, we rid 'em so hard the last few days."

John took his leave of Walt to inform Khan Singh where he would be that night. He received a sincere welcome back from Kai Singh, grabbed a fast bath, put on a change of fresh clothing, and exited the rear of the *Star* in thirty minutes. He climbed directly on the back of a waiting horse positioned by Curly Bill so that he did not even have to put his feet on the ground.

Curly Bill's hair was still damp from his bath as he rode beside John. The easygoing Texan whistled a happy tune as they trotted their horses down the street to downtown Denver, straight to Sheriff Gilbert's office. "William," John asked, "Since I was in the tub, where did you bathe?"

Curly Bill grinned over at his friend and leader. "I used the horse trough out back of the barn. Water was cool and fresh, and there was some lye soap available fer such a necessity."

John smiled. "You must be planning a real soirée. Isn't that your very best dress shirt?"

"You said it, Boss. I've been hankerin' fer some tender lovin' care from Claudette ever since we started up the road from Central City."

John glanced to the west. The dark mass of the high mountains was an indistinct blur against the moonlit night sky. "I'd say we had a rather exciting party up there, wouldn't you?"

"All in a day's work, Boss." Curly Bill was too intent on the coming attractions to give much thought to what they had so recently experienced.

Sheriff Gilbert was about to make his rounds when John and Curly Bill arrived. His worn face broke into a wide grin, and he back-slapped and hand-shook both men to excess. "Gosh damn, it's good to see you two again. Way to go, on those outlaws. Delivered 'em all quiet and ventilated, ready fer plantin'. Sure saves me a lot of work. You get the rest of them?"

John re-told the story of the shootout at the cabin and the
trial held in Central City, knowing that he had to do it shortly
when he saw Belle. The telling was beginning to become tedious,
and he hurried through it, allowing Curly Bill to add the embel-
lishments.

Sheriff Gilbert slapped his knee. "By damn, what a tale. You
boys'll be the talk of Denver fer the next month, I swear."
Gilbert's face hardened. "What ya gonna do about Loren Krammer?"

"Tomorrow will be soon enough, I think, Sheriff. I prefer not
to arrest him at his home, in front of his wife and daughter. I'll
be here with William at nine o'clock. My men will keep an eye
on him tonight. If you would, I'd like you to accompany me
when I take him into custody tomorrow."

"Be proud to, son. I'll be ready. Meantime, I gotta make my
rounds, so I'll bid ya good night. You two be stayin' over to the
Silver Bell?"

Curly Bill's surprised face was a pleasure to behold for the
old lawman. "You don't think I'm so broke down I can't keep
track of someone now, do ya?" He laughed as he escorted the
two detectives out the door. "Don't fret. I know when to jabber
and when to quiet up. I'll be a'waitin' fer ya in the morning."

John and Curly Bill walked to the Silver Bell, John grinning
at Curly Bill's face when Bill realized just how aware the sheriff
was of their off-duty activities. "Dag-gummed ole fuss-pot,"
Curly Bill finally exclaimed. "What's he a-doin', checkin' up on
us like that anyways?"

John laughed, ruefully. "A good lawman likes to know what is
happening in his town, William. He's known since the first day
we went there. We didn't exactly try and sneak in the back door
every night, now did we?"

"Well, as long as I don't catch him peekin' in the window, I
suppose I'll have to put up with him pokin' his long nose into

my business. I'll be a-lookin fer a chance to pin the rooster feather on him from now on, you betcha."

Several days' abstinence from each other fueled John and Belle's reunion. It was after ten P.M. before they sat down at her small table for the cold chicken and bean salad prepared for them by the loyal Sally. John gnawed on a leg and smiled at the lovely woman sitting across from him. Her robe was carelessly draped about her, allowing him a delightful view of forbidden temptations, as they snacked and drank the cool wine. He eagerly anticipated their return to her warm bed, so he hurried through the story of the ambush, pursuit of the fleeing outlaws, and the subsequent trial in Central City. Belle listened avidly, adding her own impressions to the sparse details. Her understanding of the man she had grown so fond of easily filled in the gaps he glossed over. As she listened, she also experienced a persistent knot of fear. His job was almost done. What would happen to their budding romance then?

"I'll arrest Loren Krammer and his son tomorrow," John concluded. "I will take personal pleasure in his apprehension, I assure you. He was the brains and master of the outlaw infestation. Sitting safely here in Denver, he orchestrated the death and suffering of many good men." John paused and looked at Belle. "When Krammer's in jail, his bank will likely fold. Do you have an account with his bank?"

Belle shook her head. "No, me and my girls all closed our accounts there the day you rode into the mountains. It was a pleasure, since he always treated us like trash even while taking our money. It will serve him right to be beaten into the dust like the cur he is."

"I feel some remorse for his wife and daughter, though. They are victims like the other innocent sufferers of his nefarious activities." John finished the glass of wine he was toying with.

Belle glanced at him sharply. "Feeling sorry for young Miss

Suzanne Krammer, are we?" Her eyebrow arched dangerously, and her cat's claws came out, ready to slash.

John was determined to defuse the potential verbal battle. "She's a sweet young child, my dear. I feel the concern of an old family friend who has to stand aside while she faces a nasty lifetime experience for the first time, nothing more."

Belle smiled sweetly, her feminine sense of competition soothed. "Well, of course. I feel badly for her as well. Unfortunately, it's not your fault. Her papa's responsible, not you, don't forget."

"Quite true, but I fear it will be me whom she blames, once tomorrow is behind us."

Belle took a final sip of her wine and rose from her chair. She moved to John and plopped onto his lap, allowing her robe to fall open. She lowered her face to his, whispering softly, her sweet breath caressing his lips. "Well, then, me loving bucko, I guess I'd better take your mind off the coming morrow, at least for a while." She did just that. Delightfully and passionately.

John had to hurry to be at Sheriff Gilbert's by nine o'clock the next morning. Curly Bill was waiting for him, along with Walt and Khan Singh. Grinning sheepishly, John delivered his final instructions.

"What's the status of our quarry?" he asked of Walt.

"Vernon and Will are a-watchin' him over to his bank. He got there about thirty minutes ago. Joe is at the house, keepin' an eye on Tom Krammer. When I left to come here, the youngster was still inside. All was quiet last night, although I got the idea Krammer was expectin' visitors. He kept lookin' out a window toward the west and checkin' the front yard."

"Probably lookin' fer the gold he thinks his scum have stolen fer him," Curly Bill interjected.

"Fair enough," John answered. "Walt, you stay outside with

your men. William, you cover the rear of the bank, in case Krammer slips past us. Sheriff Gilbert, you and Khan Singh will accompany me while I make the arrest. Sound agreeable to everyone?"

At their nods, John continued. "Walt, I'll give you two minutes to get into position before I start. As soon as I arrest Krammer and Sheriff Gilbert locks him up, we'll go to the Krammer home and arrest young Tom. Here we go now."

In a few short minutes, John, Sheriff Gilbert, and Khan Singh stepped inside Loren Krammer's bank. Khan Singh positioned himself by the closed door into Krammer's private office. John knocked and opened the door, without waiting for an answer. Loren Krammer jerked his head up from the ledger he was studying, startled at the interruption.

"What the h—oh, it's you, John, and Sheriff Gilbert." A wary look crossed Krammer's pudgy face as he swallowed hard. "What can I do for you? Is something wrong?"

John moved closer to the desk, his face firm and grim. "Loren Krammer, I'm a detective with Pinkerton's and commissioned a US marshal. I'm here to arrest you for robbery and murder. Please come with us."

Krammer's face paled, and his voice rose in volume. "What are you talking about? I'll have you know that I am—"

"Save it, Loren," Sheriff Gilbert interrupted the bluster. "We got the goods on ya. Come along with me right now and don't cause no trouble."

Krammer's face had paled to a pasty white, and he started to sweat. He licked his lips nervously and shifted his eyes from Gilbert to John and back. "What are you talking about? I'm afraid you've lost your senses, the both of you."

"I have you, Mr. Krammer. We caught your gang in the act of committing another robbery. Luke and Frank Adams talked before they were hung by the miners' committee in Central

City. Young Tom, the heliograph, the land purchases. The money you have been spending buying up land around Denver. The source of all your money."

Gilbert spoke up. "Add to that, J. B. Franks trying to kill John here. And the secret messages. John broke the code." Sheriff Gilbert started around the side of the desk, handcuffs in his hand, open and menacing in their purpose.

Almost faster than John would have believed possible, Loren Krammer's hand darted under his desk and re-appeared with a gun, which he aimed at John and Gilbert. His face was flushed in rage and fear. "So, the game's up you say. We'll see about that. Keep your hands where I can see them. Move back, Sheriff. Next to Whyte there."

"Loren, don't do this," Sheriff Gilbert tried to reason with the panic-crazed banker, as he backed away from the desk, his hands raised. "There's men all around the bank. You can't go anywhere. Put the gun down, and give it up."

Krammer shook his head. "They won't try anything with you and Whyte here. Is there someone outside?"

John nodded. "My man, Khan Singh. Also men at the front and back doors. Give it up, Krammer. Don't risk dying. Think of Suzanne and your wife."

"Shut up. Call for your man outside. Get him in here, now. Tell him to keep his hand away from his gun or I start shooting, first you, then the sheriff."

John shrugged his shoulders, resignedly. "Your call, Krammer." He called out, loud enough for Khan Singh to hear. "Old friend, come here. Leave your rifle outside. Come." John caught Gilbert's look. Khan Singh was not carrying a rifle. John gave him a slight nod. Gilbert's return nod indicated he was ready for whatever came next.

The door opened, and Khan Singh stepped inside. One glance gave him the whole story. He moved to the side, away from the door and from behind John's back, until he had a clear view of the rattled Krammer. The portly banker was trying to cover all three men at the same time, the pistol darting from one man to the next.

Krammer saw the imposing Sikh warrior was unarmed and motioned with his pistol. "Shut up and don't move, or I'll kill Whyte, understand?" He didn't even wait to see what the old warrior's response was before turning back to John. Krammer started to move around the desk, planning to position himself between John and Gilbert for his escape.

Suddenly, his mouth dropped, and he fell back into his chair, the gun dropping, with a loud thump, on the polished floor. Krammer glanced down, his eyes wide in surprise. The jeweled handle of the knife Khan Singh always carried protruded from where his vest vee'd upward, exposing his white, linen shirt. Krammer tried to speak, to breathe, to beg, but nothing happened except for the angel of death that descended like a chilling shroud upon his soul. His head flopped back until his eyes stared upward at the ceiling, and a final gurgle issued from his lips. His eyes widened at the view of the unending darkness awaiting him across the final river, and he died.

The room was silent, shock and awe evident on Gilbert's ruddy face. "Jesus Christ," the sheriff finally exclaimed. "Stuck him like a pig. Damn!" He turned around, really seeing Khan Singh for the man he was. He remarked to John, "You boys don't mess around, do you?"

John shook his head. "Not with murderers and criminals, no, we don't. We gave him a chance, remember. It was his choice." He gripped Khan Singh's strong right arm. "A good job, my friend. Summon Walt and William, will you please?"

Tom Krammer had been casually walking down the street, intending to visit his father at the bank, when he saw John Whyte, his manservant, and Sheriff Gilbert entering ahead of him. Suspicious, he turned into the nearest store, a saddle and bridle shop, and observed through the wavy glass of the front window. The owner came up and inquired, "May I help you, sir?"

"No, thanks," Tom answered. "I'm only browsing. I'll let you know if I need anything."

The owner returned to the bridle he was repairing while Tom observed the bank. He poked around a saddle sitting on a sawhorse by the front door to explain his presence in the store. He did not notice the tall man who was watching him from across the street, so focused was he on the bank. Nothing happened for a few minutes, and then several men rushed inside, guns drawn. Sheriff Gilbert emerged and communicated some instruction to a passerby, who hurried off in the direction of the jail.

Tom's breathing rapidly increased as he realized something was wrong, dreadfully wrong. His papa had assured him they had figured out a foolproof plan, and they would never be caught. The undertaker appeared and, in a few more tension-filled minutes, re-appeared, accompanied by two men carrying a body lying on a door, covered completely by a rug that he recognized was from his father's office.

The frightened young Krammer knew it was his father. He would be next. He struggled to control his fear. He turned back to the shopkeeper. "You have a back door here?

"Yep. Back through the storeroom. What's going on?" The man started to rise, wondering what Tom was staring at so intently outside.

Tom Krammer bared his teeth in a humorless grin. "Don't worry. It's nothing." He drew the small pistol he was carrying in his pants pocket. "Give me all your money. Quick, before I shoot your ears off."

The frightened sstorekeeper opened his cash drawer. "I only

got thirty dollars or so."

"That'll have to do. Now, keep your mouth shut." Tom grabbed the few bills and ran out the back. He had maybe fifty dollars now, and he had to get away, fast. He looked up and down the back street. A dun cow-pony, barrel-chested, with short, sturdy legs, was tied up at a small shop two doors down. It would have to do. He ran to the animal, leaped on its back, and whipped the surprised horse into a hard run, due south. He thundered across the wooden bridge over Cherry Creek to Auraria. He kept the animal at a dead run all the way through the town, until he was on the Pueblo Road. He'd run for New Mexico Territory. "Run, run" was all his addled brain could think of. "Run, run, never stop."

The shop owner ran outside, screeching his lungs out. "Help! I've been robbed!"

Joe Richardson, six-gun in his hand, ran into the shop and out the back, in time to hastily fire one time at Tom's retreating figure before the terrified fugitive turned the corner. Joe missed, to his disappointment. Seeing no other horses available to pursue Tom, he re-entered the store and ran out the front door to the bank, where he reported to Walt and John with the bad news.

"Don't fret," Sheriff Gilbert consoled John and Walt. "We'll catch up with him, sooner or later. The gold robbers are done for, and that's enough work for one day, I reckon."

"I suppose you're right, Sheriff. A bit short of a full load, but acceptable, I guess. Come on, let's inform Rafe Wallace of the good news. He'll be mighty happy to hear it. Then I've got to get a report off to Pinkerton's main office. I'd say my day's just beginning."

Chapter 30
A Poignant Good-bye

Rafe Wallace's meaty fist slammed down on the table with another resounding *smack!* He shouted loudly from a combination of his exuberance and the numerous bottles of champagne he had helped to drain. As host of the blow-out party for John and the rest the Pinkertons at the Silver Bell, he was well into his duties. "Where the hell is that bubbly I ordered?" He shouted even louder. "These boys'll die of thirst afore you get here, iffen you don't hurry up now." His blurred vision fell on John sitting at the far end of the table, talking intimately with Belle, who was seated beside him. "Ain't that right, John. Well, finally, here it is. Pour another round fer everyone," he imperiously ordered the harried waiter.

Rafe gripped the edge of the table to steady himself as he stood to offer another toast. "I'd like to make another toast. Everyone grab hold of your glasses: To John Whyte and the best damned detectives in the world, Pinkerton men. Great job, everyone of you."

John appreciatively raised his glass at the tipsy Wallace. "I say, old chap. That's about the fourth time you've given the same toast. Aren't you tired of it yet?"

Rafe weaved and flopped back into his chair, throwing an arm around his escort, one of Belle's regular girls, who snuggled up close to the likeable, gruff, mining engineer. "That's all right. You boys deserve it, right, Alma?" At her smile of agreement, he looked around the table to the Pinkerton men, each seated by one of Belle's girls, save Walt and Joe, who chose to stay faithful to their wedding vows. "You boys sure did it. Cleaned out the nest of rats that was drivin' me outta business, and took care of their sentences in the bargain. Not even the expense of a trial to put up with. We appreciate that sort of tidiness, don't we, Rance?"

Sheriff Gilbert chuckled tolerantly. "All I can say is stay inside tonight, Rafe, else I'll have to arrest you for public intoxication." He looked around the table at the Pinkerton men, all there except for Khan Singh, who was back at the *Star,* enjoying some time with his son and avoiding the glare of the limelight. He had repeatedly assured John he had no desire to attend and would rather stay with Kai Singh, perhaps even take him up in the foothills to do a little hunting. "That goes for all of you." The sheriff laughed.

"Hell, Rance. We'll not be outta here afore noon tomorrow, if I know Belle's gals. And come to think of it, I do."

Rafe patted his "date's" hand and turned to John, sitting beside him. "What's your plans now, John? Gonna stay awhile? Or you have to be returnin' back to the East?"

John turned from Belle to Rafe. "Oh, I shall stay here for awhile, thank you. Belle is going to show me some land she is interested in, up at—what was it, dear? Boulder Creek?"

Belle responded with a happy glow on her face. "That's right, darlin'. Boulder Creek. It's beautiful up there. You ever see it, Sheriff?"

"Nope, can't say I ever did. 'Course, I don't get far from town it seems, afore some yahoo causes a ruckus and spoils my day off."

"That must be aggravating, especially since there is so much to see around here. I'm looking forward to exploring some of it with Belle as my guide. The men could use a few days to unwind, and the home office doesn't have any new assignments

264

pending." John turned his head toward Belle and smiled at her, before continuing. "In fact, we should be making our plans right now. If you gentlemen will excuse us. Thank you, Rafe, and goodnight, fair comrades all. 'Tis sweet dreams I wish for you and the sleep of the just."

"Hell, Boss," Curly Bill chortled, "I don't know about these other gents, but me and Claudette may forgo sleep tonight, if you get my gist?"

With good natured hoots echoing around the table, John grabbed an unopened bottle of champagne in one hand and, taking Belle's slender hand in the other, pulled her to the stairs leading to her private suite. She coyly resisted, enough to leave the impression she was not as anxious as he, but following him anyway, to further ribbing by men and the knowing smiles of her girls, each aware her turn up the stairs was rapidly approaching.

John and Belle awoke in one another's arms to a day of brilliant sunshine and cloudless, azure sky. They were soon riding in her carriage north from the town toward the new settlement called Boulder City, twenty miles up the road. The road skirted the low foothills that led to the higher mountains beyond and offered spectacular scenery of flat slabs of towering rock where the foothills rose into mountains. Sally had provided them with an excellent picnic lunch, which they enjoyed. Afterwards, by the rushing waters of Boulder Creek, in the privacy of an immense pine, they made passionate and intense love once again.

Buoyed by John's enthusiastic approval of the property and their reaffirmation of their feelings for each other, Belle sat close to John as he drove the carriage back toward Denver. As they approached the town, John spoke seriously to Belle. "My dear Belle, buy all the land you can. This town and this part of the country is going to grow and flourish; it's inevitable. In a few years, you will be so wealthy you will be able to take your place among the socially elite of Denver. People will tip their hats to you when you meet and strive to be in your company."

Belle questioned John, sitting so close beside her that their legs brushed against each other's with every jar in the road. "What makes you think I want to stay here, me handsome bucko? Maybe I would rather go back East and become a fine lady there."

"No, this is the place for you, Belle. It's a new land and free from entrenched mores. You won't have to apologize for the source of your money, here. Back East, you'd face the enmity of heartless prudes who would never let you forget your origins. Women who have made an art out of cattiness and cruel rumors."

Belle spoke softly. "What about you, John? You ever think of settling out here?"

John missed the subtle suggestion. "No, I don't think so. Why, my estate in Missouri is starting to flourish. No, for me, Colorado Territory is only a place to visit, I'm afraid."

Ice formed in Belle's heart; she was numbed by the abrupt dismissal of their relationship. Her soft voice hid the pain in her heart. "Perhaps I will get to see it some day."

John, still oblivious to his insensitive remark, turned his head and smiled at his lovely riding companion. "Oh, I hope so, Belle. I think you would really like it. Someday, you'll have to make a trip to St. Louis, now that the train runs there. Hopefully, I'll not be away on a job for Pinkerton's. Even if I am, let me know, and I'll arrange a royal welcome by my household staff."

The ice in Belle's heart grew. Tears welled in her eyes. She realized that John saw her as something to enjoy, not cherish. She felt the pain in her heart and cursed herself for allowing her whore's heart to grow attached to any man. Unfortunately, it only increased her desperation. John sensed a new tension in their relationship. To his puzzlement, the strain between them only deepened as the time passed. He tried to lighten the mood but eventually gave up and matched her silence as they finished the ride back to Denver.

John dropped the quiet Belle off at her establishment after obtaining her promise to receive him later that evening. John leisurely drove the buggy toward the rail yard, contemplating what he might have said to cause the tension between them. He spotted two women leaving the undertaker's, dressed in black, clutching each other in their grief. He turned his carriage toward them. Suzanne and her mother did not see John until he was nearly up to them. Then the younger Krammer woman recognized John, and her face blanched, then turned viciously bitter.

John halted the carriage and removed his hat. "Mrs. Krammer, Suzanne. My deepest sympathies for your loss. I assure you I did not want it so . . ."

Suzanne Krammer hissed at him in feral hatred. "Damn you, sir. Get away from my mother and me. You repay our kindness to you by killing my papa and driving my brother away from us, when Mama needs him most. You used me to get to my father, damn you. I hope you burn in hell. Come, Mama."

The two women climbed into a small carriage and departed, Suzanne snapping the reins and galloping the horses up the street. Shaking his head in sorrow, John continued on to the *Star,* where he cleaned up and prepared himself for the coming evening with Belle. He hoped that whatever he had said or done to set her off earlier was over with by now.

Their evening was enjoyable but somewhat strained, as the uneasy tension between them remained, lurking just below the surface. John left the next morning feeling perplexed as the night had not been as satisfying as he had expected. He left the

Silver Bell knowing a distance was growing between himself and Belle. He rode to the sheriff's office and greeted Rance Gilbert, who was coming out the door, a piece of paper in his hand.

"Morning, Sheriff. Off on an errand?"

"Morning, John. Yep. I was comin' over to see you, as a matter of fact. A telegram came for ya, from Chicago."

John took the offered message and opened it. He read it, then passed it over to the old lawman to read. "Well, I guess this will be my last full day in Denver," he said. "I'd better return to the *Star* and prepare for the trip east. We'll take the morning train to Kansas City tomorrow."

Gilbert handed back the telegram. "Damn sorry to see you go. Me and a bunch of good folks here in Denver. Would ya have time to finish your deposition about the money Krammer used to buy his land? Rafe'll be wantin' to ask the courts fer some of it to make up his losses, I reckon."

"Certainly, Sheriff. I'll be here right after noon, if that is acceptable to you and the judge."

John's announcement of his pending departure allowed Belle a chance to shed some of her frustrations in a good cry. Their last evening together was poignant and sadly unfulfilling. Over breakfast the next morning, he kindly bid his farewells to Sally, surprised at her hostile response. A bit dismayed, he turned his attention back to Belle, resplendent in her morning gown, her face still flushed from a long night of silent grieving.

"Belle, dear, you remember what I said. Invest in land and real estate. Build a future here, and become the grand dame of Denver. You have the brains and determination to do so."

Belle nodded, brushing a wisp of hair aside, her eyes downcast and her demeanor subdued. Her grief was palpable. "When are you leaving?"

"In a couple of hours. Walt and Khan Singh said everything's ready. All I have to do is pry William from Claudette's arms and off we go."

"Yes, that's all, I guess. Do you want me to come to the train station to say good-bye?"

John shook his head. "No, please don't bother. I'll make my farewells here, in the privacy of our wonderful retreat from the world beyond. Much less commotion, don't you agree?"

"Oh, I suppose. That way, you won't have to explain my presence, in case any of your social hobnobs come down to see you off."

"Not at all, Belle. I don't expect anyone to be there, nor do I give a whit if we're seen together. I'll simply depart, and life in Denver will go on, as it should be."

"And me?"

John puzzled over her question. Did she actually think he would bring a lady of the lotus blossoms into his home as mistress of Oakview? He thought hard. He had made no promises, set no conditions. She was hinting at something more permanent, he knew. In India, you simply thanked your pleasure partner and moved on, no strings attached. How was he to answer her? "You are a special person to me, Belle. You have given me a gift of wonderful memories and a special friendship that I will always treasure."

"So, now you'll leave me and return to your fine home and friends back east, while I stay here and go on like nothing's changed. You've behaved as if we had a special relationship, but now you abandon it without regret or a second thought. Are you afraid I'm trying to step up too high from my lowly station in life? Well, why not? You think I want to be a paid companion all my life? I want a lot more than that."

"Belle, please. Not at all. You know I'm going to Mississippi, to investigate those Klu Klux Klan depredations against freed blacks. I'm not going back to Fair Oaks to be with friends. You know I care for you. You will always be a special friend to me. You know that."

"Well, I don't want you to go, John, or I want to go with you."

"Belle, Belle. Our lives run in different directions. You belong here, in Denver. I belong there, doing my job. Being a detective and running Fair Oaks, when I can. I hope to come back here soon, and we'll see each other then, I promise you."

Belle stood up and came to John, who rapidly stood as well. She kissed him hard and pulled back her head, so she could look at his face. Her eyes were brimming with tears, which she would not allow to fall. "Good-bye, me handsome bucko. You've broken the heart of this whore, and that's a rare thing indeed. Now, off with you, you cad, before I have Sally toss you out."

John left, a nagging doubt in his thoughts that he was leaving someone more special than he cared to admit. He could not imagine why Belle believed their liaison was anything more than just a passing episode. Still, leaving Belle was more difficult than he had considered.

He gathered up Curly Bill, who lustily kissed Claudette good-bye while stuffing paper bills down the cleavage exposed by the plunging neckline of her peignoir.

Together, they rode over to bid Sheriff Gilbert and Rafe Wallace good-bye. As the sun started its daily climb up to the summit of the deep-blue sky, their train chugged out of Denver, pointed toward the rolling plains of Kansas, to the East.

John stood on the rear transom with Walt Pate as the train departed the town and clattered down the shiny tracks. Without speaking, Walt offered John a cigar, and the two men lit up, savoring the pungent bite of the tobacco on their tongues. Walt spoke, but John did not hear, so intently was he staring back toward Denver, his mind wrapped around a beautiful, red-headed madam. Abruptly, Walt went inside the *Star,* leaving

John alone with his thoughts. The town receded in the distance. He strained to see Belle's balcony and imagined he did see a spot of color against the cluster of buildings where the Silver Bell should be. He hoped she was there.

"Hey, John," Curly Bill called out. "These here Kansas City slickers think they can take some of our money at poker. Get on in here, and let's have a hand or two."

John smiled sadly and glanced again at the fading outline of Denver, swallowed in the haze and dust of the late morning breeze. The spiny outline of the great Rocky Mountains seemed to swell out of the distance. John sighed and took one last drag of his cigar before flipping it off the back of the transom. He turned into the car before the smoking cigar butt hit the track bed.

The train rumbled its way on down the iron tracks, while a skinny coyote slipped out of the dense brush along the right-of-way. The animal warily stepped between the two long strips of shiny man things. Gingerly, he sniffed the smelly thing lying between the two tracks, inhaling the thin streamer of wavy, white smoke drifting upward. It was not a thing to eat, so the small animal ignored it and crossed on over to the thick growth of brush on the far side. Mice were there—the wily coyote knew it—and it was time for lunch.

ABOUT THE AUTHOR

Thomas P. Nicholson was born in Springfield, Missouri, and grew up in northern Arkansas and southwest Missouri. He graduated from Missouri School of Mines with a bachelor's degree in nuclear engineering. During the summers he worked out west for the US Forest Service in forest fire suppression.

After college he briefly worked in a uranium mine in New Mexico before joining the US Army, where his first assignment was to play post football at Ft. Knox, Kentucky. He then graduated from the officer candidate school at Ft. Benning, Georgia, where he is now in its hall of fame. After graduation, he attended parachutist training. Following an initial assignment to the mountain brigade at Ft. Carson, Colorado, he joined special forces and trained at Ft. Bragg, North Carolina.

His initial overseas assignment with special forces was with the 5th Group in South Vietnam, where he was the XO of Camp A-224, Phu Tuc, in the highland mountains of II Corps. His camp was actively engaged in interdiction operations against the Viet Cong. Upon his return he was assigned to Fort Leonard Wood, Missouri, training recruits for several months before he returned to special forces, first to Panama and then back to RVN, where he was assigned to CCN, MACV-SOG, engaged in behind-the-lines interdiction operations against the North Vietnamese army. He was the S-3 Plans Officer, then the S-1, personnel officer, followed by Company B (Hatchet Force) commander until his return to Ft. Bragg, North Carolina, where he was the chief of Phase IV training to enlisted SF soldiers.

After his discharge from active duty, he joined the 12th Special Forces (Reserve) and served in the active reserves until his retirement in 1996 as a full colonel with over thirty-three years service. He worked as a professional engineer in his civilian status, obtaining his MBA from Pepperdine University through the GI bill. He is a registered professional engineer, a graduate of the Industrial College of the Armed Forces, and an enrolled agent of the IRS. He has worked for thirty years as a football official, both in high school and college. He is married to Sandra, a public school speech pathologist, and lives with her in Highland Ranch, Colorado, where they are retired. He writes western novels while working on his golf game in the summer and skiing in the winter. They have five grown children, scattered from Washington, D.C., to Portland, Oregon.

The employees of Five Star Publishing hope you have enjoyed this book.

Our Five Star novels explore little-known chapters from America's history, stories told from unique perspectives that will entertain a broad range of readers.

Other Five Star books are available at your local library, bookstore, all major book distributors, and directly from Five Star/Gale.

Connect with Five Star Publishing

Visit us on Facebook:
    https://www.facebook.com/FiveStarCengage

Email:
    FiveStar@cengage.com

For information about titles and placing orders:
    (800) 223-1244
    gale.orders@cengage.com

To share your comments, write to us:
    Five Star Publishing
    Attn: Publisher
    10 Water St., Suite 310
    Waterville, ME 04901